Suddenly, the Radio Sputtered to Life . . .

It was PFC Grayson, out front on recon. The young Marine had found a corpse.

"ID impossible, sir," reported Grayson, his voice tense. "It's in too many pieces. I can positively say that it was a white male. It looks like . . . Jesus, sir, it looks like claw marks. And this body's been chewed."

Wild beasts on airless Phobos? The masticated body parts had been found in the processing plant. We heard Weems over the radio issuing orders to converge on that point when a burst of static interfered with the reception.

When Grayson's voice came in again, it was loud and clear. Up until that moment, the universe still made some kind of sense to me. Of all the military scenarios running through my mind, none prepared me for what happened next: "Jesus Christ! It's not human," shouted Grayson. "Too big . . . shaped all wrong . . . humanoid . . . red eyes . . ."

While Grayson was providing this fragmentary report, he punctuated his description with bursts from his rifle. Before he could become more coherent we heard an inarticulate roar of animal pain from whatever he was shooting, and then he shouted, "I can't put it down!" The next scream we heard was fully human

My whole body went

Books in the DOOM™ Series

Knee-Deep in the Dead
Hell on Earth

Published by POCKET BOOKS

For orders other than by individual consumers, Pocket Books
grants a discount on the purchase of **10 or more** copies of
single titles for special markets or premium use. For further
details, please write to the Vice-President of Special Markets,
Pocket Books, 1230 Avenue of the Americas, New York, NY
10020.

For information on how individual consumers can place
orders, please write to Mail Order Department, Paramount
Publishing, 200 Old Tappan Road, Old Tappan, NJ 07675.

KNEE-DEEP
IN THE DEAD

A Novel by Dafydd ab Hugh
and Brad Linaweaver

Based on *Doom* from id Software

POCKET STAR BOOKS

New York   London   Toronto   Sydney   Tokyo   Singapore

The sale of this book without its cover is unauthorized. If you purchased this book without a cover, you should be aware that it was reported to the publisher as "unsold and destroyed." Neither the author nor the publisher has received payment for the sale of this "stripped book."

This book is a work of fiction. Names, characters, places and incidents are products of the author's imagination or are used fictitiously. Any resemblance to actual events or locales or persons, living or dead, is entirely coincidental.

An *Original* Publication of POCKET BOOKS

A Pocket Star Book published by
POCKET BOOKS, a division of Simon & Schuster Inc.
1230 Avenue of the Americas, New York, NY 10020

Copyright © 1995 by Id Software, Inc. All rights reserved.

This work is based upon the computer software games DOOM™ and DOOM II™. DOOM © 1993 Id Software, Inc. All rights reserved. DOOM II © 1994 Id Software, Inc. All rights reserved.

All rights reserved, including the right to reproduce this book or portions thereof in any form whatsoever. For information address Pocket Books, 1230 Avenue of the Americas, New York, NY 10020

ISBN: 0-671-52555-7

First Pocket Books printing August 1995

10 9 8 7 6 5 4 3 2 1

DOOM™ and DOOM II™ are trademarks of Id Software, Inc.

POCKET STAR BOOKS and colophon are registered trademarks of Simon and Schuster Inc.

Printed in the U.S.A.

Dedicated with lust to Camille Paglia,
who smokes the same cigars as Fred Olen Ray.

Before the Beginning

Kefiristan is about as close as you can come to hell on Earth.

I say that with authority: I've spent the last eighteen months doing a tour here, trying to keep the Kefiri People's Liberation Army, who call themselves the "Scythe of Glory," from the throats of the rightist Khorastisti, who have the backing of Azeri transplants from the south (who want to keep their enclaves), who are fighting a "dirty war" against Communist Cuban and Peruvian mercs . . . Jeez, you get the picture. It's a snarled skein of a million bloody threads up here on the top of the world, in the northern extension of the Karakoram range, between Afghanistan and Samarkand, Uzbekistan.

We'd just punched through the craggy pass pleasantly known as the "torn hymen" in the local tongue and come across the small, Muslim city of pik Nizganij, perched on a mountain peak of 2200 meters.

I stared in horror. Even eighteen months of picking up after the Scythe of Glory and their Shining Path buddies didn't prepare me for what was left of pik Nizganij.

It was a Bosch canvas, severed limbs and hollowed-out trunks—eaten out by *animals,* I prayed—planted through the fields like stalks of corn, blood painting doors and walls like the first Passover . . . except it was human blood, not lamb's blood.

Corporal Flynn Taggart, Fox Company, 15th Light Drop Infantry Regiment, United States Marine Corps; 888-23-9912. Everyone calls me Fly, except when they're pissed.

Fox crept through the town, hell-shocked, trying without much success to count body parts and make a reasonable KIA guess. Fog or an evil cloud rolled across the mountaintop, shrouding the sprightly red decoration and muffling our footsteps. It was like we walked along a cotton corridor, tripping over gruesome reminders that war, especially the virulent hatred of one tribe for another, throws men back into pre-bronze, pre-agricultural savagery. I wondered how many victims were killed by the victors' bare hands.

Something moved in the mist.

A shadow, a shape; nothing more. Gunnery Sergeant Goforth froze us with a slight hiss . . . Fox is damn-well trained, even for the Light Drop.

Gates stopped next to me; he touched my arm, silently pointing to left and right. I saw immediately; whatever the shapes were, they surrounded us from eight o'clock to four o'clock . . . we might be able to retreat, but we couldn't flank.

I watched the gunny; Arlene Sanders was whispering something in his ear. She was our scout, the lightest of the Light Drop. PFC Sanders could fade into the night so not even a werewolf could sniff her out. My best buddy.

She might have been more; once, we had—no; we were buddies. We didn't talk about that night. Anyway, she had Dodd, and I don't separate bookends.

Arlene backed away, backed past me, throwing me a wink as she vanished. She would swing in a wide arc, ease around behind the still-moving shades, and report back to the lieutenant and Gunny Goforth via a secured line. I'd find out soon enough.

I hadn't moved, and neither had the rest of us; I could barely hear Bill breathing next to me and couldn't hear Dodd or Sheill at all. If we were lucky, maybe the dinks wouldn't even know we were here; they'd just pad right on by.

Then Lieutenant Beelzebub came running up, demanding, "What the hell is going on?" in his normal speaking voice, an irritating whine.

The lieutenant's name was Weems, actually. I just call him Beelzebub because he's a fat, sweaty heathen always surrounded by a swarm of gnats. They like the taste of his perspiration.

The dinks froze as suddenly as we had; no longer moving, they vanished into the swirling gray. We had just lost whatever surprise we had, lost our best chance to get out of this encounter without a shot fired . . . and all because a buffoon who had been a first lieutenant for three years now couldn't figure out it was a Medusa drill!

One of them moved; then another. They moved singly, here and there, and we no longer had a clue where the mass of them was.

Weems began to panic; we'd all seen it before. "Aren't we going to take them out?" he asked Goforth, who was frantically putting his finger to his lips. "Somebody should take them out."

Goforth put his hand to his ear; he was listening to Arlene's report, trying to stifle the lieutenant with his other hand.

But Weems saw a ghost to his left, a specter to his right. We were surrounded! In Weems's mind—I use the term loosely—they were Indians, we were the 7th Cav, and he was Custer.

"The lieutenant isn't going to stand for this!" snapped the lieutenant. "Goforth, take out those soldiers!"

The gunny broke his own drill. "Sir, we don't even know who they are . . . Sanders says they're wearing robes and hoods—"

"Scythe of Glory!" said Weems, again raising his voice.

"No sir, just robed men—"

"Gunny, I gave you an order . . . now *take down those men!*"

Arlene flashed past me again. "What the hell's going on?" she hissed.

"Weems wants us to take 'em down."

"Fly, they're monks! You gotta stop the crazy son of a bitch!"

I was the second-ranking noncom; Goforth would listen to me, I thought. I hunched over and jogged to the gunnery sergeant. "Gunny, Arlene says they're monks."

"Taggart, right?" said Weems, as if bumping into me at an oyster-shucking party.

"Sir, they're just monks."

"Do you know that for sure? Does *anyone* know that for sure?"

"Sanders said—"

"Sanders said! Sanders said! Does Sanders have to deal with Colonel Brinkle every week?"

"Sir," began the gunny, "I think we should recon the group before we open fire."

Weems looked him in the face, shaking in fury. "As long as *I'm* giving the orders here, Marine, you'll obey them. Now *take down those men!*"

Monks. Freakin' monks!

I snapped. Maybe it was the bodies, or the body parts. The mountain air, thin oxygen. A gutful of Weems, Arlene's frightened, incredulous stare, the way Goforth's jaw set and he turned to give the order—a twenty-year man, he wasn't going to throw it away over a bunch of lousy religious dinks.

But suddenly, it occurred to me that if Weems were lying facedown in the deep muddy, he wouldn't be giving no orders. Then we could let the damned monks disappear, and nobody would be the loser.

4

"Scuse me, sir," I said, tapping the looie on the shoulder.

He turned, and I Georged him. Full-body swing; came out of Orlando, where I grew up. Picked up speed over Parris Island, hooked in at Kefiristan, and turned off the lights of Mr. Lieutenant Weems in pik Nizganij.

Alas, they only flickered. Power was restored. The dork didn't have a glass jaw; have to give him that.

Weems sprawled messily in the mud, and a couple of the boys were on me like monkeys on a tree. Weems flopped for a bit like a giant spider, then he found his hands and knees. He glared at me for a moment, an evil smile cracking his face. "Later," he said. Then he turned back to Goforth. "That don't mean crap, gunnery sergeant; now take down those men—or are you going to frag *me,* instead?"

Goforth looked at me, looked at Weems, looked at the ground. Then he clicked his M-92 to rock 'n' roll and quietly said, "Fox—take down those men."

I closed my eyes, listening to powder hiss, bullets crack, the metal clang of receivers slamming back and home. The screams of the dying. The shouts of the victors. I smelled the smoke from the smokeless power, the primer, fresh blood.

I'm in hell, I remember thinking; *I'm in hell.*

We mopped up the enemy troops in record time. Strange thing; none of them shot back. Fact, no weapons were found . . . just fifty-three men ranging from preteen to seventy or eighty, wearing brown robes and hoods, shaved heads, a couple carrying prayer sticks.

The boys wouldn't get off my back. Weems wouldn't even walk around where I could see him, the murdering bastard, while he formally charged me and I opted for a formal court-martial instead of Captain's Mast.

Jesus and Mary, somebody should put a bullet in his brain. I could taste the trigger. I didn't know how I was ever going to be shriven if I couldn't feel remorse.

1

I didn't miss Earth, but I sure as hell hated Mars. Sitting in a dingy mess hall on Phobos, one of the two, tiny Martian moons, seemed like a nice compromise.

Ordinarily, the C.O., Major Boyd, would have handed me over to the jaggies for trial; but the day after Weems gave the fateful order that bought him a mouthful of fist from Yours Truly, the 15th received orders to answer a distress call from Phobos. Fox Company was due to rotate back to the world anyway; Boyd decided to mail us to Mars.

They poured me onto the transport along with the rest of Fox; plenty of time to fry my butt after we figured out what the hell the UAC miners were squawking about this time.

The Corps, the Corps, all glory to the Corps! I don't think you know what the Marine Corps truly means to me. It has a bit to do with my father; no, he was not a Marine, God no. Maybe something to do with growing up in Orlando, Florida, and Los Angeles, seeing first the ersatz "Hollywood Boulevard" of Universal Studios East, then the even phonier real thing out west. Glitter and tinsel . . . but what was real?

7

Everything in my life rang as hollow as the boulevard until I found my core in the Corps.

Honor wasn't just something you did to credit cards. A lie wasn't called spin control, and spin was something you only put on a cue ball. Yeah, right, you think you know more about it than I? I know it was all BS, even in the Corps. I know the service was riddled up and down with lying sacks of dung, like everything else. "There is no cause so noble it will not attract fuggheads;" one of those sci-fi writers Arlene is always shoving at me, David Niven or something.

But God damn it, at least we say the word honor without laughing. At least we have a code—"I will not lie, cheat, or steal, nor tolerate those among us who do"—even if individuals don't always live up to it. At least it's there to reach for, even if our grasp falls far short. At least decency has a legal definition, right there in the Universal Code of Military Justice! At least respect means more than leaving the other guy's graffiti alone. At least we do more crap by six A.M. than most of you civilians do all day. At least the Corps is the Corps, semper fidelis—damn it, we know who we are and why we are! Do you?

Arlene never saw it the way I did; hell, no one did. I was a majority of one.

But you can't understand me unless you understand this much: there is a place in the world where decent men walk the streets, where water flows uphill, where miracles happen behind enemy lines and without air support, and where a guy (boy or girl) will stand on the wall that divides you people from the barbarians at the gate, take a bullet, and shoot back at the son of a bitch what fired it.

Unless you've been there, you'll never know. I want to take you there.

The long trip to Mars was dull, and the little voice in the back of my head had plenty of time to ask whether I would do anything different if given the chance. I had to honestly answer no.

Funny thing is, I always hoped I'd go to space one day . . . but not like this. My idea was to be on a deep-space exploratory ship, pushing out beyond the bounds of the known solar system. But when I scored only a 60 on the MilSpaceAp test, the chances of me receiving a deep-space assignment ranged somewhere between infinitesimal and "forget it." The big surprise was that one right upper cut to the concrete jaw of Lieutenant Weems opened my pathway to the stars.

Not only would I do it over again, I'd still enjoy it!

I stared at the two men whose job was to guard me, and had a strange feeling of unreality. "Want some coffee?" one of them asked with something that sounded like actual concern. His thin face reminded me of one of the monks.

"Yeah," I said. "Black, if you don't mind." He smiled. We'd run out of cream back in Kefiristan, and when he hopped up to Phobos, the supply situation was no improvement.

The guard's name was Ron. The other guard's name was Ron, too—I called him "Ron Two," but they didn't see the humor in it.

We didn't talk much. It seemed a little insulting only having two Marines protecting such a dangerous type as Yours Truly; but the other men were busy figuring out what had gone wrong on Phobos.

After we up-shipped to Mars Base, we sat for a solid day, trying to find out why the UAC miners on Phobos had sent a distress call—and why they didn't answer now. In the Marines, you spend eternity so bored you'd look forward to your own court-martial as a break in the tedium. Then an unexpected danger with huge, jagged edges comes rolling over all the set routines, a reminder that the universe is a dangerous place.

The last message we received from Phobos was: "Things coming through the Gate." When something that serious hits the fan, boredom is returned to its proper place as a luxury. The court-martial of a corporal was deemed less important than a potential threat to Mars—and not important at all compared to an immediate threat to the profits of the Union Aerospace Corporation.

With a ringing cry of "sounds like they're smoking something up there," Lieutenant Weems boldly led his men into the transport. At first I thought I'd be left behind on Mars Base; but either Weems thought I might prove useful to have along, or else he just didn't want a loose end. I volunteered to go along. Sometimes I'm not very bright.

Major Boyd did his best to brief us by video feed, under the obvious handicap of complete ignorance. He made the best of it. We were issued pressure suits, in case we had to leave the immediate vicinity of the Gate. You couldn't stay very long outside the pressure zone, and you'd get mighty cold, mighty fast. But at least the suits gave you a fighting chance to get to a ship or a zone before you were sucking vacuum. I was pleased to be issued a suit; I was less pleased that Weems didn't issue me a weapon.

While I contemplated the lethal uses of common household articles, PFC Ron Two brought the promised cup of coffee. It tasted bad enough to be a strategic weapon of deterrence. The expression on the guard suggested that he might have sampled it before passing it on to me; but maybe he was just plain scared of the situation. I couldn't really blame him.

A word about these Gates on Phobos and Deimos, the two tiny moons of Mars; you've probably heard about the Gates, even though officially it's a secret.

They were here when we first landed on Mars. It was a hell of a shock, discovering that someone or some thing had beaten us by a million years to our own closest neighbor! It was long before I joined up, of course, but I can only imagine the panic at the Pentagon when we found ancient and wholly artificial structures on Phobos, despite the complete lack of any form of life on Mars.

It was pretty clear they'd been placed there by some alien intelligence. But what? All my adult life, I'd heard speculation: all the usual UFO culprits . . . Reticulans, Men-in-Black, ancient Martians—that was the most popular theory, despite not working at all: there was no native life on Mars; but try to tell that to generations raised on Martian Walkabout, Ratgash of Mars, and Mars, Arise!

Me, I figured it was a race of alien anthropologists; they got here, said, "Hm, not quite ready yet," and left a "helipad" in case they decided to return . . . which they might do tomorrow or a hundred thousand years from now.

Somebody decided to call them "Gates," even though they just sat there doing nothing for as long as we've known about them. But surrounding them was a zone of about half Earth-normal gravitation . . . on a moon whose normal gravity is just this side of zero! In addition to the big, inert Gates, there were also small pads scattered here and there that instantly transported a person from point A to point B within the area, evidently without harm . . . teleports, if you will. I had heard about them but never seen one; damned if you'd ever get me into one, either.

When the United Aerospace Corporation bribed enough congressmen for the exclusive contract to mine Phobos and Deimos, they built their facilities around the Gates, taking advantage of the artificial gravity . . . except for those parts of the operation that wanted low gravity, which they built outside the "pressure zones." After the big reorganization, the Corps got the task of guarding the Gates.

Well—it looked as though the big Gates weren't quite so inert as we all thought.

Once we landed on Phobos, the gunny dropped me and my two guards at the abandoned Air Base depot (in the "western" pressure zone—antispinwards) and took the rest of Fox Company on to the UAC facilities, Weems in tow, to reestablish contact and "secure the situation." All my friends went with Weems, leaving me with the two Rons for company.

The Phobos facility is built like a gigantic, underground cone extending many hundreds of meters into the rock. There are a bunch of levels, I'm not even sure how many. Eight? Nine? The whole thing is built in the center of the solar system's largest strip mine, which would be terrible for the Phobos ecology—except that Phobos doesn't have an ecology, of course; it's an airless moon of ice and rock.

The facility was on the opposite hemisphere from the base. Big deal . . . the entire moon is only about twenty-five kilometers in diameter. You can walk from one pole to the other, except most of it is disturbingly close to zero-g, outside the pressure zones.

We had the radio on in the mess hall and were periodically picking up messages from Weems's Weasels. We'd about given up hope of hearing anything from the UAC guys who used to be on Phobos. As I sipped the scalding wake-up-call, wondering who I could sue if I burned my tongue, I couldn't help but scrutinize the two Rons. Neither gave the impression of being on top of the situation. They kept glancing at the closed cafeteria doors, at the radio, at each other . . . They weren't paying much attention to their prisoner.

They were also having the same conversation every twenty minutes or so. It generally started like this: "What do you think's happening?" one would ask the other.

I was tired of listening to variations on I-don't-know, so I volunteered a theory: "Somehow the Gates turned on, and whoever built them decided the UAC was trespassing. Maybe they were wiped out."

"But who attacked us?" asked Ron One. Funny; I never thought of Union Aerospace as part of "us."

"They said monsters were coming through the Gate," said Ron Two with the same sense of surprise he'd displayed the other half-dozen times.

"They said 'things,' " I corrected. Neither heard me. Things or monsters, I had faith in Arlene and the rest of the guys.

The guards didn't strike me as being overly interested in the subject of high order physics. They had reached firm conclusions in the realm of the biological sciences, however. They didn't believe in monsters.

The truth is that neither did I.

In one respect I was as bad as the PFCs. There were questions that couldn't be answered yet, but they wouldn't stay out of my mind. Who was the enemy? How had they reached Phobos through the gateways? And most troubling of all, why hadn't Fox found any bodies yet? Major Boyd and even Colonel Brinkle back on Earth would want answers to these questions and a lot more.

Suddenly, the radio sputtered to life, grabbing our attention, an invisible hand reaching out to choke the breath from us. It was PFC Grayson, out front on recon, reporting to Weems, who was elsewhere in the facility. The young Marine had found a corpse. Weems radioed back the obvious instructions.

"ID impossible, sir," reported Grayson, his voice tense. "It's in too many pieces. I can positively say that it was a white male. It looks like—Jesus, sir, it looks like claw marks. And this body's been chewed."

Wild beasts on airless Phobos? Judging by the sickened expressions from Ron and Ron, it was all too evident that neither of these specimens had ever seen combat. I've seen my share . . . and all at once, the idea of living long enough to attend my own court-martial seemed very appealing. Even five years at Leavenworth looked good. The fact that I didn't have a gun crawled around deep inside my gut like a tapeworm. Right then I decided to remedy the situation.

The masticated body parts had been found in the processing plant. We heard Weems over the radio issuing orders to converge on that point when a burst of static interfered with the reception.

When Grayson's voice came in again, it was loud and clear. Up until that moment, the universe still made some kind of sense to me. Of all the military scenarios running through my mind, none prepared me for what happened next: "Jesus Christ! It's not human," shouted Grayson. "Too big . . . shaped all wrong . . . humanoid . . . red eyes . . ."

While Grayson was providing this fragmentary report, he punctuated his description with bursts from his rifle. Before he could become more coherent, we heard an inarticulate roar of animal pain from whatever he was shooting, and then he shouted, "I can't put it down!" The next scream we heard was fully human.

My whole body went cold. Jesus—Arlene was down there.

Keep cool, keep your head—she's a Marine, damn it!

One of the Rons looked like he was about to throw up. "Okay," I said, "this has gone on long enough. We know we're in this together. Give me a gun and let's make some plans." If Arlene were being shot at, God damn it, I intended to shoot back! The honor of the Corps was at stake, not to mention my best buddy's life.

The radio was reduced to background noise for the moment as Weems the Weasel tried to control the situation. The nervous looks exchanged between the dynamic duo in the mess hall made me wonder about training that completely destroys initiative. On the brink of death, all the Rons cared about was going by the book—even if that book printed their own obituaries in flaming letters.

One finally generated the initiative to say, "We can't give you a weapon!"

I tried again. "Staying alive is the objective here. We've all got buddies down there. They don't court-martial the dead! You can't help anyone or defend anything if you're dead. Now give me a piece!"

If either of them had shown a glimmer of intelligence

14

or guts, I wouldn't have taken the next step. But they insisted on being idiots.

Jesus Christ! As the Godfather said, there are men who go through life begging to be killed.

2

Shut up," said the first Ron.

"You're going back to detention," said the other. This was a truly pathetic spectacle. Suddenly, I had become the threat in their eyes, simply because I was forcing them to face an unpleasant situation head-on.

A number of things happened at once: more screams and gunfire came over the radio, and *I thought I heard a woman scream*. The nearest Ron unholstered his 10mm pistol and pointed it at me—then the poor jerk gestured the direction he wanted me to walk. He gestured with the hand holding the pistol. With an invitation like that what could I do?

I caught his arm, moved the gun aside, and rabbit-punched him in the kidneys; the gun slid across the floor. The other Ron was still fumbling with his holster, so I turned and jabbed him in the throat . . . not hard enough to kill, but with enough impact to keep him busy trying to breathe.

Sorry, Rons; Arlene PFC Sanders means more than the both of you rolled together!

I turned back to the first one, who surprised me by regaining his feet and making a grab with his good arm. Too bad for him, he was off balance and fell toward me, providing another irresistible target. I flat-palmed the back of his head, and he was out like a light. The other Ron was still doubled over, trying to breathe as I collected their weapons.

"You guys aren't exactly cut out for Light Drop Infantry," I said in as kindly a voice as I could muster.

Now I had a problem. They weren't bad guys, but I couldn't trust their goodwill not to come after me. Their fear might be enough to keep them out of my hair, but I couldn't count on that, either. Nor did I want to leave them sitting ducks for the hostile forces that were loose in this station. So I helped the one who was still conscious to his feet and waited for his glazed eyes to clear a bit.

"Listen, Ron; we've got a situation here. So far as I can tell, we only have these two sidearms between the three of us. This is not good. The lieutenant should have left us with some weapons, don't you think?" It was a rhetorical question, so I kept on. "I'm leaving one of these guns with you, unloaded." I let him sink back on the floor and slid the ammo clip across the floor. "When you feel well enough to reload, I suggest you barricade the door better than I can lock it from the outside, and wait for orders."

He looked sick as a dog but nodded, and I left him to his own devices. I pocketed the remaining ammo clips. I wanted all the edge a few extra rounds could provide until I could find an armory and lay my hands on some real firepower, if the factory had any.

As I locked the mess hall doors behind me, I heard the radio sending out useless static crackle; no Weems, no Goforth—no Arlene. Well, last I heard, we were all going to have a party, with Grayson's remains as the Guest of Honor. I didn't like that particular train of thought so I derailed it. Time to get serious.

After ten minutes of humping around the compound, I found a landcart—the last one. That was thoughtful of them. Phobos is so small, a diameter of only twenty-two kilometers, that I almost could hoof it to the factory . . .

particularly in the ultra-low gravity. But I might need to evac the survivors; and in any case, speed counts.

Although I'm not claustrophobic, I'd lately had my fill of blank walls. The spaceship was the worst. Traveling through a million miles of nothing in a little cubicle just so you can reach another cubicle at the end is not my idea of the conquest of space.

At least for the one day we spent on Mars, we had a view. The domes were made of super-thick, insulated plastic, but were cleverly designed to give the illusion of being thin as a soap bubble. The only trouble was that the view wasn't very impressive—a blank expanse of empty desert broken by an equally barren, dark purple sky. I was only so thrilled with looking at stars. I liked something bigger up there. Although we could see Phobos from Mars base camp, it was so tiny it almost looked like a bright star trucking across the sky. Not enough moon for a melancholy mood.

But now as I crawled the land-cart out under the black, airless sky of Phobos, I enjoyed my first genuine feeling of freedom since I left Earth. Mars loomed in the sky, three-quarters full, larger than any moon and burning red as all the blood of all the armies ever spilled in uncountable battles across the stupid, drooling face of eternity—the face of a monster.

By contrast, the gray, dull surface of Phobos looked like brittle, laundry soap or dried oatmeal; the only variation was Stickney, the huge crater that covered a quarter of the moon's surface and filled the rest with impact striations.

At that moment I thought that Mars might be the last beautiful sight I would ever experience. Ahead lay nothing good. The thought that I might shortly die didn't bother me nearly so much as the dread of letting down my loved ones . . . again.

There weren't that many back on Earth, but there was one here on Phobos that meant everything to me.

Maybe I did love her; I couldn't say. I mean that

literally . . . I *couldn't say it* with her hooked up with Wilhelm Dodd, the dirty bastard. But that didn't mean crap; if Arlene were in trouble, then putting my life on the line was the easiest choice I'd ever made. Doing my duty didn't mean I had a death wish; it meant that I would have to stay alive as long as possible to find her and hump her out. All right, and the rest of Fox, too.

So with Mars looming gigantic and our sun a shrunken, distant ball of flame, quickly setting as I crawled toward the factory, I sped through Phobos daylight, across the terminator, and into the black night.

My stomach started roiling the moment I left the zone and entered the correct gravitational field of Phobos— not quite zero-g, but close enough for a queasy stomach. I had to watch my speed carefully here; I wasn't sure what the escape velocity from Phobos was . . . probably a lot more than a crawling land-cart could make. But I sure as hell didn't want to end up in orbit—the tractor treads didn't work too well out there!

I wished I could drive the land-cart right inside the refinery, but I had to leave it in the garage on the surface. It sure felt good to get back under even the half-normal gravity in the refinery zone. The silent station lurked below the surface, containing what was left of Fox Company.

As I began the long descent, I promised to keep very, very quiet. Early in a career in the Light Drop Infantry, you learn the absolute essential of lying to yourself. Sure enough, there was noise, and I was the source of it. Even in the low-g, my boots squeaked slightly. Each squeak was magnified in my imagination as if giant rodents nibbled at my heels. The rectangle of light beneath me grew in size as there was no turning back.

I thought about using the lift, but there was no telling who I'd find inside. The access-tube ladder looked a safer bet.

A popular feature of these permanent stations is how

there's always light and air so long as the small reactor is working. Imagine my disappointment on climbing down the ladder into the hangar when I noticed the first signs that something was seriously wrong: the lights were flickering, and I didn't hear the whine of the air recirculators.

The light was adequate to show empty corridor stretching in front and behind me. This section didn't seem to show any signs of recent conflict . . . and no sooner did a small part of me make the mistake of relaxing than I heard a sharp hissing sound. Before I had time to think, the 10mm was in my hand and I had spun around into a defensive crouch. I'm sure I scared the leaky pipe real bad. At times like this, nothing is more welcome than an anti-climax.

As I examined the damaged pipe, mindful not to be scalded by the escaping steam, I realized that I might have found something interesting after all. The pipe had been dented by a blunt metal object of some kind, and there was a rusty stain on the floor underneath it.

There was really only one direction to go, so I went. That direction would also take me toward the hangar control room, where I could swear I heard low, growling noises. Somehow I didn't feel like reholstering my gun. I didn't like the way my palm was sweating, either.

Taking it nice and easy, I proceeded down the corridor. I had a good, long view ahead of me. No room for surprises. I didn't hear the animalistic noises again, but that didn't make me feel any better. Finally, I reached the control room. Right before I pushed the door open I felt a sudden shiver on the back of my neck and spun around, trying to look down both directions at once, like one of those crazy cartoon drawings of a double take. But there was nothing. At least nothing I could see. No casualties yet, thank God.

The control room was empty, but it had a peculiar odor like sour lemons. After months in a barracks, whether in Kefiristan, on Mars, or in space, you get used to the smell of paint and gallons of disinfectant. But this was nothing like that. I didn't like it one bit.

It took only a few minutes to establish that all the equipment was in working order—except for the communications system, which was smashed into nonexistence. Then I had a brainstorm. There might be a gun locker here, something left over from when Phobos was an Air Force outpost; something a bit heavier than a 10mm pistol would greatly improve the adjustment to my new environment.

I found the locker and jimmied open the door fairly quietly; but there were no weapons. Bare cupboard. Not even a slingshot. But so it shouldn't be a total waste, there was a nice selection of last year's flak jackets; not combat armor, but better than skin and a pressure suit. One looked like it fit me, so I put it on.

There seemed nothing else to do but resume my journey along the corridor that must ultimately take me into the rest of the station. I was reaching that dangerous psychological state when you feel that you are the only living person in what had been a battlefield situation. Another word for it is carelessness.

Reconnoiter, you bastard! My little voice was telling me to get back with the program. And not a moment too soon. A human figure came striding purposefully in my direction from just around the curve of the corridor.

I almost shot first, and asked questions at some undetermined future date. Reminding myself that Arlene and my buddies were here, as well as UAC civilians, I relaxed the old trigger finger that crucial centimeter. But I kept the gun on the human shape and experienced a sickening moment, not of empathy, but of reluctant understanding of Lieutenant Weems and the monks.

When the fearsnake slithers around inside your gut, it's pretty damned easy to just start squeezing off at anything that moves.

Then I recognized the shape as one Corporal William Gates.

"Bill!" I shouted, relief flooding me at contact with a fellow Light Drop. "What the hell's going on? Are you all right? Where's Arlene—the rest of Fox?"

At no moment was there any doubt that this person approaching was the corporal with whom I'd played poker, drank, and told nasty jokes. We'd been through enough together that I didn't even mind that he was one of the monkeys who jumped on my back when I popped Weems. Bill had a very distinctive face with eyes spaced wide apart and a scar that ran from his prominent chin into his lower lip.

He was walking in an erratic manner; fatigue, I assumed. Men in combat situations can get very weird, and I'd seen plenty worse than this.

Battle fatigue might even have explained the strange words coming out of his mouth, stuff that sounded like an old horror movie. Bill was staring straight ahead; but he didn't seem to recognize me as he chanted, "The Gate—the Gate is the key—the key is the Gate." I didn't like the spittle on his chin, either.

As much as I wanted to run over to him, I held back. There was something really wrong here, nothing I could put my finger on yet, but it was like that smell in the control room—little hints that something was FUBARed on Phobos.

"Bill," I tried again. "Bill, it's your cuz, Fly."

This time he noticed me. I could tell because he grinned the most evil grin I've ever seen in my life.

Then he raised his rifle and opened fire!

Even then, I didn't want to believe what was happening. Fortunately, my bodily reflexes were more realistic. Diving behind a pillar, I was already preparing to return fire.

I had to try one more time. "Stop firing, Bill! It's Fly, goddamn it. Stop shooting!"

3

Bill didn't stop; he came closer. Desperate, feeling like Cain, I returned fire. Given the half-dead condition Bill was in, killing him all the way should have been easy. The first bullet took him in the throat, above his kevlar armor. That should have done the job, but he kept on coming. I pumped more rounds at Bill, and finally one connected with his head. That dropped him.

But even as brains and blood oozed onto the corridor floor, his body continued to flop around the way a chicken does when its head has been removed. Humans don't do that . . . and they don't have a sour-lemon smell either, which was suddenly so overpowering that I could barely breathe.

I stared, shaking like a California earthquake.

I was looking—at—a zombie.

That was all that kept racing through my head, screaming the word over and over again between my ears . . . *zombie, zombie, zombie!* What utter shit. Maybe Arlene could believe in all that crap and bullroar; she watched those damned, damned horror movies all the—I wasn't never going to watch anything like . . . a freakin' *zombie?* I was crazy, buggin', freaked like some hippie punk snot flying on belladonna.

There are no goddamned zombies! This is the real world, this is—"

Gates flopped some more, then stiffened up so quick, it was like he'd been dead for hours. Scared, but drawn

22

toward him like iron filings to a magnet, I crept forward and touched his corpse.

Billy Boy was ice-cold. This meat was decidedly not fresh.

I gagged, then turned aside and vomited. He was blue. His skin was tough, like leather.

Private Gates was a freaking zombie. Walking dead. They'd killed him, then sucked the life out of his body, so that in just half an hour, he was many days dead.

Arlene . . . !

I knew what I had to do next. I was crying while I did it. I hoped I'd find some magazines to go with my new acquisition, a 10mm, M-211 Semiautomatic Gas-Operated Infantry Combat Weapon (Sig-Cow, we called it). Bitch of a way to get one.

Gates only had a single spare mag, and the one in the rifle was dead. Still shaking, I reloaded the rifle, dropping rounds left and right, and crept on, wondering who would come running at the sound of me murdering my dead chum.

Leaving Gates's body, I started walking fast, then a little faster. Suddenly I was running . . . not in fear, but sick rage. The little voice in my head that usually keeps me on track was screaming about discipline and strategy and keeping my cool. The voice wanted me to make a nice, practical analysis of the evidence.

I had every intention of listening to reason, but my feet and brain stem had other ideas. They were running from the face of a man who used to be a human being; running toward the bastards who reworked him.

I've always had good survival instincts. They'd never abandoned me before, not even in the worst firefights in a career that had seen its fair share of combat. But here and now, in a dull, gray cavern under the craggy surface of Phobos, my body was betraying me. If I could just stop seeing the slack jaw, the dead eyes, I could get control again. But the face wouldn't go away; even the characteristic twitch of the right eye that used to annoy me when Gates was alive unnerved the hell out of me now. I couldn't stand to be *winked at* by a zombie.

Yeah. Zombie. Putting the word to it helped. At least I was running a little slower and started paying attention to my surroundings. I saw the walls of the corridor instead of a phantom mask of death; and I heard the loud echoing of my footsteps, my labored breathing . . . and the shuffling noises of *other* feet.

Four of them were waiting for me around the bend— four zombies. They stared at me with dead, dry eyes . . . and one of the zombies was a woman.

I didn't know her; UAC worker. Thank God it wasn't Arlene. I didn't even want to think about Arlene with gray flesh and a sour-lemon smell, sneering and pumping bullets at me without any recognition.

I felt a rage I'd never felt before; my blood was on fire and my skin couldn't contain the boiling, liquid anger. I shook from hate so deep that military training could never reach it.

I didn't want to shoot these travesties of human life. I wanted to rip them apart with my bare hands! They shuffled toward me, fumbling their weapons and pumping shots like their rifles would never run dry. What did I do? I staggered directly toward them, raising my own M-211 and taking one of the walking dead in its shoulder . . . a useless shot.

It was the girl that broke the spell. Some little piece of who she once was must have been left in her brain, a faint echo or resonance of human thought. She didn't charge blindly like the other three; she turned and fell behind cover to plink at me.

My higher brain functions kicked in. I shook my head, then strafed while sidestepping to a pillar; once behind cover, I aimed a shot into Zombie One's head. It roared, then danced like a headless chicken and collapsed. I got the message: only head shots got me any points. Just like in the movies.

The citrus stench almost overwhelmed me. I snuck a quick glance at the zombie I'd just smoked . . . *something squirmed inside its brain.* Swallowing nausea, I took a bead on Zombie Two.

The zombie-girl chittered, and the other two headed jerkily toward the console behind which she crouched. I caught Zombie Two before it made it halfway; but the other one took a position behind cover, and both it and Zombie Girl returned fire.

A standoff. I was trapped behind the pillar, two zombies behind an instrument console marked UAC and covered with sticky-pad notes, the three of us separated by no more than twenty meters. Swiveling my head, I stared wildly around, trying to spot something useful.

Five minutes deep into the Phobos facility, and I was pinned down inside a mortuary in hell. A dozen bodies sprawled on the floor from the open control room in which I stood all the way to a curve in the corridor beyond which I could see no farther. Recognizing a few of them didn't do my stomach any good. The others were probably UAC workers.

I thought I'd seen war in Kefiristan.

The undead and I played a game of tag around the pillar; I popped out to fire off a shot, and they sprayed my position a moment after I abandoned it.

There wasn't much time to appreciate the fine details; the third time I popped around for a shot, I slipped on fresh blood. Even as a kid, I was good at turning mishaps into advantages; special training merely augmented my natural instinct for survival.

I hit the floor on my knees, then dropped to my belly to aim a shot while braced against the floor. The third male zombie rose to fire down on me, and I caught it in the throat, knocking it backward; before it could reacquire its target, Yours Truly, my next shot took Zombie Three in the right eye.

The female wasn't wearing a uniform or armor; I realized she must have once been a UAC worker, not a soldier . . . which might account for her bad aim. She fired off a couple of rounds that missed by a wide margin.

I can fight this war forever, I thought, rage starting to creep back. Then it struck me: I *could* fight this war forever, at least until I was finally blown away, and never even come close to figuring out what had happened here at Phobos Base.

I had to take one of bastards "alive," if that was the right word.

The plan flickered through my head between one shot and the next; and now that I finally had a plan, I was Light Drop Infantry again!

Quickly, before she could adjust and acquire me, I bolted around the pillar, head-faked to the left, then cut right and hopped over the console. Zombie Girl swiveled the wrong direction, and before she could turn back, I swung the butt of my Sig-Cow into her temple.

She dropped like bricks on Jupiter. The rifle sailed from her hands across the floor. I slung my own M-211 across my back, flipped her over and shoved my pistol in her mouth.

"What the hell's going on?" I demanded.

"Mmph hmmph rmmph," she said. I pulled the gun out of her mouth, but she kept talking as if she had not even noticed it. "—is the key. Gate is the key. Key is the gate. Coming. Kill you all."

Zombie Girl's eyes shifted left and right; she was preternaturally strong . . . but not as strong as big Fly Taggart. My hand drooped as I stared at her, and she snapped at it like a rabid dog, trying to bite me.

Abruptly, I realized why the zombies' eyes were so dry and their vision so bad: they never blinked.

I pushed the pistol against her forehead. "If there's any piece alive inside of you, you know what this thing will do to your shriveled, little brains. What the hell is coming through the gate?"

"Great. Ones. Gate ones." She focused her eyes on me,

seeming to see me for the first time. She didn't answer, but for a moment her face was filled with such torment that I could no longer stand the interrogation.

I cocked the hammer; her eyes rolled up, looking over my head. "You *want* this?" I asked.

Zombie Girl closed her eyes. It was the only kind of prayer left to her by the reworking that made her what she was.

I closed my own eyes when I squeezed the trigger. The gunshot snapped me awake again; I jumped up, slid the Sig-Cow into ready position, and backed away from the undead dead.

What the hell was going on? I started to think I had an answer . . . part of an answer.

"Who built the Gates?" The question endlessly on everyone's lips might be about to be answered. Maybe. But were the "Great Ones" coming through the Gates the ones who had built them? Or had the builders already been overrun by some even more powerful, horrific critter, who was now joyfully following Gate after Gate, finding and overpowering all the colonies of the builders' "empire"?

Neither thought was pleasant: humans were either trespassers who were about to be run off the property or dessert after a main course of Gate builders.

I got the shakes, real bad. I backed into a dark corner, M-211 pointed toward the corridor, the unknown, the way I hadn't been yet. I had not seen a particular body I'd half dreaded, half *hoped* to find. Christ. Arlene was still Somewhere Out There, one way or the other.

I prayed she was lying dead on the deck, not stumbling toward me with dry, unblinking eyes and a sour-lemon smell.

I might soon be the only living human on Phobos, I realized. I had little faith in the guards I'd left back in the mess hall. First contact with zombies, and they'd role over and, to coin a phrase, play dead. I could imagine a rotting corpse that used to be Lieutenant Weems telling them to get with the zombie program; the Rons would salute and "Yes sir!" themselves straight to hell.

The old survival mechanism was definitely starting to kick in for Yours Truly. I'd never been completely comfortable as a team player. I could see myself doing the job of zombie exterminator until I was the only biped left standing on Phobos. These living dead characters weren't very good soldiers. Yeah, I could dust them all. Except for one little detail.

I couldn't bear coming up against what used to be Arlene Sanders. No, that wasn't very appealing at all. It's not like she was my girl; she had her Dodd, and it seemed to satisfy her. Dodd and I didn't really like each other, but we tolerated for Arlene's sake.

Not love, I swear. It's just that Arlene lived in the same world I did, and I mean a lot more than just wearing the same uniform. She wasn't like any other girl I'd been . . . I mean, any other girl I'd known.

Arlene remembered being awakened by a D.I. heaving a trash can down the hall, same as me. She remembered the jarhead getting all over her; "on your face, down-up-down-up-down-up—you keep pumpin' 'em out until *I get tired!*" She knew about reveille at 0500, PT (Physical Training), or a dainty, eight-mile run at 0505.

Arlene knew the smell of disinfectant. She knew all about scraping two years of accumulated crud off a wall with a chisel so the next guy could slap on a quarter-inch-thick splash of anti-corrosion paint.

She'd spent just as many months as I wrestling a goddamned floor buffer up and down a corridor, while already dog-sacked from hours of PT, obstacle course, combat training, small-arms, endless, mindless instruction on how to break down and reassemble a Sig-Cow while blindfolded, and lectures on the exotic venereal diseases of Kefiristan, Mars, Phobos Base, and Ohio . . . hours that always seemed to add up to twenty-six or twenty-eight per day.

Arlene figured out a lot about me in record time. She was bright, and just as committed to a military career as any other man in the outfit. She'd become my best buddy in the platoon.

As I sat there, wiping blood and crud from my face in the eye of an impossible hurricane, it helped to think about Arlene. Recalling her features drove the monsters from my mind. I played a little game with myself, not letting the horror rise up and engulf the picture I was drawing.

I don't think I've ever seen a better-looking woman than Arlene, objectively considered. She wasn't drop-dead gorgeous in the conventional sense. To use an older phrase from a braver age, she was "right handsome." Five-ten and compactly built, she worked out more than anyone else in the platoon. She had beautiful, well-cut muscles.

(Once, when for a few days she thought she might be "with child"—not mine—Gates had said, "She's such a man, I bet she got *herself* pregnant." He didn't say it loudly.)

I liked how she looked at everyone through slitted eyes, giving her a hooded serpent look. She was not to be trifled with, as one skank found out when he thought it was funny to sneak up behind her and pull down her pants.

The rest of us were certainly interested in seeing all we could of her well-shaped posterior; but we weren't idiots. Without turning around, she backhanded him perfectly and broke his nose. At the time all I could think of was how much I enjoyed seeing her move. We're talking ballet here.

Of course, there was a lot more to Arlene; she had a brain. Those are in short supply in the service, even in Light Drop, and I hated to see one go to waste. I took her to Corps music concerts, and she dragged me to old sci-fi movies. We got drunk together sometimes. We played poker, too; but my only chance against her was when I was stone-cold sober.

One night we got so drunk that we fumbled our way into a kiss. It just didn't feel right. We were buddies, not lovers.

Arlene and I reached an unspoken agreement where we didn't talk about that night. As if to prove what a pal she could be, she started setting me up with dates. She had girlfriends who were always first-rate in one way or another, and they liked to oblige her by hanging with her pal. I didn't kick. I just didn't seem able to return a commensurate favor.

Arlene told me once how she wanted to save up some money and go to college someday. I didn't hold that against her. I wished the best for her.

The best. That thought shot down my reverie in flames. What could the best be for her now, in this place? Death, I guessed; anything would be better than gray flesh, dry, unblinking eyes, and jerking limbs.

"No," I heard myself talking to no one, "she'd never allow herself to be turned into one of *those.*"

But what if this reworking took place *after* death?

Swallowing hard, I stood up and decided to get back to business. I needed ammo; a wild shot had destroyed the magazine and receiver of one of the Sig-Cows; the only thing a zombie could use it for now would be as a war club, so I left it on the floor. Nobody had a select fire weapon, which was too bad; I sure missed the luxury of launching three or four rounds at a time toward a zombie head . . . much better chance of a bull's-eye. On the other hand, if they *had* had one of the two select-fire M-220 Dogchoppers that a squad carried, I might not be alive to pick through the weaponry.

I shoved some magazines into my ammo pockets and loaded up both weapons. No sense carrying another Sig-Cow. I really wanted to get my hands on the riot gun that Dardier usually carried, though—except it would probably mean ripping it out of her twitching fingers after blowing a hole in her pretty, blond head.

I followed the trail of corpses another two bends of the corridor, taking as much ammo as I could carry without rattling like a medieval knight. We were all supposed to carry head-talks, so we could communicate . . . but I didn't find *any,* which was pretty suspicious. No ELFs or MilDataBuses, either: *nothing whatsoever* that might be used to communicate what the hell was going on.

And I always made time to check the faces. So long as one, particular face wasn't there . . . I knew I could stand it.

4

I almost felt relief when I ran into two more zombies. Now that I knew what to do, it was just some sickening sort of exercise. I only "killed" one of them; the other, I just popped its rifle, then shot out its knees and hips; I wanted it alive, maybe to answer some questions before I smashed in the curling mouth with the yellow teeth.

I didn't recognize this one; it was a former UAC worker, used to be a man. It didn't have even as much mind left as had Zombie Girl; but this time, I let it babble for some time:

"Big, coming through, big, Gate is the key, killing, killing, all the killing, coming through, coming to kill you all, the Gate is the key, the key, hell and damns is the key, coming through the Gate . . .

"Phobos! Fear, fear, fear, fear, fear!

"Coming to Phobos, coming from Phobos, crossing the Styx, pickup Styx, Styx is the key."

I waited until it started repeating itself; after a moment, a chill crept down my neck: the thing was repeating itself *exactly,* like a tape loop. Suddenly more scared than I had been in hours, I put it out of its misery (and mine).

I backed up into a dark alcove, praying nobody had a light-amp glasses or an infrared sensor. I needed to think this through.

A single strip of hellishly bright luminescence flickered off and on high in the center of the ceiling; a bare sun bulb was all that was left of the lighting system. The strobe effect made shadows look like monsters, creeping toward me. But I didn't smell any rotten citrus, and heard none of the characteristic zombie gibbering . . . just a strange clicking sound ahead, like a dolphin with laryngitis. I figured I was safe for the moment.

Phobos was pretty obvious; they were here, at Phobos Base. They came *to* Phobos . . . but what did the thing mean saying they were coming *from* Phobos?

I started feeling nauseated. My skin began to creep up and down my bones . . . If the zombie didn't distinguish between yesterday, today, and tomorrow, then maybe it was telling me that Phobos was not the final target of the invasion; they were going to cross the River Styx, the river of the dead in Greek mythology.

And what was on the other side? Well, hell, I supposed. Hades. But wait—if you were *starting* from hell, then "crossing the Styx" took you to . . .

I swallowed the nausea back down. Sweat dripped down my forehead, stinging my eyes.

The target was Earth. Terra mostly firma. Home sweet hovel.

I accepted the fact that I was a dead man. After four years of Catholic school, run by Father Bartolomeo,

Society of Jesus, I had always thought I was pretty much "prayed out." Certainly, even after four years in the Corps, the last three in Light Drop Infantry, I hadn't had a word to say to the Big Guy, if He were even listening.

But now, for the first time, after a cumulative seventeen weeks of actual combat intercut into four years of military life, I finally understood that stupid line about there being "no atheists in foxholes." I didn't use the words that the Jesuits taught me, but I know who I was talking to, begging for the guts and skill not to hose up.

"Suicide mission" was a weak term for what I was doing. I'm as afraid to die as the next jarhead; but goddamn it, I didn't want to be damned as a walking dead!

I told the Big Guy what I'd done wrong in the last, ah, seven years and promised him a lifetime of penance if He'd just forgive me and send me into battle shriven. It was a hollow offer, I knew; that "lifetime" was probably measured in hours. Thank God it's the thought that counts.

Taking a breath, I swung my rifle around, finger outside the trigger guard, and stepped out of the alcove. I continued around a corner toward the clicking noise.

Suddenly I saw what looked like a working radio! Hurrying over—too quickly for caution's sake—I saw that only the front part of the mechanism remained. The back was ripped out in a way that showed clear sabotage. Up to that moment, it had seemed possible that the radios were destroyed accidentally, casualties of battle; but this was clear evidence of at least human-level tactics, far beyond what I'd imagine the zombies could do.

There was somebody else wandering around here. If I hunted long enough, I figured I'd find it . . . if it or they didn't find me first.

Turning a corner in the corridor, I saw more evidence of some kind of strategy: on the wall, a map to the installation had been burned beyond recognition, while the space around it was only slightly singed. Whoever that other something or somebody was, it knew that more of us would be coming after it; it didn't want us to be able to find our way.

Ahead was a hatchway, the door open. The light directly over it was broken; but a steady, green glow emanated from beyond the narrow opening; the glow did not come from any electrical source I could think of. Even as I moved toward the entrance, I knew I wanted to be anywhere else but here. A new odor assailed me, far worse than the sour lemons. This was the loving, sweet aroma of something that should have been buried, or better yet, flushed. It literally burned my nostrils.

I fumbled for the mask that accompanied the combat armor. *Jesus,* I thought, *what I wouldn't give for a working environment suit!* My hands shook as pulled it over my mouth and nose, wondering what horrible, toxic fumes I was breathing.

The surge of air from the suit augmented the bad air; but it did little good. The molecules of the toxin were evidently smaller than oxygen molecules and didn't react to any of the filters; I could still smell them right through the mask.

Every warning klaxon in my body was screaming; my skin tingled, and the proverbial hair on the back of my proverbial neck jumped up and did some PT. I took a few tentative steps farther in, then I came up short; I'd found the light source.

Pools of thick, green liquid bubbled on both sides of me. The stuff was luminescent, probably radioactive. It looked like boiling lava on Saint Patrick's day. I wasn't going to stop and run any experiments; but I had no doubt the gunk would eat right through my combat suit, given enough time. The prudent decision was to stay as far away from the green slime as humanly possible.

No sooner had this thought crossed my mind than a

ton of bricks slammed into me from the right, knocking the 10mm pistol out of my holster and into the green toxin. Something had decided to run the experiment after all.

The 10mm made a hissing sound as it disappeared from view. I didn't care. I had problems of my own.

Flipping over, I struggled to get to my feet and bring my big Sig-Cow into play, if I could figure out what the hell hit me. The impact had blurred my vision. I stood up, dizzy, shaking my head. The figure that had hit me so hard stood just out of sight, in the shadows. I assumed it was another zombie, but a stronger one than I had encountered before.

Then it cut loose with a hiss, and more of that clicking sound I had been hearing. Well, one little mystery solved.

The strength in this—zombie?—inspired greater caution. I rolled my M-211 around and skated to the side, waiting for the creature to come to me. He did.

As the large body moved into sight, I saw brown, leathery skin, rough like alligator hide, with ivory-white horns sticking out from chest, arms, and legs. The head was inhumanly huge, with maddened slits of red for eyes. It was a monster!

It was a demon.

5

My first reaction was to laugh. This was a childhood nightmare, a bogeyman. The part of me that had worked so hard to grow up just couldn't believe in something that looked like this.

Only trouble was, the damned thing didn't appreciate its own absurdity. It took a few steps toward me where the light was better. Movement made the figure less ridiculous. Shadows played across its rough hide, and I saw that the wrinkled flesh under the eyes were wet. I hated to admit that it really was flesh. The eyes flickered with an angry red light. The worst features were the lips curling back to reveal ugly, yellow canines. This was no Halloween mask with a rigid grimace. Inhuman as this monster was, I couldn't confuse it with an animal.

Just an alien bastard, I told myself over and over; I was a lot more comfortable with the idea of an alien, even an alien soldier—a cosmic grunt. Not a . . . a *demon*.

The extraterrestrial stopped advancing. It turned its head at an angle no human could copy, but kept its eyes fixed on me. Mexican standoff.

Despite it having attacked me first, I couldn't shake the thought that it was my responsibility to try to make contact. No communication seemed possible with the hollow shells who used to be my buddies or UAC workers; the most I could drag out of them was simple parroting of what they had heard, before or after death.

But this one was different . . . this one was—how

could I fire up a conversation with an alien "demon" whose interest in humans seemed purely nutritional?

"Who are you?" I asked. I figured it wouldn't know English, but might at least guess from the tone what I had asked. But it threw me a curve by smiling wide and silently mouthing the same question, Who are you, seeming to mock me.

I tried again: "Human being," I said, tapping my armored chest. "Understand? Do you talk?"

Nothing. Nada. I took a calculated risk: I wasn't about to put down my weapon; but I slowly extended one hand, palm forward, in what I hoped was a universal symbol of nonaggression.

There was a response but I didn't quite know what to make of it. The grotesque humanoid slowly lifted its right hand up to its shoulder and stroked the white protrusion of bone, allowing its thumb to linger on the sharp point. The sight was very strange and it did not suggest peaceful intentions. Definitely a Mexican stand-off.

I suddenly got nervous about leaving my hand exposed. The sharp teeth suggested a healthy appetite. I became acutely aware of my environment. The bubbling, green sludge behind me burbled louder, and for the first time, I thought I heard the monster breathing.

The breathing stopped.

Pure instinct took over. Soldiers sometimes take a sharp breath just before attacking . . . some hold their breath as the floodgates open, releasing enough adrenaline to turn coward into hero.

The monster attacked so quickly I couldn't have gotten a shot off even if my Sig-Cow hadn't jammed.

Whatever the thing was, it was not stupid. It charged me, clawing for my throat with one set of nails while the other hand fended off my bayonet.

That was the only good news; if it was afraid of my blade, then surely the alien would bleed if I stuck it.

If...

I stopped pushing and suddenly pulled with the monster, instead of against it. I fell backward, and four hundred pounds of leathery skin and iron muscle dropped on top of me—and right onto my bayonet. With an inhuman scream that nearly ruptured my eardrums, the demon died, convulsing a few last times before instantly stiffening into what felt like a stone statue.

I was mighty damned glad to learn that demons *did* bleed, at least on Phobos. I was relieved for some reason that the blood was red.

I was less pleased to feel the stone weight of the monster crushing me into the floor. Jesus and Mary, did I wish I could turn off the Phobos gravity generator, just for a moment!

Years spent in Catholic school came back to me; I remembered an old penguin, Sister Beatrice, who was obsessed with the biblical injunction to avoid unclean things. *Unclean things!*

My stomach heaved; shaking the body off me with more strength than I'd ever experienced before, I almost vomited on the very spot where blood pulsed out of the alien's belly wound.

Jumping too quickly to my feet, I slipped in the slick, red goo—right next to one of the bubbling pits of green sludge. Heat poured from the boiling, green liquid waste. I didn't want that stuff any closer to my face than it was already; I had a feeling the luminescence was not harmless phosphorous, and this didn't seem the time to run any tests.

I took a moment to catch my breath. It had been difficult enough to accept the fact of people—buddies!—turned into zombies; but this *thing* at my feet meant anything could happen next. I didn't want to let my imagination run wild. Reality was bad enough at the moment.

Not since childhood had I really felt a desire to pray.

The first monsters of my life had been stern nuns refusing to answer the questions of an inquisitive mind. But now I felt a need for God, if only to have a power big enough to swear an oath on.

"I'll stop you," I promised, "whatever you are, however many you are." It helped to say the words out loud, even if one of the bastards heard me. Hell, they could hear my footsteps, anyway. "If there is a God, please let me live just long enough to stop these monsters from dropping ship to Earth!"

The small voice of reason was growing smaller all the time; scientific knowledge! Physical law! Like the song says, biggest lie you ever saw.

Survival came first; killing lots of monsters. Learning something useful about the enemy was just fine, so long as it came third. And there was the problem of how I would communicate any useful discovery; and to whom.

Ahead were the remains of yet another smashed radio. A human hand still touched the controls. The hand was not attached to an arm. The best explanation was that the body probably lay dissolving at the bottom of the pool of green slime.

Making my way out of this section seemed the most important move for all three goals, if only to get away from the hot, green liquid. The monster had thrown me off. I couldn't help imagining the creature from the black lagoon, or green lagoon, waiting at the bottom of every toxic pool.

If I could meet one two-legged nightmare, I could meet more. And I don't just mean more like the ones I'd already fought; there could be worse things, anything! What were the laws for monsters? Thoughts of horrors crawling around on the bottom of radioactive sludge pools gave way to even more unlikely scenarios. How about creatures that could exist outside the domes, in airless space? And if they didn't need to breathe, maybe those aliens didn't bleed, either.

I made myself stop. If I kept this up, I wouldn't need to be picked off by the enemy; I'd be saving them the trouble.

I heaved a sigh of relief to leave the toxic-spill room, clearing the jammed brass from my Sig-Cow receiver; it made little difference—I only had two or three rounds left and nowhere to stock up.

As if being rewarded for a bad attitude, there was another collection of inanimate dead just through the doorway, awaiting inspection. For the first time since this nightmare began I actually felt relief at the sight of human corpses. At least they were human. Not zombies, not monsters. If I'd been more careful—or paying more attention to my imagination—it might have occurred to me that one of the zombies could be pretending to be a corpse. But somewhere in the back of my brain I had already figured out that the zombies were no-brainers. They weren't about to pull tricks.

There was something very reassuring about thinking about things that weren't possible (or at least not very probable). Sure beat the hell out of imagining super-monsters that could do anything! As I surveyed the dead men, the damaged weapons, the lack of ammo, and for dessert, a smashed radio, I finally understood what must have been going through the minds of these soldiers as their lives were ripped out of them.

I understood why they hadn't done the intelligent thing and withdrawn, regrouped, reported: they'd been so overcome with revulsion, just like Yours Truly, that they'd simply charged into the mob (of zombies? monsters?) in a berserker fury, killing anything that got in the way. They stopped *thinking* and started reacting instead —and were cut down, one by one.

A heavy rumble from behind grabbed my attention. Setting a new record for spinning around, I realized I had to go back into the blasted toxic-spill room to check this out.

So I did.

The latest surprise: when I killed the monster, it evidently fell across a lift lever I hadn't noticed. I arrived at this conclusion because of the large, metal platform which finished lowering itself right in front of my nose. Beyond the lift was a brand new corridor I hadn't seen before.

To enter or not to enter? That was as good a question as any I'd had all day. Staying behind meant facing inconceivable danger and unimaginable odds. Whereas going forward meant facing unimaginable danger and inconceivable odds. Or something.

The corridor ahead had two appealing features: there were no slime pits and the light was brighter. The latter decided me. There had to have been some good reason to make the choice I made.

I backed up and took a flying leap; fear lent my feet wings . . . but not jet engines, unfortunately. I landed short and teetered on the edge of the biggest pool of green crud in creation. I windmilled my arms . . . if I hadn't stepped back, I would have fallen back.

For a second all my foot felt was icy, icy cold, as if I'd stepped into liquid nitrogen. Then the pain struck. I tried to yank my foot free, but my muscles wouldn't respond!

My leg was on fire from toe to thigh. I lurched forward, falling on my face; my foot was free of the toxin, but I shouted through clenched teeth.

Fighting a suicidal impulse to grab my still-wet foot, I wrapped my arms around my gut instead. If a zombie or monster demon had stumbled across me then, it could have snuffed me with my blessing. It was minutes before the throbbing pain in my leg subsided. I scraped my foot against the floor, rubbing off as much of the toxin as I could; but my leg swelled tight and angry red inside my ruined boot.

But at least, thank God, the pool was behind me.

The new corridor seemed antiseptic and clean after what I'd just stepped in. If there were unpleasant odors, they didn't penetrate my visor.

I followed the corridor until I came to a room on the right. Something made me hesitate about going in. It wasn't a sense of danger or anything like that. Maybe it was because the door was closed. Mostly they'd been open. I don't normally credit sixth sense stuff or mysticism; but I've learned in combat that you ignore your instincts at your peril. There are human "predator senses" that normal, civilized life pretty much breeds out of us.

I had my weapon at the ready even though two shots from now the Sig-Cow would be nothing but a fancy spear.

Kicking the door was easy; looking into the room was hard. There was one lone body on the floor, female, her back to me.

6

For a cold-gut second, I thought she might be Arlene. The impression lasted only a few seconds; then I saw it was Tij "Dude" Dardier. We'd fought together pretty closely in Kefiristan, and you get so you recognize a buddy from behind, especially females in a crack fighting unit.

Her face was unmarked, still cute, still a little girl with red hair who had a big surprise for any man who thought she was easy pickings. I wondered if a monster or zombie had gotten her. The ugly wound was in her stomach.

There was something funny about her posture; she lay as if she had a secret.

I stared for a moment, coaxing her dead body to talk to

me. Then I figured it out: Dudette was lying on top of something, shielding it from dry zombie eyes.

I touched her gently, then gingerly slipped over her corpse. Dude Dardier was lying on top of the pump-action riot gun I'd been wishing for earlier—her death-day present for Yours Truly.

I felt like a ghoul, but feelings were a luxury. With a shotgun in my arsenal, my survival rating took a big leap up the charts.

I checked the bore and found no obstructions. There were plenty of shells in the bandoleer around her body. I thanked Dudette for being a Marine to the end ... semper fi, Mac.

Back in the corridor, I found remains of a map on the wall. The Bad Guys evidently followed a plan, proven by destroyed radio gear and vandalized wall maps. But this time there was just enough left of the map to figure out the basic direction toward the lift, which I prayed was still working. Being properly armed did wonders for my psychology; I decided maybe I would do well to generate a tactical plan.

There is no north or south on Phobos, but I oriented myself along the facility's major axis. Getting to the nuclear plant was the next logical move; it had the largest concentration of equipment ... and perhaps even an untrained engineer like me could jerry-rig some gear into a working radio.

I found the lift without further molestation; naturally, it was broken, shot to hell—the hydraulics leaked away from numerous gunshot holes. But the manual escape hatch still worked. Placing myself back into a narrow, confined space was about as appealing as it sounded, and my damned imagination started bugging me again at precisely the moment duty called. My imagination was not very patriotic; it needed six weeks of boot camp.

There was a dim light in the shaft, very, very dim. Every square foot of the base was supposed to be constantly lit, bright as day, except for the barracks.

Someone in charge must have been mugged by a flashlight when he was a kid and wanted nothing more to do with them. Maybe I shouldn't have complained; light was light.

As I climbed down the long shaft, it occurred to me to think about something cheerful, a silver lining that must exist somewhere in these storm clouds. There had to be something.

And there was. I hadn't found Arlene's body yet . . . and so long as I didn't know what had happened to her, there was hope.

I figured the nuclear plant must be at least six stories down. Just keep climbing, that was all I could do. Climb. Hope. Watch out for demons. Real simple. I preferred thinking about Arlene.

I remembered the day she showed up from Parris Island and joined the real Corps, the fighting Corps. I looked up from monkeying with the sticky belt-advance on a .60 caliber auto-stabilized, and I saw a brutal babe in cammies, spats, webbing, and sporting a newly shaved high-and-tight. Catching her eye told me all I had to know. She knew what she was doing, all right. The Corps is protective of its haircut, flat on the top and shaved on the sides. We're talking a sign of distinction, a challenge thrown at every other service. God help the Navy, Army, or Space Force puke who shows up on one of our bases in a high-and-tight! What happens afterward is why God made Captain's Mast.

But Arlene was no innocent. She wore her cut high and proud, and wore a single, red, private's stripe.

Lieutenant Weems (pre-punch) took one look at Arlene Sanders, a long, hard look, and curled his lip. He watched her hand her packet to PFC Dodd, who stared at her like she had two heads. So far as I know, that was the first time they ever met, they who were destined for . . . well, not love, exactly; extreme lustlike. (After about a year of ignoring him with all her might, then another six months of despising him, she shamefacedly confessed to me that she'd spent the night in his flat.)

All in all, not the best-foot-forward on this first day for the first woman in Fox Company.

Of course, the opinion of Lieutenant Weems was already a debased currency by this time. But the opinion of the other men mattered. And no one could express that company opinion with more eloquence than Gunnery Sergeant Goforth, the company's "grand old man." Hell, he was in his late thirties, an eighteen-year Marine, the last ten in Light Drop.

Goforth looked like Aldo Ray in those old John Wayne movies. He was heavyset, muscular but not fat; he shaved his head but would probably be bald anyway. Goforth was a Franks tank with legs, a few freckles mixed in along with the Rolled Homogenous Armor.

The gunny made a big deal of sauntering over to Arlene and let loose with his thick, Georgian drawl: "Hooo-eeee! Where'ud the *lay-dee* get thuh purty *'do?'*"

She looked him in the eye. That was all. Not a bad answer, really, but I thought that under the circumstances a few words of reason might be in order.

I volunteered myself for the task. Partly because I liked a woman with guts; partly because I respected the men in the Corps and felt their position could be expressed in a more thoughtful manner than Gunny Goforth was likely to manage. But mainly I spoke up because at some deep level I hate all rules, symbols, rituals, fighting words, gang colors, routines, decorations, medals, trophies, badges . . . and anything else that suggests one human being is to be taken more seriously than another in a given situation simply on the basis of plumage. Besides, I was making no headway with the damned .60 cal.

I was sitting on the mess hall table and felt very much above it all as I said, "Private, a high-and-tight is not a fashion statement. You gotta earn it."

That seemed a nice ice breaker. She must have agreed because she spoke to me, not Goforth. "I'm as much a

Marine as the next man," she said, glancing at me before returning her steady attention back to the gunny.

The first retort that crossed my mind was to take a big bite of the red apple that happened to be in my hand. The longer it took to chew and swallow the piece of apple, the more profound would be my clever rejoinder, it seemed to me.

So I did. And Goforth took a step closer to Arlene, deliberately breaking her space. Arlene stood her ground, not budging an inch.

In between bites of the apple, I thought I would essay another arbitration. "You know," I essayed, "a high-and-tight is not mil-spec for ladies."

"It's not regulation for men, either," she shot back. There was no arguing with that, but there was plenty of apple left to crunch.

Gunny Goforth didn't have an apple. "Any Muh-reen who wears thet 'do," he said, "sure as hell *is* gonna earn it, missy." I thought the "missy" was a bit much.

Arlene Sanders leaned forward into his space, close enough to either kiss him or bite off his round knob of a nose. Instead, she said two words: "You're on."

Goforth was just as stubborn. He was native to Georgia but might as well have been from Missouri when it came to matters of proof. "Every Muh-reen is a rifleman fust," he said. "If'n you want to spoht thet thang, missy, then you had best pick up yer cute lil' buns and follow me tuh the rifle range."

She gave him a curt nod. Challenge accepted. They started to leave, then Goforth noticed my juicy, red apple, which had tasted much better than the discussion, far as I was concerned.

"Hey, Fly," he said, "howzabout grabbin' thet sack o' apples?"

As I hoisted the apples and made tracks, I could honestly say that I didn't have a clue what old Goforth was up to.

The range was a short walk. Every man who had been

present for the exchange of words followed along. No one wanted to miss entertainment of this high a caliber, no pun intended.

Goforth walked on over to Arlene and said, "Private, you need a whole helpin' o' guts to wear thet 'do. Takes more'n jes' a steady *rifle* hand, thet it do!" At least he didn't call her "missy" this time.

Holding up his hand, palm toward me, he shouted, "Fly, toss me one of those apples. Ya'll watch a history lesson." Now that I finally had the idea, I was none too happy, but Arlene just smiled—a little, thin smile. I think she guessed what the gun' was scheming.

I slapped the apple into the gunnery sergeant's paw. He casually tossed and caught it a few times, then asked Arlene: "Yuh lak historee, lil' lady?" He was laying the accent on so thick I could barely understand him.

"Let me guess," she said with a thick grin. "You like William Tell."

Goforth looked crestfallen that she had outguessed him, stealing some wind from his sails. But if verbal teasing wouldn't do the job, he was more than ready to push this thing on to the real thing. I could see it in his face; there was no humor left.

When I had first joined Fox Company, Goforth went out of his way to make me feel welcome. About the worst he did was to tag me with the nickname Fly. He didn't bag on me the way he was doing to Arlene. He gestured to Dodd to bring over the artillery, and Dodd brought a .30-99 bolt-action sniper rifle, top of the line. Goforth flashed Arlene a big, soapy grin; but she held her ground.

Made me wonder, not just about the gun', but the other guys, who leered and chuckled unpleasantly. Plenty of men are solid guys, decent fathers and husbands, but revert to Wolfman when confronted by physical prowess in a woman.

As Goforth lived up to his name and went forward with the William Tell bit, I was getting panicky . . . but I kept it to myself. She was going to play this one out to the bitter end. I figured that from the way she planted her feet, put her arms behind her and said, "Go for it!"

Abruptly, everybody stopped laughing. Gunny Goforth noticed but wasn't about to back down with eight, I'm sure it was, eight guys watching. With an almost delicate concern, he carefully placed the apple on her head. Then he took the .30-99 and slowly backed away from her. He aimed just as carefully and said, in a voice that had lost all the sarcasm, "Last chance, honey." I thought "honey" sounded better than "missy."

Arlene didn't move, but I could see that she was trembling ever so slightly beneath her bravado. I sure as hell didn't blame her. Goforth took a deep breath and said, "All right, darlin' . . . I suggest in the strongest terms thet you don't flinch none."

I was the one who jumped when he squeezed off a shot—and damned if the apple didn't split perfectly down the middle, each half falling on either side of her head! Everybody let out his breath, and a ragged cheer erupted.

"Way to go, Gunny!" said one man.

"Fox Company *ichiban!*" said another.

We'd forgotten one item. We'd forgotten that Arlene had put her skull on the line. The drama wasn't over until she said it was.

As Goforth basked in his moment of glory, the boys all praising him, Arlene walked toward him. Her hands were behind her back and she was smiling sweetly.

I saw what she was carrying before the gun' did. She held an apple up until he saw it; then she tossed it to him.

Silence again; nobody moved. Then just as smoothly as you please, Arlene Sanders picked up the .30-99 from the table, staring expectantly at Goforth and cocking one of her eyebrows.

I never doubted what Goforth would do. His basic sense of fair play could be counted on; and he had guts. He wasn't about to lose his men's respect. Not Goforth!

So, in the words of the old-time baseball player, it was déjà vu all over again.

He put the apple on his head, his icy eyes boring into Arlene's. She watched him just as intently; no lovers were ever more focused on one another.

She cocked and raised the rifle, which wasn't even fitted with a scope, just iron sights. A few of the men backed farther away from the cone of fire surrounding the gunnery sergeant. That pissed me off, so I deliberately took a few steps closer to the duel. Something about this girl inspired confidence that she was no more likely to blow away a spectator than the gunnery sergeant.

Goforth had his own concerns: "If you have to miss," he said so softly that it didn't even sound like him, "please tuh make it high?" He smiled with an effort. The request seemed reasonable enough.

Arlene said nothing. She lifted the rifle nice and slow. She didn't make us wait; she pounded out a shot, and the apple was blown off Goforth's head. Corporal Stout ran over and picked it up. It was still mostly in one piece, but there was a gratifying furrow a little high off the center.

After a long moment, during which no one said a word, Goforth walked up to Arlene Sanders. Putting hands on his hips, he made a big show of inspecting her high-and-tight, while we all held our breath.

Goforth bent down, examined her right side, left side, back, front, then looked her evenly in the eye, winked and nodded. "It's *you*, Private," he said. And I was pretty damned sure he wouldn't be calling her "missy" again. She didn't *miss*, you see.

Some of the boys took to calling her Will, though.

7

The odds against Arlene's survival in this hellish maelstrom were astronomical; but then, so they were against mine. Hope that she might have made it kept me going; fury at the thought of her death spurred me to action. Maybe just when I was running out of steam, the need for revenge would inspire Yours Truly.

As if to test my newfound resolve, Phobos threw some more at me. Glancing down, I saw that the access shaft did not descend the full six stories required to reach the nuclear plant. The ladder ended in a few ragged shreds of metal; an explosion had cut off the rest of that route.

Of course, I could always get to the nuclear plant level really fast, so long as I didn't mind the sudden stop at the end.

"Damn, I knew this was too good to be true," I said out loud. Just before running out of ladder, I saw a thick, metal hatchway leading to the next level down.

It looked solid, heavy; a pressure lock held it shut; I would have to spin the wheel to open the door, a happy trick when the ladder ended a couple of rungs above the hatch.

For a moment I was stymied. I could just barely reach the wheel by hanging one-handed from the last rung; but I had no leverage . . . I couldn't turn it to save my life. I took a deep breath, closed my eyes, and thought for several seconds.

Jesus—what am I, stupid all of a sudden? I rotated around the ladder, lowered myself until my lower legs poked through the last hole, then slowly let my body down until I dangled upside down from my knees. Now I had the leverage; all it took was muscle.

I cranked the wheel clockwise, loosening it until it spun freely. I wrestled open the door—and now for the hard part.

Holding tight to the wheel of the now-open door, I straightened my legs, dropping heavily as the wheel spun. I clung to it grimly, swinging back and forth until I finally stopped swinging.

I edged around the door, caught the corresponding wheel on the inside and swung myself up and into the shaft. I lost nothing but any desire I might have had to take my name to heart and become a Human Fly as a career path.

The access shaft led me into a tunnel where the light was crappy again, flickering on and off like some sicko nightclub. It was tall enough to stand, and I did.

After five meters I decided this was the weirdest stretch of architecture yet. The light was lousy, but it was good enough to make out the walls—plain and gray with an oddly rough-hewn surface, as if hacked out of the rock with a magic ax.

Large, rectangular designs everywhere gave the feeling of a colossal cemetery. More than anything else, the strong impression of something truly ancient and evil permeated the narrow corridor. Alien, and yet familiar somehow. It was as if I'd been cast inside the oldest labyrinth in the universe and would spend the rest of my life trying to find my way through the maze.

Damn imagination acting up again . . . memory was better; at least it gave me something to hold on to. A link to the past, a better past.

Then I saw old Gunnery Sergeant Goforth, walking down the corridor in my direction. The failing light made it difficult to make out skin tones; but the smooth, purposeful way he walked made me think he couldn't be a zombie.

It was Gunny Goforth—and he was alive!

"Gunny!" I shouted, ecstatic to have finally found another live one in this nightmare.

He didn't answer; my God, that should have told me something.

He raised his old .30-99 and aimed it right at my chest. I threw myself to the floor just as the bullet seared over my head.

"Damn you to hell!" I shouted, outraged that the universe had decided to foist a new, improved zombie on me. Too late; I'm sure he already was—and me with him.

This new horror seemed even more unfair than that crazy brown monster with the spikes. I'd settled into a nice, predictable pattern about what to do with zombies. No fair changing the rules now!

Hey, Gunny, you're still a pal.

He marched straight for me, no deviations, no ducking, no turning sideways to make a more difficult target. An obliging guy in his way. Of course, he was working the bolt on his sniper rifle, trying to blow my head from Phobos back to Earth.

I didn't just lie on the floor, waiting for that unacceptable outcome. I had plans of my own.

In life, Gunny Goforth could shoot—hell, could shoot the apple off a young Marine's head. In death, he shot better than all the other zombies. And he *blinked.*

I rolled back and forth, waiting until he was ten meters away; then I shouldered the riot gun and squeezed.

It was the biggest mess I'd made on this godforsaken rock of a moon so far. The splatter was sort of an artistic statement. But I must have gotten something in my eye. I kept blinking, but it wouldn't go away.

Somebody was laughing, sort of a crazy, whacked-out cackle. "Shut up!" I screamed at the jokester, wiping my cheeks. The laughter stopped, and only then did I realize the mirth was courtesy of a poor jarhead named Fly.

This was no good. I had to get a handle on the situation. Running multiplication tables in my head helped me chill while I scavenged Goforth's pack for ammo. My breathing slowed to something sane, and my heartbeat took a licking but kept on ticking.

In fact, I was so calm I barely blinked when a whirring, metallic skull sailed past my head.

This time I was sure my imagination was off on a wild toot. I'd never done hallucinogens as a kid, and it just wasn't fair for my imagination to suggest a giant, white skull had gone flying past (on its way to the demonic head shop, no doubt). So I made a deal with my imagination: if it didn't throw any more Halloween balloons at me, I'd give it a break when it wanted to go traipsing down memory lane. I can be fair.

I ran like a madman up the corridor, jogging a couple of times. Whatever it was, I'd lost it for now.

Emerging into a big open room made me feel more claustrophobic. That might sound fairly nutty but you'd have to see this place for yourself. I wasn't bothered by the incredibly high, arched ceiling, supported by grotesque pillars that would be more at home in some ancient palace in India. No, what bothered me was that this huge room was full of barrels of that noxious, green liquid I thought I'd left behind—and good riddance.

The empty, cavernous room was a perfect place for a congregation of Halloween goblins and all species of zombie, fast and slow, dull and the cognitive elite.

No sooner had this unpleasant thought crossed my cranium than the floodgates opened and *they* started pouring into the room from all directions.

I shrank back into the shadows, trying to look dead and mindless; it worked for a few moments . . . none of the zombies seemed to notice me.

There really wasn't time for a sanity check, but I ran a quick one anyway. I'd read about a mental condition or a philosophy (I forget which) called solipsism: you think of something, and it happens. The ultimate case is when you think you're all that exists, and the whole universe is your dream. Man, I was ready to buy into that, if only I could dream away these monsters as quickly as I seemed to be filling up this room with them!

Well . . . what can I lose? I closed my eyes and concentrated real hard, wishing away the bogeymen.

While I was thus occupied, I was blown off my feet by an explosion and searing heat right over my head. Opening my eyes to excruciating pain, I discovered I wasn't alone on the floor: whatever had blown me down got the nearest few zombies as well.

I decided that solipsism was a load of crap.

And when I looked up, my old friend was back, the crusty, brown monster with ivory-white spikes . . . and he'd brought his buddies. They watched me stagger to my feet, *and they laughed.*

Then one of them wound up and threw something, some sort of mucus ball that burst into bloodred flames as it left the creature's hand. I dived across a burned zombie, and the flaming phlegm spun me buttocks over boots.

I looked for a weapon, a glint of metal, a tube, something! But no, these demons were actually producing the fire with their bare hands . . . and their aim was deadly.

The monsters hissed, pointing directly at Yours Truly; then the zombies noticed me for the first time and began shooting. They weren't too particular about innocent zombies getting in the way, either—and whenever one zombie would shoot another, or a demon would pelt a bunch with a flaming mucus ball, the monster victims would turn on their monster allies, completely forgetting about me. While I ran screaming from one side of the room to the other, I filed that little datum somewhere in the back of my brain for future use.

Now the room was really filling up with at least a dozen zombies and three leathery demons . . . and again I dived to the side as a whirring, screaming hunk of steel buzzed my helmet. This time there was no mistake: it was a goddamned *flying skull* with flaming rocket exhaust spewing out the back. It turned and banked, trying to mow me down and chew me up with razor-sharp, steel teeth, like one of those wind-up "chattering skulls" gone mad.

But the fireballs were the main problem; the brown demons were a lot tougher than the zombies. Suddenly, I was grateful for the pillars; they provided cover, at least. Making a mad dash for the nearest, I fired off the shotgun at the remaining zombies.

Catching my breath, I risked running to the next pillar. This time a fireball almost fried me. There was just no way I could get to the demons from here without being toasted . . . and the shotgun range was too short to pop them where I crouched.

While I dithered, I heard a whirring behind me, then a harsh, iron screech. Sure enough, the flying skull had sailed around the pillars and spotted me again.

I can take care of you at least, you F/X reject! I whipped the riot gun around and fired from the hip, not even taking time to aim.

It was the best mistake of my life.

The little bugger skittered out of the way; I tried to track as I fired, and I popped one of the toxic barrels instead.

It exploded with a terrific concussion, kicking me in the body armor like a mule and tearing off a chuck of my kevlar vest. The skull vanished in a spray of metal gears and exploding JP-5.

Almost immediately, my bruised eardrums were assaulted by another explosion, then another and a fourth. Five or six more barrels touched off in rapid succession. All I could think was thank God I was on the other side of the pillar.

An acrid cloud of blue smoke swirled around the walls and floor . . . residue from the explosive oxidation of the toxic goo. Gasping, I peeked around the pillar at a scene of astonishing carnage.

Zombies and demons alike had been torn to shreds

and strips of gray flesh, their parts mingling in a hellish mulligatawny. The stench of a thousand sour lemons permeated the room, even driving out the horrible, burning smell of the toxic fumes. *Jesus,* I thought, *I hope the cameras got the shot.*

I climbed shakily to my feet and padded toward the door, chastened by the awesome destructive power in those forty-gallon drums. At the edge of the room I found the only other survivor.

The demon crawled along the ground with its hands, one leg blown entirely off and the other twisted into a crazy angle. It leaked yellow pus, globules that burst into flame as soon as they dripped off the monster's body.

I leveled my shotgun at its head. "Die, you dumb animal," I said with a smile.

"Aaanimaaal," repeated the demon, "not . . ."

I paused, startled. I didn't know they could talk. "You're right," I prodded, "at least animals kill you clean or leave you alone."

It twisted its head all the way around to stare up at me while lying belly down on the floor. My stomach turned at the sight. *"You*—are aanimaals when we fix planet."

I curled my lip, but my heart leaped. Which planet was that? Mars? Or did the aliens' plan include Earth? "We'll mow you down as fast as you bubble up out of the sewers, you piece of filth."

The alien monster laughed, opening its mouth wide enough to swallow a man's head. "Weee throw rocks . . . big rocks."

The image was ludicrous; but I got a premonitory shudder. Somehow, I guessed the emphasis was on the word "big."

8

Despite my better judgment, I was too intrigued for the moment by the sound of pure evil pleading its case. "Why haven't the others spoken to me? Can you all talk?"

It opened its mouth wide, exposing gums full of squirming cilia and teeth that rolled and shifted position. "Not . . . all ssssame, like you-mans not sssame."

The alien crawled on a bit farther. I don't think it was trying to escape; it knew that was impossible. I began to worry that it was leading me toward something. Ahead of me was a greenish stone wall carved in bas relief with a hideous, demonic face. Somehow, I doubted that was an original furnishing in the Phobos base of the Union Aerospace Corporation.

"How aren't we the same?" I prodded. I felt in my gut that I was on the verge of something important.

"Sssome . . . fear," it gasped. Its face showed no sign of distress, but I knew from the shudder that wracked its body that it was very near death. "Othersss sssstrong . . . you ssstrong."

Good Lord—was this alien *thing* admitting a grudging respect for Fly Taggart?

"Few ssstrong, like you ssstrong . . . mosst good for ssslavesss. You-man ssslavesss."

A thought buried deep behind my ears thrust itself forward. I wasn't too fatigued to pick up that slip of the tongue; even a tongue as thick and brutish as this one.

Few strong—*others* strong . . . there must be other humans who were still themselves and still breathing!

When hell came to Phobos, I had to keep hope locked up in a small space without a zip code.

I kept a poker face; the monster might be smart enough to spot my eagerness at the possibility that one of the living might be Arlene.

Any human survivor would change the Phobos situation dramatically: food and water were minor problems, but I could only operate so long without sleep. With no one to stand guard, giving in to exhaustion was suicide. But I couldn't keep going forever; and if I couldn't rest, all the ammo in the solar system would not save me.

"I'm touched by your concern for my survival," I said.

"Deal," he unexpectedly offered, ignoring the sarcasm. "You . . . live; you work; you help."

All I had to do was work with the alien invaders and help them conquer the human race, and they might graciously allow me to live as a slave. *Jesus, how tempting,* I thought.

I decided that I liked the ones who grunt better. What did these creeps want from me? "I've got a great idea. Why don't you tell me what the hell you're after?"

The thing laughed. The sound grated on my nerves like a ripped bagpipe. "Hell . . . we after," it declared. "Ssssurrender . . . help; you live, you-man."

"As a zombie?"

"You live, not deadwalk; you sssee othersss."

"What others? Who else survived? Did a girl survive?" Great, Fly; nice and subtle. Does it even know what a girl is? Does it care?

"You help . . . you sssee othersss."

I stared down at the loathsome thing. I knew I had gotten all the intel from it that I could. "Let me answer," I said at last, "louder than mere words can do. Tell me if this is tough enough."

Without another thought, I pointed the shotgun at the monster's upper chest and pumped a round at point-blank range. The alien jerked—then amazingly, stared up at me, still alive by a thread.

The alien grimaced, facial muscles finally growing rigid. Then for a moment it relaxed. "We could eat anybody onccce," it declared. Then it stopped moving; even the cilia in its mouth stood up straight and froze. The demon was dead.

After catching my breath, I started getting angry. It was one thing to fight a human enemy, but battling malignant *demons*? Every time I killed one of these humanoid things, I felt like doing a hundred more. That might be the only good to come of this latest encounter. Give no quarter and kill, kill, kill. Kind of reassuring to learn that all that Marine training hadn't been a waste of time.

Of course, the rational portion of my brain still made plans. I wanted to climb down and out of this hangar and reach my next objective, the nuclear plant. The plant was the most dangerous item to fall into enemy hands. Better it should fall into my hands.

Making one last circuit of the zombie bodies, I scavenged for blessed ammunition. I'd have killed for a decent backpack; come to think of it, that's probably how I would have to get one. I was running out of pockets for the ammo.

So, how to get out of the hangar? My playmates found their way in; all I had to do was reverse the process. First thing was to hug the wall and make a nice, slow circuit of the big, ugly room.

The damned monsters bothered me a lot less than the architecture changing on me. I'd never been in Phobos Base before, but I'd talked to guys down on Mars who knew these installations; there was no way this place hadn't undergone a change as bug-nut crazy as the demonic characters themselves.

And what made that more upsetting than the monsters was the idea that the floor you walked on, the wall you brushed against, the damn *place* could turn on you and become something else. Like a cartoon world that suddenly turns everything into rubber . . . except you.

If this kept up, Yours Truly was going to place his imagination on short rations.

I leaned against the wall, and suddenly it was like those old Abbott and Costello movies back Earthside: the wall had a hidden door. I even tripped going through the blasted thing. In my mind a laugh track played and played and played.

I fell into a new corridor, which I followed to a rising wall at the south end of the hall. There was another of those crazy platforms near at hand. Instinct told me to give it a wide berth, and who am I to argue with my most cherished faculty? When I reached the wall, I found another switch, which I flipped.

The wall *shoooooshed* up, revealing a down staircase; it was an encouraging sign—the nuke plant was down another level or two, I vaguely remembered. Cautiously, I started down the stairs, grateful for steady light. My reward was the biggest slime pool yet, waiting at the bottom. If only I'd remembered to bring swimming trunks, I could have gone in for a dip. Best toxic sludge in the whole solar system right here—come one, come all.

Skirting the pool, pressed against the wall, I finally ran out of hangar. Along the narrow corridor past the toxin, I found the shredded body of another one of those brown-leather, spiky demons. If it were a talker, someone had already silenced it forever with seven or eight rounds from a Sig-Cow. Score another for the Corps.

The bug lay against a sliding door that belonged on a dumbwaiter. I yanked it open, happy to take out my frustrations on something that didn't shoot, claw, or flame me back.

Sure enough, it was a lift, barely big enough for a big guy to squeeze into. I spotted a funny mark on the wall, as if someone had started to draw a map using a bright, red paint stick—we use them to blaze trails in forests or urban environments. Whoever it was had been interrupted in mid-map. I studied it for a bit, then shrugged; whatever he was trying to tell me got lost in the translation.

I scrunched inside the tiny lift, wondering which of the two buttons would take me down to the plant. Staring at the labels, I decided to push the one marked "Nuclear Plant." And they say you don't get an education in the service!

With a jerk, the tiny lift sank, swerving and rattling all the way, as much as screaming out *Here I come!* to the whole world. Well, to the whole Phobos pressure zone, I guess.

I didn't have to guess whether this important part of the base had fallen into enemy hands. The minute I stepped off the platform, I was in the soup up to my neck. This particular recipe called for more zombies than I thought could be crammed into such a small space. Come to think of it, the space wasn't all that small. I guess when it's wall-to-wall corpse-sickles, it's easy to lose track of the finer points of design.

For the first time in my life I felt what it was like to be claustrophobic from being surrounded by walls of human flesh—well, formerly human flesh. I couldn't understand why I wasn't dead meat.

Two things worked in my favor: first, so many zombies were sardine-canned in the room, they could hardly move, and most of them didn't even know I was there. Second, it had become clear to me by now that the only use for brains in a zombie was for gray and white color contrast when you blasted their heads like rotten fruit. Even Gunny Used-to-Be-Goforth had been operating on motor reflexes, and he was the most dangerous one yet.

There was plenty of time to think about such things because there was really nowhere for me to go, and I was waiting for one of them to notice me. Then one of those wonderful moments of dumb luck added the final spice to the soup. Another contingent of zombies trooped into storage, and one of the shambling creeps elbowed aside another, simply trying to find somewhere to stand. In the tiny, new space created, I noticed an undamaged map on the wall!

By this time, I'd arrived at the conclusion that zombies were not responsible for the destroyed radio equipment, the vandalized maps, the deliberately wasted weapons. The advantage of attending my first zombie convention was that there apparently wasn't room for the demon monsters to get in here and do their damage; the space was being used for zombie storage.

Trying to look dead on my feet—not difficult—I shambled a few meters to where I could get a better view of the map—it was a full schematic of the entire station seen from the side. Unfortunately, it didn't include overhead views for each level; but at least I could see how far down the station went. My God, it even had a *You Are Here* arrow!

I was indeed at the nuclear plant level; above me was the hangar, while still below were the Toxin Refinery— didn't that sound appetizing—Command & Control, the labs, Central Processing, and MIS. Jesus . . . only six more levels to clear; I was afraid it would be thirty!

Funny how what I was seeing triggered memories of malls and shoppers. Best not to dwell on that . . .

Somewhere in the back of my head a shrill voice screamed for me to get the hell out of that room. I figured this situation was too lucky to last.

Without false modesty, I can say I was proven a prophet. In that sea of pale, dead faces, two dry as dust eyes came to rest on Yours Truly. Hoping the unfocused eyes would continue their survey of the room, I didn't move a muscle . . . which was normally what the zombies did when they had no orders and had not spotted a human: they stood and did nothing.

Except, that is, for the one who wouldn't stop staring at me. I wasn't about to make the first move. I'd been through a lot lately but I could still count.

It seemed like this could go on forever; but then, out of

nowhere, a *zombie-child* separated itself from the rest of the throng and stumbled toward me.

Jesus! For a second I didn't recognize that she was as dead as the rest. Seeing plenty of zombies recruited from soldiers made it easy to forget the UAC civilians that had been on this base. But somehow I'd never dreamed there would be *children* here.

The kid headed straight for me, mouth opening and closing but no sounds coming out. Then those soft, wet, cold hands were rubbing on my arm . . . and I couldn't stifle my reflexes. I put my arm around her to comfort her.

All hell broke loose.

Staring-boy opened his mouth, too; but instead of words, he belched an inarticulate roar. But he was so hemmed in by his fellows, he couldn't raise the pistol in his right hand. Impatient guy that I am, I acted: I tilted up my shotgun and squeezed the trigger.

A dead-center blast helped a lot. I pumped the slide, then pounded home another shot to clear a path.

Then I was running as fast and hard as I could to the left. In close quarters like this there was no opportunity to use the rifle. My best bet was to find elbow room where I could at least make a stand but that wouldn't put me in a cul de sac. The sounds pounding in my ears told me that they were following me, but I wasn't about to turn around and take a head count.

I ducked into an open doorway, then turned like Custer at bay. Three of the creatures shambled past, not even noticing me—the fourth was not so obligingly stupid. It pushed through the doorway, and I raised the shotgun.

Just before I turned that face into an explosion of red, something about it reminded me of my grandfather. I wish that hadn't happened. I was doing all right until then.

The trouble was that every time I made careful calculations about what I could do in terms of stamina, willpower, and even strategy, the old emotions got completely away from me. I'd thought I was a better Marine than this. Then again, they'd never trained us for a nonstop horror show.

I needed a break. I needed to lie down for five minutes because my lower back was killing me and there was a muscle spasm in my right shoulder blade. A nice cold drink of water would have gone a long way toward cooling the fire in my brain. But seeing old Granddad's face on the umpteenth zombie was the latest straw breaking the latest camel's back.

I couldn't shoot. I just couldn't! I grabbed it by its coveralls and shoved it backward with superhuman, adrenaline strength.

It bowled over some of its buddies; then one in the back rank raised a lever-action rifle and tried to blow my fool head off.

I slapped the deck face first, and the bullet scorched the air, blowing apart one of the zombies that had missed the turnoff a few seconds back, splattering the other two with what passes for zombie brains.

The creatures went mad. That shot must have kicked their IFF off-line, because they opened up on their zombie brethren, who cheerfully returned fire. In seconds, every zombie was shooting wildly at anything that moved!

I stayed very, very still, frozen on the ground, trying as hard as I could to look like a "dead" zombie.

9

When the ammo finally ran dry, the jerking bodies above me started tearing each other limb from limb, as if auditioning for modern ballet. I seized the opportunity to roll out from under the forest of legs; the rifle was strapped to my back, but in the chaos of the moment, I left the shotgun behind.

I ran, and this time I wasn't followed. After thirty heart-pounding seconds, I was alone with me, myself, and I. And somewhere along the route, I had stooped and grabbed a pack, one of Fox Company's—but I had no memory of having done so!

I was utterly lost. I silently cursed at being reduced to the Sig-Cow and wandered more or less aimlessly . . . terrified of shadows, where half an hour ago I stalked with confidence. With just a pistol and a semi-auto rifle, I avoided confrontation wherever I could.

With no map, I wasn't sure what part of the plant I had reached; then I pushed through another of those trick doors—I would have missed it had I not been sliding along the walls like a mouse—and found the computer room. The lights were blinking on and off, just what I needed for a headache after everything else. When the light was on, it had a sickly blue-green color that didn't do my empty stomach any good.

So far as I could tell, I was alone here, at least in this section. I wasn't happy about the way the corridor went up a little ways and disappeared around a bend. I decided then and there if I ever try to be an architect, all my buildings would borrow from my old high school gymnasium—a big, empty space where you can't possible hide anything. May not be much in the way of privacy, but there are advantages all right.

Placing my back firmly against a wall, I took inventory of the contents of my new pack. First thing that jumped out at me was ammo for the missing shotgun. I was going to have to replace that as soon as possible. Dude Dardier would have wanted it that way. I had some 10mm rounds for the Sig-Cow that also fit the pistol, a bit of water or other liquid, chewing gum . . . and a small, little metal object that appeared to be a shiny flashlight battery. I had no idea what the last was; the UAC logo was printed on the side, not the globe and eagle of the Corps emblem.

First order of business was checking the liquid. I was worried it might be vodka or gin or rubbing alcohol or something other than what I wanted it most to be. But at long last I was in for a bit of good luck: it was water. While I took a first grateful sip, repressing the desire to finish it off with one gulp, I picked up the batterylike object with my other hand. Then I realized what it was. I'd heard about, but never seen, a rocket this small.

Correction: I had seen one in a UAC weapons demo video when they were trying to sell it to the Pentagon. (We didn't buy it—I wish we had!) Yeah, these were special little babies, all right. But no one from Fox Company had been carrying any rocket launchers. This kind of ordnance was for desert fighting. Where had this rocket come from?

I laughed out loud. Not smart in this situation, but it was becoming a bad habit. If evil demons could be lurking anywhere, and the walls and floors were metamorphosing into Halloween decorations, why couldn't there be a state-of-the-art tac rocket in a forgotten backpack? Maybe I'd find a tomahawk next.

At least I'd stopped laughing. The rational part of my brain was trying to figure out where I might find a rocket launcher. Made sense. I was trying real hard to listen to the little voice that made sense. Only trouble was that a much louder voice was roaring from somewhere lower in the brain. It wanted me to find the rocket launcher, too, but for a less defensible reason.

I guess I'd been more upset by the roomful of zombies than I'd realized—or maybe I'd been this freaked-out all along, and was only now realizing it. My God, did I really want to find that missing launcher just so I could eat a rocket?

Suicide isn't in my nature. I'm an extrovert type, more likely to frag someone, say a certain butthead lieutenant, than snuff Yours Truly. That's sort of a job requirement for the Marines. The battlefield doesn't cure depression.

But the tac-sit here on Phobos was a lot worse than a battlefield. Having to go through the same crap over and over is just part of life. I know guys who have been married.

But what had happened on Phobos was so far beyond normal repetition that it turned me totally cold and numb. If I could just find one living person! That thing had said . . . had *implied* that someone still lived. Jesus, if there's such a thing as the soul, then mine had been beaten black and blue.

Maybe I wasn't being completely honest with myself. I could have killed myself with the rifle. There are other ways, too, God bless our training. Waiting for the launcher could have been just a good excuse for postponing the inevitable. Maybe. Or maybe if I found the launcher, I really would put the tube in my mouth and, as they say, "fire and forget."

Fortunately, I never had to make that decision. I found something else instead.

I stood in a long, steel corridor that curved off to the right; the only light came from a bluish, fluorescent tube that curved along the left wall and a sporadic white overhead spot. I crept as near as possible to one of those white-light areas . . . somehow I felt better surrounded by more natural colors, even though it made me more of a target.

Then I glanced to my left and saw it.

I didn't trust my eyes at first. They hadn't been doing much to encourage trust lately. But if what I was seeing was real, then I wouldn't be fooling around with any more self-destructive fantasies.

Directly in front of my nose, scrawled with the same red paint stick that had started drawing a map in the dumbwaiter, were two capital letters: A.S. An arrow was drawn by the same dye marker, pointing to the right at a downward angle.

I stared at the mark, memory working furiously. Two years back I had gone to see the old James Mason movie, *Journey to the Center of the Earth.* I didn't know who Jules Verne was—but Arlene had insisted. She loved sci-fi of any type.

We made a big event out of it. We had just come off a three-month stint in Peru, torching coca-leaf fields so they'd never be processed into cocaine, and we were ready for an old-movie orgy. We didn't usually eat junk, but for this special occasion, we gorged on the unhealthiest popcorn we could buy, even including black market liquid grease-butter. I can honestly say that I have never enjoyed a trip to the movies so much.

In the movie, Arne Saknussem, world's greatest adventurer, was the first to explore the secrets of Earth's inner world; he leaves his initials marked in candle soot at different levels, so anyone coming afterward can follow his route. The arrows point out the path he took when the caverns branched off.

I stared at the mark. A.S.—Arne Saknussen; A.S. . . . *Arlene Sanders.*

My gut dropped to my boots. *Arlene!* Arlene was alive? It had to be . . . what other explanation was there? She was alive . . . and she was doing just what I was doing: going deeper into the station, hoping to find a radio or another living human, or maybe her old pal, Fly. She was drilling deeper into this hell, hoping to find a way out!

There was no doubt in my mind: A.S. meant my bud was still alive . . . or at least, she'd been alive *up to that point,* alive and still herself. She must have survived the firefight that killed her platoon.

All thoughts of self-destruction were wiped away in an instant. I felt supercharged. For the first time since stepping foot on this damned space rock, I was happy! I moved forward, military discipline reasserting itself, putting some breaks on the warrior who would still be needed for the killing time.

Following the arrow led directly to an exit to a patio. I took it. As always when entering a new locale, I braced for a potential zombie attack or another encounter with the monsters. But now I had a new objective: to find Arlene—and for that, I had to find a new shotgun. Neither waited for me on the patio; something brand new was there instead.

This one took the cake, and it was nobody's birthday. Picture a perfectly round sphere floating in the air. No strings attached here. A blue sphere, as pure a blue as a perfect spring day back home, with one extra touch: there was a face on this ball. I didn't have very long to appreciate how butt-ugly the mug was because no sooner had I registered all this in the brain department than the sphere rushed me and smashed into my head before I could even twitch, bursting all over Yours Truly.

I figured I'd had it. For a moment I couldn't breathe with that weird glop all over me, running down the length of my body, reaching the floor so I could conveniently take a header, which I did. My first thought was *poison!* I could still breathe, though, once my mouth and nose cleared.

With the first swallow, I felt something cold and invigorating rush through my body. Taking a deep breath, the air seemed cleaner and tasted better.

Suddenly, I felt great. If this turned out to be a strange

symptom of the alien poison, I could recommend it. Special Endorsements available from Flynn Taggart's coffin . . . reasonable rates. Sitting up, I expected an attack of dizziness; but it never came. The liquid had mostly evaporated by now or maybé absorbed into my body.

With another deep breath—which felt better than ever—I stood up. I hadn't been poisoned—just the opposite, in fact. This crazy floating sphere had been good for me! It was perfectly reasonable to assume that any weird creature coming through one of the Gates would be bad, and worse, deadly to all things human. Discovering that lovely A.S. had been the most pleasant surprise of the day (yeah, I know day and night are pretty tricky concepts when you're stranded on a space rock the size of an average-sized garbage dump); but the second piece of good news was how this blue sphere had just made me feel like a billion dollars.

Now that I was feeling like a new man, I was more dedicated than ever to the proposition of finding Arlene and exiting the nuclear plant. Easier said; Arlene's arrow pointed me to the blue sphere—but was that all? *Maybe I should follow the arrow down the computer-room corridor,* I thought, *and forget the door leading to the patio.* Then again, maybe she didn't even see the hidden door, and I just stumbled through it, misreading her arrow.

I returned to the computer room and headed in the direction of Arlene's arrow. After twenty minutes of winding through the maze, I ended up right back at the arrow again! "Well, that was a real brainstorm," I grumbled.

I decided to leave a small mark of my own, a simple **F**, next to her initials whenever I found them. This would prevent my mistaking one mark for the next—and anyone else, Arlene or maybe the "Ron" twins, who came this way again would know he was not alone.

I followed her mark again, this time picking a different

route; and at last I made eye contact with some company, however unwelcome. One of the familiar brown monsters with the painful, white spikes was eating something, its back to me.

Up to now I'd been spared seeing them eat. It sat on a table, hunched over, making hard, crunching noises. I caught a glimpse of something red in its jaws as it turned its head to the side; fortunately, it didn't check its six.

If I'd found another shotgun by now, I would have blasted the blasphemy from behind . . . but sometimes frustration is the father of fortune, for suddenly I heard a whole bunch of the bastards walking right past me—on the other side of the thin, computer-maze wall.

If I had followed my gut instincts and shot the demonic son of a bitch, I would have been ambushed. Shaking from a retroactive adrenaline rush, I silently told myself that my objectives were to find Arlene and *get the hell out of here,* off Phobos, and find a radio somewhere!

Then a thought hit me like a ton of slag. Arlene wouldn't bother taking time in this hellhole to scribble her mark unless she had a damned good reason. Not just to point out the sphere—if she knew it was there, she'd have used it herself like a good soldier.

The only logical conclusion was that the arrow pointed the way out of the nuclear plant—the way Arlene Sanders had already gone. Like Arne Saknussen, she marked her own trail for all who followed.

So why hadn't I found it? Same way Arlene missed the patio door: there had to be another hidden door nearby that *I* had missed.

Third time's the charm. The damned door couldn't have been more than five feet from the one I had found. One good push and it was open, leading to a beautiful piece of straight, well-lit corridor that reached its end with a clean, massive metal door that had printed on it the welcome letters EXIT—obviously a holdover from the plant's mundane days as a hangout for humans. Feeling bold and unstoppable, I walked right up to that door and discovered that it required a computer key card before it would bless the lonely traveler with an *open sesame*.

Great. Now I could be miserable again.

10

Something I'd learned at age fourteen: when your mind is working, don't give it a reason to stop. I'd reasoned it out this far, fitting pieces into place. Why should I be stopped by one minor impediment?

When you welcome thoughts, they come. There had been something wrong about the sound of the crunching from the monster that was eating. At first I was certain it was chowing down on the remains of one of my comrades; but now I realized the sound was all wrong, too high, too sharp. And when I saw the color code on the EXIT door—bright red—I acted on my hunch.

I didn't want to run into any more of those monsters, so I took it nice and easy getting back to the one having its Happy Meal; with that troop trooping around somewhere, silence was definitely golden. My main concern was that he might be gone. I needn't have worried.

Now I know why God invented bayonets.

The thing died gurgling without a scream, a roar, or a gunshot to call monsters from the vasty deep. I missed my chance to find out if I had another intellectual demon.

Flipping it on its back, I saw something red in its mouth—a clear, red, plastic computer key card on which it had been chewing. Next to it was a pile of plastic cards, mangled beyond repair, small red and blue globs suggesting the remains of more key cards. Fortunately, the one I carefully fished out of its mouth was still in one piece.

The red card worked; the exit door slid open, revealing an access ladder. I climbed down as quietly as I could . . . but I still hadn't found a new shotgun.

The toxin refinery; such a lovely name. The dump was another step down, in more ways than one. At first it seemed as though I'd entered a zone of peace and tranquility. Greeting me was a wide-open space lit by a sun lamp so bright that for a moment I thought I was back on Earth in the middle of a pleasant afternoon. The abundance of weird-looking machinery raised my suspicions, however; I could easily imagine monsters and zombies lurking behind equipment of that size.

As I began to explore the area, I was grateful for the first sight of a barrel full of the toxic sludge. I'd certainly changed my mind about green slime! Now that I knew the stuff was as explosive as nitro, finding it was like coming across another weapon.

I searched frantically for another mark by Arlene. I remembered another afternoon we spent at the rec-hall flicks. We watched one of those mad scientist movies, and the laboratory was stuffed with more switches and levers than humanly possible. The more I checked out the toxin refinery, the more it seemed like that make-believe lab.

Not all the switches had to be activated by hand, either. I made that discovery when I walked past a green section of wall, the color of a ripe avocado. The immediate whirring sound had me spinning around and ready for action. But nothing was coming to get me this time. The motion detector I had just activated stimulated my memory. CNET used to show us training videos, and I remembered that Union Aerospace used movable architecture to transport the liquid metals extracted from Phobos ore.

I watched the corridor behind me slowly shift out of

sight; it sure beat the hell out of coming into a room and finding stone and metal that had grown scales or pulsing veins. No horror faces here! The bad part was that as the physical layout changed, the corridors would realign; the route in was no longer the route out.

With so many hidden triggers, I never knew when I was going to shift everything all over again. Stepping on a land mine would be a lot worse; but this situation was still unpredictable enough to be a major pain in the ass. I tried avoiding the sensor eyes, but they were too well hidden. Once a motion detector activated, I couldn't undo it; I had to love it or lump it.

When I tossed out the old religious baggage, I thought my superstitions had gone with it. Well, Phobos might not drag me back where the nuns wanted me, but it did reintroduce me to every superstition I ever had as a kid.

So the first thought that leapt to mind when something cold brushed my face was *Ghosts!* Peripheral vision warned me something was definitely there; but when I turned to face it, all I saw was a blur.

I was still debating when something big and fast knocked me on my ass. I still couldn't see it, but I figured any ghost that can knock you down is a ghost you can return the favor to.

Jesus and Mary, did I miss that shotgun now! The wide blast dispersion was tailor-made for shooting something you can't see. But if the rifle was all I had, the rifle was what I'd use. I was a Marine, damn it—and every Marine is a rifleman first.

Scrambling back from where I'd been attacked, I readied my Sig-Cow, aimed at nothing in particular, and waited for the first blurring of vision that meant either I was having a stroke or I'd found a new kind of monster.

The wall in front of me went a little watery, like something insubstantial was in front of it. Without staring and losing it, I fired four quick taps.

I expected to draw blood; I didn't expect an explosion. The ghost screamed and seemed to collapse; I wasn't sure. Then something hot and heavy pounded me from behind, and I finally tigged what had really happened: more damned fireballers! The first shot had missed me and killed my "ghost."

I whirled around, diving sideways; two spikys, two zombies, one big barrel of sludge. Ignoring the monsters, I concentrated fire on the stationary barrel. It took a couple of rounds then exploded spectacularly.

I wondered if my "intellectual" demon could spell KA-BOOM?

I approached cautiously and examined the remains. At least the aliens' blood was red and the internal organs bore a strong resemblance to human plumbing. Just beyond the primary gore site I noticed another tangle of human arms and legs.

Catching my breath, I went closer. It was a relief when I saw the bits and pieces were from zombies; for a moment, I'd been worried.

It was Christmas when I saw the riot gun clutched in one severed hand . . . but it was Valentine's day, hearts and flowers, when I spotted the missing rocket launcher!

The shotgun was a little fancier than the last riot gun, a more old-fashioned model. It took the same twelve-gauge, but it also had a muzzle device so you could adjust the pattern spread for close work or far.

I allowed myself to feel real gratitude for the zombies, who were turning out to be my best pals. If not for them, I wouldn't have a single functional weapon. Even when the aliens deliberately destroyed radios, maps, and anything else decorative or useful, they had to keep their zombies armed. We don't come equipped with claws or armor plate. At least, not we *guys*.

Looking around, I was disappointed there was no one else to shoot. Then, as if receiving a good grade for a job well done, I spotted the glimmer of another A.S. on a distant wall.

I ran to look. It was! Arlene had come through again. Once again the arrow showed me where to go, and I wasn't complaining. It seemed like she had an uncanny knack for shadowing the demons until she found the way down.

Clipping the rocket launcher to my webbing gave me an odd feeling. I had thought to use it to frag myself; but Arlene and her Magic Markers changed that plan.

The rocket launcher was serious firepower. This one looked in good shape, but it didn't have the two pre-loaded rockets that were standard issue. I was going to have to make my one rocket round count. I loaded up then let it dangle.

Armed for very big bear, I followed Arlene's arrow through a narrow opening; I could barely squeeze past. The UAC designers evidently did not have big men wearing combat armor in mind when they built the "Manual Vertilift Bypass Route."

The doorway led to a spiral escalator down. It was not operating, so I crept down as silently as possible . . . not very.

The escalator led down to the Command Control level, as I recalled from the map I had seen above. C&C was the nerve center; if there were any working radios in the facility, that's where I expected to find them.

Once there, I wondered if it had been worth the trip. The architecture of this place was the most depressing yet, heavy, gray, very much in the style of military garrisons from World War II. I had to wonder why any human would build thick, fortified walls deep inside Phobos—if a human had. Maybe we inherited this, too.

Making my way down the longest corridors I had seen yet, I was struck by the grotesque combination of black moments from human history with the inhuman qualities of the invader. A heavy whiff of diesel fumes had me coughing so badly I had to stop and catch my breath. Diesel fumes? That couldn't be right. But that's what I had smelled.

My footsteps echoed so loudly, they sounded like mortars. I was glad when I reached the first open space, if only because the echoes wouldn't be deafening. The kind of stone forming the floor changed, and the higher ceiling gave the sound somewhere to go.

I was at the edge of a huge room, shrouded in darkness except for a couple of shafts of bright light shining through glass skylights. I don't know whether there were spots behind the glass or whether I was seeing actual daylight; but the squares of brilliance lit up two spots as bright as freeway construction sites.

One of the two bright-lit squares contained a table; on top of the table was an AB-10 machine pistol. God, did I want that pistol! I could almost taste it. I stared from the doorway, trying to estimate the odds that the pistol was bait for a trap; I kept getting an unacceptably high probability.

Turning in the opposite direction, I crept along the wall, rolling each step, just as they'd taught us in SERE School and SurvInfil. Every few steps I stopped abruptly, listening for someone shadowing my footsteps.

I tracked the wall to the left, followed it for a right turn, and finally approached a hulking machine of some sort that almost touched the wall, leaving a slight gap. I slid through the gap as silently as I could and poked my head out.

What I saw made me smile grimly. Behind a pile of boxes, ten feet past the machine pistol, were no fewer than a dozen of those brown spinys who would never make Smokey the Bear's Christmas list. They were hiding behind the boxes, staring greedily at the well-lit gun and waiting for someone stupid enough to march up and try to grab it.

Allow me to introduce myself . . .

I let my new shotgun dangle, shouldering the mini-rocket-launcher instead. I only had one round, and I had never fired one of those things before; my first shot would have to be a damned good one.

I closed my eyes and visualized the UAC sales video: raise range finder; grab plastic propellant tag and pull—

which mixes the volatiles and incidentally engages the primer firing pin; thumb-off safety; aim and squeeze trigger. Pulling the trigger halfway produced a tiny, red laser dot; I lovingly moved it across to sit directly on the rump of the biggest demon.

One of the other demons noticed the spot and reached out to touch it. I squeezed the trigger the rest of the way.

The rocket exploded with a bang so loud, I thought I would be permanently deaf. While my ears still rang, I dropped the rocket-launcher and retrieved my scattergun.

I humped toward the remains of the ambush crew; there were a few survivors, crawling along the ground looking for their legs and arms. I put them out of my misery.

I counted thirteen heads and fourteen left arms, so I must have slipped a digit somewhere. Shotgun in hand, I slowly approached the AB-10, alert for a second line of attack.

I was still seven meters away when I heard the sound, and it was a bad one; the worst one yet . . . a low, piglike growl, a snuffling sound turning into a wet, animalistic grunt. I froze, the image of a giant boar filling my mind. Slowly, I backed away from the AB-10. I did not want to meet whatever made that noise.

11

Damn! I thought, furious that even after expending my only rocket, I couldn't get the machine pistol; I was right back where I started, except one rocket lighter. I had squandered my gift! I felt like the guy who found a lamp that would grant one wish, and he says, "Jeez, I wish I knew what to wish for."

I moved on, warier than before. The simplicity of the layout and the big blocks of stone made secret doors less likely here, although I would pause occasionally and try pushing against anything that looked remotely promising. The fact that the alien monsters had set a trap worried me; as I went deeper into the base, it seemed like they were getting smarter.

I was becoming concerned that I hadn't found any more messages from Arlene. Was I still following her trail, or did I take a wrong turn?

Through a doorway arch, I found another room with a light blue motif. The UAC logo was repeated regularly, over and over, in the floor; evidently, I was back in original, human architecture.

The room contained a number of kiosks, four that I could see. As I neared the center kiosk I must have triggered another of those motion detector switches. All the doors began to rise as one. A filth of aliens tumbled out, and this time I had no rocket and no convenient barrels of toxin.

I fired a quick shell, dropping one; then the rest fell on

me like ravenous in-laws. I dropped the shotgun to the ground and barely managed to swing my semi-auto Sig-Cow up to take the shock as the first alien hit me.

The damned thing impaled itself on my bayonet—but it was too stupid to die! It clawed forward, stopped only by the bayonet hilt, and grabbed my padded shoulders with death-grip talons, dragging me back against the wall.

Saved my hide, it did. The alien's broad back shielded me as its brethren flung their fiery, mucus wads; the fireballs burst, spraying flaming, red liquid that dribbled down my dance partner's legs to pool on the ground, lighting the room with a hellish, red glaze. I fired nine or ten times, finally blowing a hole clean through the alien . . . a gory loophole through which I turned on the rest.

I guess they refused to believe that the firewads weren't frying me; they stubbornly kept throwing them, ignoring the burning pool around the feet of the first, dead monster. I got lucky; two of the aliens jostled, then turned on each other, fang and claw. The weakened survivor fell to a single shot from my Sig-Cow . . . abruptly, I realized I was alone with two hundred kilos of alien brochette on my bayonet. What a life!

Evidently, I had not met all my playmates yet. I decided I liked it that way.

The room had a central kiosk, which I entered. There was a blue security card in there. I grabbed it on the chance I'd find a use for it. Then it was back to the search for signs of Arlene.

Edging up a shallow set of steps, I finally found Arlene's next A.S. and arrow. Grinning, I followed her trail through a room stuffed with computers. Most of these centers had the same basic floor plan; but I was absolutely, one hundred percent unprepared to encounter a freaking swastika! Some sick joker had arranged eight Cray 9000s to form the "crooked cross" that a certain Austrian corporal had appropriated in the middle of last century. Maybe it was a coincidence, but I doubt it.

This was all getting a little too weird for me. The River Styx, zombies, demons, flaming skulls . . . what kind of intelligence was behind this? Whatever it meant, I decided not to think about it.

I could easily have gone through the computer room without noticing, but an undamaged map to the section made it impossible to ignore the swastika floor plan. My adventure with the kiosk had been dead center in the largest circle. Above it and slightly to the left was the swastika of the computer room. Walking through, one might figure it out. At certain angles one couldn't help but recognize that the bloodred design of the floor had a certain association. The map was like a slap in the face.

It barely bothered me when I triggered another of those damned motion detectors. They were becoming routine by now. Of course, there was always some element of surprise. In this case, the swastika-crays lowered into the floor, real slow with a grinding sound like the bones of a million dead being rendered to powder, and I expected to see soul-shattering horror. Instead, I won another jackpot.

I'd just found two boxes of rockets, five to a box. And I found a yellow security card with a note that if I were trying to find the card where it was supposed to be, north of the "maze" at the northwest corner of the installation (maze? talk about feeling like a trapped rat), well, I wouldn't find it there because it was here instead. Safe and sound with the rockets. The note was signed A.S.!

Man, I was going to have a lot of questions for that girl when I found her. It was hard enough staying alive without going to a lot of trouble for a hypothetical fellow soldier, who on a wild off-chance might still be breathing and putting one foot in front of the other. She had performed incredible feats here. As Arlene found supplies along the way—everything from weapons and ammo to these ugly key cards—she took only what she could carry and stowed the rest where a thinking man might find it.

Anyway, the least I could do under the circumstances was load the battery-sized rockets into my pack (aside from the two I loaded into the launcher), pocket the yellow card next to the blue one, and blow this horror show.

I ran into one minor obstacle along the way. I should say I avoided it; I was just about to barge through a flimsy, narrow door, en route to the exit from Command Control, following Arlene's latest arrow, when I heard the horrible pig sound to which I'd taken an instant hatred. This time it was accompanied by heavy footfalls suggesting tons of flesh waddling ponderously in the artificial gravity of the base. These pig noises were sloppier, wetter, deeper than before.

Part of me wanted to kick in that door and face the creature; part of me had had enough. I had rockets; from the sound, this pig thing was made of flesh and blood—plenty of both to spare.

The rational part of me said I'd probably find out sooner rather than later whether I could kill this new monster or not. Why race it to the grave?

While I was having this debate with myself, the pig thing thumped-thumped on past the door. I waited a few more breathless minutes, then opened the door a crack and listened. Nothing.

But the instant my book crossed the threshold, I heard a warning grunt from my right, down the black-dark hallway, followed by a heavy, meaty tread accelerating toward me like a main battle tank.

I could barely make out a bulky shape shambling out of the night to starboard; but directly in front of my nose was a heavy, armored door, a pressure hatch, rimmed with blue lights. I bolted across the corridor, jamming my hand in my pocket and fishing out both key cards.

The first one I tried turned out to be yellow. The door buzzed angrily, and I began to smell the rotten stench of corruption that comes from animals that chow-down on decayed carrion.

Swallowing panic, I yanked out the yellow and inserted the blue. The door chimed and ponderously rolled up; I darted through, unslung my scattergun, and waited, shaking, for the Thing Without a Name.

The heavy security door rolled shut, mocking me with its lethargy. Fortune loved me this time; slow as the door was, the nightmare was just that much slower. The door shut, and the frustrated pig-thing beat on the heavy metal and howled its rage and hunger.

And *still* I hadn't seen even one of the things in the light.

Knees weak, I followed a trail of three marks and three arrows to the next door—which wanted the yellow card, surprisingly enough. This door led to a lift that wasn't working, naturally; but the open shaft had guide cables along the sides, and that was good enough for the human Fly. I slid down almost fifty meters before finding another open lift door.

I swung through the hatch and saw the level-schematic on the wall; Welcome to Phobos Laboratories.

Five minutes in the Phobos lab convinced me that Command Control hadn't been all that bad. It didn't escape me that every time I went to a new center, it was a level farther down than the previous one. Living conditions were not improving, not by a long shot. However, none of that really mattered. If Arlene had come this way, then so would I. I had to find her; I had to find any other human survivors.

All of this made a lot of sense to me intellectually. Emotionally, I was willing to jettison honor, duty, and loyalty and run like a thief as I contemplated my first real swim in the toxic goo. *Semper fi, Mac.*

I'd talked myself into wading through the toxin way up above, and the protective boots that were part of the armor sizzled like bacon on the griddle. But the material was plenty thick, and the corrosive liquid hadn't reached my tender flesh yet. And like last time, there was no way around the horrible stuff.

Got to be some way to avoid full body immersion, I thought. But without a heavy-duty flashlight that I didn't have and wouldn't dare show if I did, damned if I could find it.

Arlene's arrow pointed across the pool. Grudgingly, I had to admit there was no way to proceed without a little swim.

I was damned glad for the edge that blue face-sphere had given me when it exploded all over me, making me feel healthier than I have in years. If ever I needed that edge, it was now.

I took a deep breath. Then I took a few more. Man, I did not want to do this! But it was the only way to get past a wall that blocked me from going any farther along the trail Arlene blazed; I had to go *under* the damned thing. Thinking of how much I hated monsters from beyond the stars, I splashed down.

Only one advantage over before: this time, I was prepared for the freezing pain, so it wasn't quite as unexpectedly horrible. Just a throbbing ache that sapped my strength, leaving me enervated and gasping for breath. One way or the other, the swim wasn't going to last very long. The toxin glowed with an eerie, green phosphorescence, and the light helped a little. It showed me a metallic object that I would have missed otherwise.

I snagged it in passing, a small, hand-sized television thing, showing a ghostly schematic.

If I struggled, I could pretend the liquid was nothing but an algae-infested swimming hole I'd haunted as a kid. Yes, I wanted to think about water instead of the thick, toxic crap I was in right now.

The wall did not extend all the way to the bottom of the pool. I pinched my nose, squeezed my eyelids tight, and ducked underneath. I was starting to tremble in the icy liquid; I felt sick, like a monster flu.

Then I surfaced as fast as the law of buoyancy allows,

grabbing the opposite catwalk, and the swim was over. Air never tasted better, even the stinking stuff in this place. Two or three breaths later, I put the breathing filter back in place. Too bad I hadn't had a full environment suit with its own oxygen supply, but I'd already regretted that absence before and nothing came of it. A Marine couldn't have everything.

For example, I couldn't keep the blue glow forever. I had taken it for granted until I realized what this swim could mean. Now I felt sapped and drained. I was all set to curse my lousy luck until I realized something very important: without that earlier boost to my system, this dunk in the sludge would have killed me.

So what about Arlene? Could she have come this way? Could I have passed her body in the green murk? Had to think this through—there was no arrow immediately beyond the toxin; maybe she found a better route. She might have a decent flashlight or light-amp goggles so she could see. Or she might have had a full environment suit.

Or what the hell, maybe she had a touch of the blue medicine show. There were all kinds of ways she could have survived.

But maybe she didn't. I refused to think about it.

It was time to move on.

12

I was back to trusting the old Fly instincts again. There were plenty of more unreliable things, such as any decision by Lieutenant Weems. Hadn't thought of Weems for a while. My lip curled; Weems was probably the first zombie; reworking him would take the least amount of effort.

I felt something in my hand. I stared—the thing I'd fished out of the sludge! I held it up close, staring in confusion. Then it clicked—it was a map, a video schematic of the labs. Jesus and Mary . . . I guess even the greenest cloud can have a silver-screen lining.

I decided to follow the same road map I'd been on for several levels now: down, down, down . . . no reason to stop. I might as well see what was at the very bottom level—which, according to the map I'd seen in the nuclear plant, was the main computer station, two floors down. But in the absence of Arlene marks, I'd have to plan the route myself . . . just as soon as I could make tops and bottoms out of my new toy.

I suddenly felt a wave of weakness and fever; I hoped I hadn't already given myself a death sentence from the toxin.

Phobos Lab was dark. Phobos Lab stank like an open sewer. But if there was anything left of the original installation here, then medical supplies had to be near at hand, if they hadn't been left in the typical condition of guns and radio sets. I picked that as my first priority; I needed an all-purpose antitoxin and a stimulant.

Leaning against a wall for support, I found a weapons locker the hard way: I leaned against it and the door collapsed inward.

Guns! I pawed through my treasure trove, scooping up as much ammo as I could shovel into my pack. Then I stared in reverence; beneath the shells and bullets rested a state-of-the-art, AB-10 machine pistol. The question was, did it still work after scores of zombies and spinys had monkeyed with it?

I checked it out, cleaned the barrel, then reloaded it. I almost pulled the trigger to do the only test that really counts, but stuck to my original policy of not making any more noise than was absolutely required.

I cleaned the machine pistol as thoroughly as I could before adding it to my arsenal. There was little doubt of this lethal package receiving a test real soon, with a real target, and hopefully with a margin of error to try something else if it failed. The best choice might be to have the pistol in one hand and the shotgun in the other. Nothing wrong with insurance, even if it made me feel a bit like a Wild West gunfighter.

As I stood, shifting the backpack to be more comfortable and finding a place for all the weapons, a sudden attack of dizziness hit me like a grenade. Medical attention had just become my number-one priority again.

I studied my hand map, working the buttons to make the pretty picture slide up and down. First task was to find *me*—no helpful "You Are Here" on this puppy. At last I found the wall crossing a trench . . . no sign of toxic sludge on the map, of course.

I must have been living right, because the nearest infirmary—marked with a red cross—was located just a quarter klick away, spitting distance. I found it, and there wasn't a single monster doctor or devil nurse. Here I'd been expecting a typical medical establishment and was pleasantly surprised.

And there were lights, the first fully operational light I'd found in the complex. If the lights had survived, maybe the doctoring stuff was still here and intact.

I resisted the impulse to cross my fingers as I unlatched and opened the first promising cabinet. Mother lode . . . thanks, Mom. I removed a Medikit with the seal still unbroken and popped her open. Inside were bandages, antitoxin compounds, even ointment for burns. (My face still felt as hot as if I had a sunburn, for which I could thank a fireball instead of a weekend at the beach.)

I found a clean room, a metal table next to a mirror, all kinds of light, even a shower cubicle. It was time for Dr. Taggart to make a house call.

I didn't do too badly, really. First off, I locked the

doors, turned out all the lights except the one in the room with the table and the shower, placed the shotgun right up against the stall, where I could grab it in a second, and, facing the closed office door the entire time and leaving the shower door ajar, I took the risk of bathing.

Sick as I'd been feeling since immersing myself in the ooze, the mere act of washing it all away made me feel considerably better. I turned the nozzle for Hot up as high as I could stand it and felt the cuts and bruises sting, then feel better. My burned face didn't get anything out of the shower but pain, but the rest of my body was doing too well for me to care.

If the shower was heaven, then the fresh towel was a piece of Eden. Here I had struck a mortal blow against the shores of hell. The rest was pretty simple. I put antibiotic and bandages on the worst of my wounds and cuts, taped my bruised ribs (didn't even remember where I got them), and took my time smearing the cold, soothing ointment on the burns.

The only moment when Doc Taggart almost failed his patient was when he—when *I*—noticed thirty or forty hypodermics, all neatly labeled GENERAL STIMULANT. I don't like needles. Never have.

But there was good reason to pick up one of those needles and give myself a shot. Just as good a reason to pack some in shock-proof carriers and take them along. I could run into Arlene, and she might need a lift. I might run into some other survivor. And if I were going to do all that, the only reasonable thing was for me to give myself an injection first.

You don't need to do that, said the little voice in my head. *Just find another blue-faced sphere.*

I argued with the voice: "It might be a once in a lifetime fluke. I can't count on that happening again." That's when I noticed that I was talking to myself. Sheeesh, all this just to avoid sticking myself with a needle!

No more. I bravely wielded the needle, got out the alcohol and cotton swab. This couldn't be any worse than what I'd been going through lately. Well, not by much anyway.

I wolfed some food from the small refrigerator, then hunted for a flashlight. Alas, all I found was one of those pencil-beam lights; if I wanted to find out if a zombie had a sore throat, or any throat at all, I was set.

According to my map, I had to go north to find some sort of route down. At least my compass was still functioning. I hated to leave, but the infirmary had done its job. I was tired, not exhausted, hungry, not starving, and not shaking like I had amebic dysentery. The only problem, aside from demons, two-legged pigs, and murderous corpses, was that I had lost Arlene's trail; if she were hurt, laying up somewhere, I might accidentally leave her behind on an upper level. The point was that I could concentrate again.

The last thing I did before stepping out again into the dark was check the boots. They'd held up better than I thought, but I stuffed some pillowcases in for added insulation.

Outside, it was just as dark as before, but I wasn't as bothered this time; the human race may not have blue spheres, but we do all right. I stayed in that frame of mind as I went north. I scuttled along the corridors, letting my shotgun peek around corners first, until I reached a huge chamber. It was dark, but not the pitch-black I had just come from. At least I could tell I had entered a larger area.

The next moment I was under attack. Claws raked across the shoulder plates of the battle armor I had just reinforced. When I tried to fend off the enemy, I half expected to feel the crocodile-type hide of the spiked monsters; but instead, my hands sank into a pulpy mass. And the contact made my flesh crawl even through my thick gloves.

The light was on, and I should have been able to see the scum, but I was getting nothing. Then as I pushed against the jellylike stuff and took a few faltering steps back, I saw a familiar shimmering. The same thing I'd seen when I thought I was fighting a ghost. That time, the issue was resolved by a miracle fireball; this time, I was on my own.

Didn't this goddamned, jelly-shimmering, half-assed, invisible son of a bitch know the rules? Ghosts can't hurt people—they can only scare them to death! Then the Caspar pounded me, knocking me back on my butt and kicking the wind out of me. I thanked Mary for the armor as I shoved the barrel of the shotgun right into the shimmering effect and pulled the trigger, hoping that if this thing had a mouth, that was exactly where he was going to get it.

I don't know if I killed it. I don't know if it can be killed. But it didn't bother me anymore after that. Not liking the idea of being followed by more invisible spooks, I jogged for a while, hoping to be done with this part as soon as possible. I also kept both eyes open for a pair of light-amp goggles, but I'd used up my good luck quotient at the infirmary.

To exit the labs, I had to enter the darkest room yet, black as coal. I wasn't surprised. This was at the north end of the installation, where, after groping in the dark by touch and even daring to use my tiny penlight, I finally found a small opening. This led down a narrow corridor to a tight, metal, spiral staircase going down—way down. I started to get very dizzy, spinning around so many times.

Central Processing had more tight, narrow corridors than anywhere else on Phobos. Good thing I'm not claustrophobic. The light was better than the labs; but that's like saying L.A. cab drivers are more polite than cab drivers in Mexico City.

And at long, long last, I found another A.S.! I stared at it, overwhelmed by inappropriate emotion. She was alive! She got this far! Relief was a physical thing, perched on my back.

The arrow pointed to a branching corridor that seemed small enough to give a midget a backache; but crawling down it was a good move. At the other end was a completely intact map of this section. The bad guys must have been getting careless lately. If this kept up, I might find a functioning radio.

Central Processing was laid out in a rough triangular shape. Made me think of a robot riding a motorcycle. Maybe I was more wasted than I realized.

The southeast corner was made up of four interconnected rooms. A warning note was attached that three motion detector triggers will close any door in the facility for a span of thirty seconds as a security precaution. I could just see myself getting caught in a room with wall-to-wall enemies while I counted off: "Thirty, twenty-nine, twenty-eight . . . notify next of kin."

Unfortunately, I couldn't take the map with me, unless I ripped it out of the wall and dragged it along, and my hand map still showed the labs above; if there were a way of changing the view, I couldn't find it.

It occurred to me that we humans needed to learn everything possible about these bastards; otherwise, Earth was a sitting duck. We couldn't shoot it out with these things and expect to survive. We had to outsmart them—or die.

I was surprised that I had survived this long. I was a pretty good Marine. There was no false modesty about that. But Arlene was remarkable; if I could survive, surely she could! Hoped she would keep it up. Hoped I would, too; but this nonsense couldn't go on forever.

As I looked at the map, I knew, I just knew, that the thirty-second security rule about doors meant there was a welcoming committee waiting for me. *Well, you knew the job was dangerous when you took it, Fly. They'll get you in the end.*

But who were "they?"

They weren't the pitiful wrecks that looked human though dead inside. They weren't the spinys or metal skulls or ghosts, either. The one making snuffling pig sounds gave me the creeps; but somehow I knew the creature was mentally no more than an animal. If I hadn't encountered the one monster who enjoyed talking, I'd be tempted to conclude we were being invaded by an alien barnyard.

But the intelligence *was there;* just well-hidden. Even without the talking demon, the alien technology itself was proof of a "mastermind."

So why didn't the intelligence simply organize the monsters and zombies into a naval search pattern and be done with it? Why were Arlene and I being allowed to play Gypsy, entering one level after another, shooting it out with pretty much the same cast of characters, encountering the same hazards . . . and beating them over and over and over again?

Maybe it was all a pre-invasion test, or worse still, a sadistic game. But test or game, it had to be teaching the Enemy Mind something important. The important question for the survival of the human race was: What the hell was I learning?

I hated to admit it, but so far the answer was not much.

13

One thing I was learning, though: speed. While I debated the finer points of philosophy with myself, a mob of zombies and spinys burst through the door at the back end of the corridor, the one I'd come through myself, as if they owned the damned place; they noticed me and tore down the narrow corridor. I did not take longer than a microsecond to resolve the question—I ran like a bat out of hell, a bat trying to get the hell *out* of hell. Although finding the commanding officer of the invasion was an important issue, I decided it could wait until later for review. Much later.

With this many of the enemy breathing down my neck, the shotgun was useless. Maybe my new machine pistol would have worked . . . but what I already had in my hands was the rocket launcher.

For an instant I considered the narrow corridor that might channel the blast right back in my face, the proximity of the nearest spiny . . . for an instant. Then I dug my heel in and spun, ready to rock 'n' roll.

The explosion was so loud that I didn't hear it. I felt it. A giant, invisible hand threw me to the ground. My eyes were open, and I saw the whole contingent that was on my tail vanish in a spray of blood and fire.

The sight was something to think about; especially since it was the last sight I saw.

I must have lost consciousness. An indeterminate time later, I began to hear a sound, too loud and annoying to sleep through. Like all the church bells the penguins ever rung at me, all the bells in the world in my head. I still couldn't see anything, just a bright afterimage.

It was about fifteen minutes before the bells were replaced by a buzzing sound, then the slosh-slosh of blood in my ears. I would have been easy pickin's, as Gunny Goforth would say. Maybe I was saved by looking as dead as the rest of them.

When I was able, I crawled along the corridor, dragging my feet. There was no time to examine my possessions. One thing for certain: if those glass syringes were still in one piece inside their supposedly shock-proof container, I'd be giving more product endorsements.

Shaking my head clear and staggering to my feet, I finally made it to the one long, spacious corridor in the otherwise cramped, tight, ore-processing center. This one was well marked on the map I'd studied—the only route to what the map indicated were the stairs down. Judging from the red and gold and brown streaks on the rough walls, this corridor had been carved right out of the rock of Phobos. I liked it and hoped it wouldn't be reworked into something sickening.

Halfway down the corridor, I suddenly felt light-headed and my stomach broke loose from its moorings. At first I thought I was experiencing more symptoms from the rocket blast. Then I realized what was happening. No one goes to space without experiencing zero-g, and you never forget it. This was damned close enough! I should have studied the map more closely when I had the chance . . . the middle section of this corridor must pass outside the ancient, alien gravity-zone.

A handrail was installed for the obvious reason. Grabbing it, I pulled myself along; a single tug was enough to overcome friction in Phobos's minuscule natural gravity. I'd spent enough time on the ship to Mars that this was simple enough, unless I had the bad luck to be attacked right now; I'd never taken zero-g combat training.

Pulling myself around a corner, I floated practically into the arms of a triplet of spinys. Luck has never been my long suit. But these leathery bastards were *walking on the walls and ceiling,* as if they enjoyed their own, personal gravity that followed them around, each oriented in a different direction.

One more piece of evidence that they were unbeatable. Then one of them looked right at me and spoke: "Gosh —are we having a *ball,* or what?"

It hocked a loogie into its hand, where the mucus immediately burst into flame.

My hog leg was tucked in the webbing at my back, and there was no room to draw it in this corridor, no time to work it free. The demon raised the flaming ball of snot, grinning like a goblin.

I threw my head back, rotating my body in the microgravity. I didn't bother *drawing* the shotgun; when I rotated my body so the barrel was pointing at that cracked and grinning face, I fired.

A lucky shot. Blew its head clean off. Guess my luck's not so abysmal after all.

The blast acted like a rocket, propelling me backward. When I stopped spinning, I grabbed the rail, drew the shotgun free, and pulled myself back where I'd left off.

The two remaining monsters had forgotten all about me; they were fighting each other, claws dug into throats, bloody drool trickling down wrinkled chins and bursting into flame.

Was it possible, just one "brain" to a set? Kill the mastermind, and the rest turn on each other?

Evidently, the Mind behind the invasion had the power to manifest itself through only one or two individuals in a group.

I tucked that one away in the hindbrain; I would use it later.

I waited politely until one brain-dead spiny offed the other; then I rewarded the victor with the spoils: a twelve-gauge blast to the face, this time with my back braced against the wall.

I hauled ass along the corridor to the gravity zone. At

the far north end of the facility, I found a switch that opened a door leading to the stairway where I could process myself right out of Central Processing.

Down one flight on the spiral, metal-grate stairway, the Computer Station welcomed me with a thin layer of green sludge. At this point I just didn't care. I was willing to jump into the ooze and slog through it as long as my boots held out. I wanted out of here! I ran without stopping until I discovered that whatever crap-for-brains idiot designed this playground set it up so you go around in circles before noticing you were going around in circles.

The Computer Station was a haze of forgetfulness. It started out badly when I couldn't find an Arlene mark. I hunted along every passageway without luck; either she followed a totally different route and our paths did not cross, or more likely, she had a reception committee waiting for her when she climbed down the ladder, and she was in a running firefight until she found a bolt-hole.

The damnedest part was, *this was the lowest level,* so far as I knew. If they finally ran her to ground, I should have found her . . . or her remains. There was nowhere else for Arlene to go.

There were few monsters on this floor; I shot a couple of spinys in the back—hey, I'm not proud—but mostly avoided the patrols.

En route, I picked up two blue key cards and three yellows, plucking one off the "dead" body of a zombie. Something or someone had gnawed off its legs and one arm; it was still animate as I approached, and tried to bite me; but I was faster (and more ruthless). I blew its brains out, putting it out of misery, and took the key card tucked into its belt.

I found two maps, both burned beyond recognition. But by sheer persistence, I finally found it: one of those big, metallic doors that like to stand between me and where I want to go. One of those key-card teases that demand you stick it in.

But this bitch had a special feature—an irritating, unisex, nasally, parking-lot ticket-machine voice, the kind that says "Please take the ticket," as if you're a bumpkin from Mad Dog, Arkansas, who's never seen a car park before. No monster could ever create such a surreal torture device of art. It took a human touch.

"Hello," it said, "to exit the Computer Station, please insert your gold security card now."

All right; I supposed yellow was as good as gold. I inserted the card, and the cheap trick chirped "Thank you. To exit the Control Station, please insert your blue security card now."

I began to hear screams behind me, up the corridor; the damned door had probably notified "security" while it deliberately delayed me. I fumbled the blue key card into the slot—but I knew exactly what was coming.

"Thank you. To exit the Computer Station, please insert your red security card now."

If there were a red key card anywhere on this level, I was a purple-assed baboon.

And I didn't become a Marine to put up with this crap. Even the spinys were less frustrating than this!

But I had a solution. Last time I'd fired a rocket, I'd made the mistake of standing too damned close. So I made sure I got far away from that smug bitch of a door, placing myself squarely behind a column and part of a staircase.

I fired both rockets from the launcher simultaneously. Just to be sure. The result was outstanding, excellent, a credit to the Corps. As loud as it was, it didn't deafen me this time. At this distance, the head gear worked like it was supposed to.

I walked through the smoking ruins of that bloody door with a sense of satisfaction greater than when I'd winged that toxin barrel and taken out a roomful of zombies with one bullet. I'd struck a blow against the True Evil, the chowderheaded humans who designed these installations!

From now on I refused to worry about plastic cards and security keys. Nothing could stop me. Then I found the lift that should have taken me out of there—the lift at the very end of the facility, my reward for having all the stupid cards.

The entire shaft was filled with human and animal remains, a hellish grain elevator. I don't know how long I stood there, staring stupidly. Then nausea overwhelmed me and I vomited for several minutes. Weak and shaky, I thought for several more minutes that I had climbed the farthest down I could go in the Phobos installation. A dead end. Nowhere to go but back the way I came. I knew I couldn't make it, but I was long past crawling into a corner and playing fetus. I'd go down fighting if I went, hoping somehow Arlene had escaped what was a death trap for me.

Even though it was a long shot, I thought again of the possibility of blowing up Phobos. Better that than let these bastards win! Then I noticed a foul, bloodred, evil-glowing circle in the floor; it had not been there a moment ago. A ghastly stench arose from the orifice, like human flesh frying on the griddle. I once missed getting firebombed by a Kerifistani terrorist; I was on guard duty at the Marine Corps compound when the main barracks went up. Thirty-three buddies burned to death. You never forget that smell.

They transferred me to Fox Company within forty-eight hours.

This hole pulsed like a heartbeat. There was a "ladder" made of light pink, fleshy cords that appeared to sweat.

I didn't have to be a rocket scientist to know that no human ever made this baby. Besides, this wasn't a job for a rocket scientist; this was a job for someone rock stupid enough to be a Marine. Resigned, I slung my shotgun and rifle, holstered the machine pistol, and started climbing down the sticky, wet, springy ladder.

At the bottom there was plenty of light, at least; a sickly reddish light. The flesh-pit ladder dropped me into the largest corridor I'd seen yet. I would have said it was carved out of the rock of this moon, the same as Phobos Lab, but the inside of the walls seemed to perspire, like the ladder. Holding my breath and looking close, I saw hundreds, thousands, of small orifices opening and closing to the same steady beat as the red circle above. I decided that I'd done enough close examination for a lifetime.

Then, by God, I saw it—another A.S., biggest one yet! Even in the heart of hell, I was cheered to know I wasn't alone. I didn't exactly whistle a tune, but I smiled grimly.

Arlene's mark was accompanied by a crude drawing of a skull and crossbones with an arrow pointing straight ahead. A second arrow pointed out a narrow slit in the wall, a slit that was a friendly hole-in-rock, not pulsating or anything disgusting; a slit into what looked to be the *outside.* We were hundreds of meters below the surface of tiny Phobos, but there was goddamn *daylight* coming through that opening.

But that was one mother of a narrow crack. Could I get through that? Could *Arlene,* even? I touched the edge of the slit—tacky blood, a couple of hours old, tops. *Mary, Mother of God . . .* I had a vision. She had gone out, right there. She shoved herself so hard, tearing at that crack, that she flayed off huge strips of skin—but she didn't care. She wanted out; she wanted out bad; she wanted out *right then,* not five seconds later.

Leading me to the obvious conclusion: Arlene had seen something up ahead that even she was too terrified to face.

14

I stared at the skull and crossbones. Whatever was up ahead was bad enough for Arlene to claw her way through a tiny crack in the wall rather than face it. Yet she wasted precious seconds leaving the warning for Yours Truly.

Thank God I didn't have to solve the mystery of the skull and crossbones. Getting through that crack would be an achievement all by itself.

Ahead I began to hear a low, slow pounding, almost like someone beating on a monster drum a mile distant. Well, I could take that—so long as it stayed there. I struggled out of my armor and pressed my right arm and shoulder into the crack.

But there I stuck. I braced my foot against the floor and shoved; several minutes and several pounds of flesh later, I was utterly convinced I could never fit through that crack unless I dismembered myself and threw the pieces through one at a time. *Wonder if I'll seriously consider that option when I see what's ahead?* I thought.

So now what? I sat on the floor, pounding my head with my hand in frustration. If I went forward, I was on my own. Arlene was no coward . . . if the Thing ahead scared the bejesus out of her, enough that she forced her way through a crack several sizes too small—then what in God's name *was* it?

Numbly, I stood, pulling on the armor again. As Mehitabel the cat said to Archie the cockroach, *wotthehell, wotthehell.* I already roamed the halls of the damned; what did I have to lose? *I suppose I could sit here and starve to death.*

Shaking, I moved forward at snail speed, loaded rocket launcher in hand; but what if I found myself eyeball-to-eyeball with . . . with whatever It was? A rocket up the nose might piss it off—but at point-blank range, it would also fry Corporal Fly!

Ahead, I found an old-fashioned wooden elevator next to an old-fashioned rusted button. Somehow they seemed to fit right in here. In a place with living ladders, a few museum places were hardly out of line.

I pushed the button. With a slow grinding sound, the lift began to descend. So far so good. It reached ground level, and I clumped aboard. What the hell else could I do? There was one button, and I pushed it.

The lift creaked and groaned, like it was a hundred years old, announcing my arrival to anyone inside. I braced, wondering whether to shift to the shotgun. Then it stopped up one floor . . . and my God, I saw what was inside!

On a pair of iron thrones sat the largest, reddest, most horrible demons I could imagine, compared to which the other guys were fit for hosting kiddie shows on Saturday mornings. Giant minotaurs with goat limbs for legs, and curling, savage horns on the top of their flat, broad heads. The chests and arms were carved from pure muscle. Their claws were so vicious that there was no comparison to the puny stuff I'd seen up until now.

Princes of hell . . .

And they were looking directly at me. So far, so bad.

I froze, whimpering like a Cub Scout. All I could think was, *Oh Lord, the sisters were right all along!*

The hell-prince on the left rose, trumpeting a marrow-freezing roar of discovery.

Come on, come on, come on, *Fly! Snap out of it; get the hell out of Dodge!* I hated every minute of every day of basic at Parris Island—and I bow at Staff Sergeant Stern's feet and kiss his shiny boots for every second of it: my training kick-started my paralyzed legs even while my brain was struggling to remember the Lord's Prayer . . . all I could get was "Hail, Jesus," and I *knew* that was wrong.

Faster than I thought myself capable, I bolted—but *forward,* right at the things—and skirted between the forest of red legs and into the black-dark beyond! If they'd been any smaller, they would have had my head for lunch.

I ran across a long stretch of floor and heard the familiar pig snorts left and right. I ran through utter blackness until I hit a wall, banging my shins. I hardly noticed. There I spun, snarling, fishing for my riot gun.

If the porcine sons of bitches wanted Fly Taggart, they could bloody well take him . . . but not cheaply!

They were converging on me; I could hear their snufflings and hungry growls. What the hell; I was dead anyway, right? I raised the shotgun and pounded a shell straight in front of me.

One of the pig-demons screamed in pain. Oh . . . you mean they *can* be hurt? I'd been wondering.

I scuttled right; the wall came to a point, folding back on itself. I slipped around and immediately barked my already-bruised shin on a barrel of that green, toxic mess.

Staring into the sickly glow, I had a shimmer of an idea. Quickly, before I could think twice and decide against it, I heaved over the barrel. The goo spilled out of the 120-liter drum . . . and now my whole corner was lit by a hellish, green glow. I could see!

I was in a pointy corner amid a forest of toxin barrels; but the monsters coming after me were still invisible. I was under attack by ghosts . . . and the ghosts and the pig-things were evidently one and the same.

But Yours Truly, Flynn Taggart, never forgets a scam. I backed away from the flickering shadows, into the actual point. Maybe I couldn't see them, but they sure as hell could see *me;* they charged.

I shot. Not a ghost; I shot a barrel.

The explosion chain-reactioned, and I dived for the deck. Too late, I remembered the ten or eleven rockets in my bandoleers. Luckily, the explosion stopped just short of me.

When the acrid rain of toxic waste stopped falling, I jumped to my feet. My entire body resonated, and my inner ear was confused; I balanced precariously on my hind legs, shotgun wavering up, down, and sideways . . . but my ghosts appeared to have died—again. At least, they didn't attack.

Staring wildly around the room, now lit by the green glow of ten thousand droplets of toxin sprayed far and near, I realized to my surprise that the room was actually a huge, star-shaped chamber. That seemed right in line with everything else. If they could have swastikas, why not star-chamber proceedings? Alas, my restful reverie was short-lived; the hideous hell-princes had seen my explosion and come to investigate.

But this time, I knew what to expect. Nuns or no nuns, I told myself over and over that these were *alien life-forms,* not demons. They couldn't be real demons, could they? Hell was a myth—wasn't it?

I raised my rocket launcher and let the first hell-prince have it at forty meters. The blast blew the motherless bastard backward, but it *got to its feet.* I couldn't believe it!

I fired a second time, pack-loaded with one smooth move, and shot a third rocket. The giant got up again and now it was joined by its comrade. This was not going according to plan.

They pointed their clawed hands at me; but instead of the usual balls of flaming snot, these "demons" fired green energy pulses out of wrist-launchers. I hugged the dirt as the stuff crackled over my head and made every hair on my head stand on end. Not very demonic, but pretty damned deadly!

My turn again; in desperation, I pumped rocket number four at the first hell-prince, and at last it seemed to do some damage. It got to its feet slowly and seemed confused about where I was. There was no reason to even try bothering the new one if I couldn't find out what repeated hammering did to the first minotaur. Yeah, minotaurs. They weren't demons; that Greek, Theseus, killed one.

Reload, rocket five, and *finally* that did the trick: number one went down and didn't get up again. But with behavior I was starting to expect from all godless creatures, it reached up a clawed hand and grabbed the other hell-prince.

Number two struggled to free itself, and I seized my opportunity. Screaming like a banshee, I charged to just out of range of its reach. Enraged, it slashed furiously; but my prayers were answered, and it was too mad to think of shooting energy bolts. I leaned in to shove the launcher right down the creature's enormous, howling mouth. And Fly let fly . . .

I won't even try to describe its breath.

The minotaur swallowed the little rocket, about the relative size of a multivitamin, and was literally blown away. I was knocked silly by the blast at such close proximity.

I came to, surprised to be coming to. Losing consciousness in a place like this seemed like a one-way ticket to oblivion.

I was lying on the floor of the same enormous, star-shaped chamber; but the walls had fallen, crumbling into constituent bricks outside, leaving the way clear to the outside. That whole concept of "outside" bothered me. Why wasn't I a corpse-sicle, floating in space?

There was air to breathe. There was an overcast sky to watch, complete with low-hanging clouds; dark clouds before a storm. Wherever I was, it sure as hell wasn't Phobos.

I found a platform behind the building. There was a switch. I pressed it and watched a stairway slowly rise. *Wotthehell, Archie, wotthehell . . .* I walked up the stairs.

At the very top was a Gate . . . a *working Gate*. It was marked by a flickering symbol that gave me a splitting headache when I tried to concentrate on the design. I approached it, eyes averted.

And damn me if there wasn't Arlene Sanders's last mark, right next to the Gate, pointing directly at the symbol. She'd written a single word: **OUT?**

I didn't know. But I didn't hesitate a moment. If that were the way Arlene went . . .

Then that was where I was going.

Without a glance back, I stepped aboard.

15

Time had no meaning for Fly Taggart—the memory of being Fly Taggart. He had no body but retained a consciousness somehow, somewhere. A sense of motion, but that might only be another memory.

Remembering a hand created a hand. Remembering a foot resulted in the sensation of a foot, a painful sensation from where his ankle had been bruised. Memory of a backache condensed into a patch of flesh and blood that was a back.

Memory of breath turned emptiness into a pair of lungs. Recollections of hot days on a summer beach left their imprint on a forehead slick with sweat.

Then he had a whole body, floating in a warm current of air slowly cooling; an upside-down vertigo turning his stomach, which meant he had a stomach. The fall wasn't long, and he skinned his knees on a hard metal surface before falling forward on his face. The air was cold.

He blinked eyes in an aching head. He couldn't see anything but white and red spots chasing each other across a field of darkness. The man panicked at the thought that he'd been blinded; but gradually vision returned. There wasn't much worth seeing.

The light was dim. He wanted to breathe fresh air again, as he had before stepping on the platform. He'd been breathing the stale air of spaceships and the Mars station and the Phobos installations for so long he'd almost forgotten what fresh air was like. Even if it had been fake, he wanted it again. But when he filled his lungs, it was that disgusting sour-lemon smell he had first noticed when he killed his first zombie. He was a man again, but he didn't want to be back in hell. Yet he had traveled somewhere, hadn't he? He felt he'd come a very long way just to reach . . .

I didn't know where I was. Instinctively, I reached with my left hand for the machine pistol, the weapon I could most quickly bring into play. My hand slapped bare flesh. There was nothing on my chest but air. I looked down and saw that I was naked.

Jesus and Mother Mary. And after all that work gathering shotgun, Sig-Cow, and rocket launcher.

Having lost my clothes during the strange journey didn't bother me, except for the drop in temperature; but I didn't want to turn into dead meat because I didn't have weapons. A naked man is an unarmed man.

I wasn't going to waste another second before reconnoitering. If there were monsters anywhere near here, then I had to get my hands on a firearm right away. The sour-lemon smell was a dead giveaway—zombies lurked somewhere in the shadows. I'd come through a gateway with nothing but my body, but at least I was breathing. I wanted to keep it that way.

The gravity was Earth normal. As my eyes adjusted to dim light, I saw I was in an oblong, rectangular building. Having had the experience of being "outside" before the transfer, I didn't look forward to roaming corridors again. I almost hated that idea more than the prospect of fighting monsters.

Suddenly it didn't feel merely cool any longer. It had gotten downright cold. Being stark naked presented other problems; with all the disgusting ways to die I had recently discovered, I'd be damned if I wanted to catch my death of cold.

Adrenaline pumping madly—my drug of choice—I ran in the most promising direction. A red light pulsed dimly in the shadows directly ahead; and the flat, slapping sound of bare feet against the metal floor seemed almost as loud as my boots had earlier.

If this setup were anything like the one I'd left, I actually *wanted* to find a zombie! "Alive" or dead, they were armed with what I needed, and a lot easier to deal with than the spinys or ghosts.

I found the source of the red light: an entire wall emitted crimson illumination; at the bottom was an inverted-cross cutout, just big enough to serve as a doorway. It was directly in line with a square platform on the ground. The platform was red, too. The symbolism was blasphemy—anyone walking through the "doorway" would have the privilege of being crucified. The religious imagery was starting to piss me off; whoever or whatever was behind this had learned things about human psychology that I preferred it not know. I slipped through, feeling dirty and corrupted.

I felt an unholy chill as I walked through the inverted cross in the red wall, the color of communion wine, the color of blood from fallen comrades.

How right I was to think of buddies lost in battle. Directly on the other side of the opening was the dead body of a UAC technician locked in mortal embrace with a soldier I recognized from Fox Company. I wasn't likely to forget Ordover.

The youngest kid in the outfit, we'd bagged on him something fierce. He was patriotic to the "Corps" and easy to rag. As I looked at the remains of this friendly private, the boyish face that hadn't been altered even in death, I regretted the times I'd helped get him drunk.

Finding out that Johnny enjoyed singing old ballads, badly off-key, when he was honed and capped was too much temptation. I thought that was as funny as everyone else did.

"Sorry, kid," I muttered to his corpse, relieved that at least he'd received the gift of a clean death. He hadn't been reworked. Now it was Johnny's turn to provide Fly Taggart with a piece of serious artillery. He was lying on top of a Sig-Cow with a fifty-round magazine. Thanks to him, I might still be a naked savage, but I was back in the game. I was a Marine once more.

As I examined my surroundings, I had the feeling I'd been dropped into a giant warehouse. There were huge boxes, or crates, all over the place with UAC stenciled on them. I began to explore and noticed a red, glowing square that emitted a curious heat. I avoided it for the moment, welcome though the heat would be.

Having gotten in the habit of following Arlene's arrows, I started hunting. And looking for more weapons, as well as food, water, and an unbroken radio. I was so intent on all this that I barely noticed it when I turned a corner and was back in zombie country.

I shouldered the rifle and fired while they wasted time roaring. The shot was good; the nearest head exploded like a ripe melon. That startled me; it was a single bullet, not a grenade! This zombie had to be especially ripe.

The next one reacted more typically; the bullet made a normal hole and the creature fell to the floor, twitching. But I was already pounding a round into the head of number three, scutting sideways, firing two or three shots at a time. I lost count of how many zombies went down. A few had weapons, but none had taken a shot at me yet.

It was all too easy; then something on the other side returned fire—actual fire. The damned, brown spinys were back, complete with their bizarre ability to toss flaming snotballs like warm-up pitchers for the devil.

The easy zombie pickin's had made me careless. The first fireball was too close, far too close, to my face and neck. The stuff stuck to my skin like napalm, burning like hell and reminding me that I had no protection over any part of my skin or vulnerable parts.

But I was pumped. With a roar to match a hell-prince, I charged the nearest spiny and let my bayonet do the talking. The blade split thick neck like a cantaloupe, and the demon dropped, bleeding a deep, ruby red.

But even with a bayonet stuck in its windpipe and blood pumping out in buckets, it stretched a clawed hand up toward me. With a thrust and a yank, I tore the neck so badly that the head was hanging lopsided. It would take a lot more work than that to actually decapitate the mother, but at least it wouldn't bother me anymore. I needed the bayonet back. I had other fields to plow.

A number of zombies had gathered around as I was busy taking care of the demon that I hoped had been the one who burned my face. More spinys loitered by the weirdest piece of wall I'd seen yet, with human skulls stuck all over it like raisins in a cake.

A thin female zombie went first, a fat male second, an ex-PFC third. I used the bayonet on all of them because there wasn't room to shoot.

Pivoting, slashing and stabbing, shouting gleeful curses—this was the way to kill! The feel, the smell, the blood pouring out of them beating through my veins, all linked. A world of blood. Some had to be mine; but this was no time to worry over details.

Then there was one zombie left. I recognized its face. Recognition slowed me down . . . this was a good face, honest and stern, like the men who'd settled the frontier.

Corporal Ryan. Dead eyes in a face I once respected were an invitation to do more than kill. I had to *erase him from the universe.*

I pinned him with the bayonet; but he was made of stern stuff, even as a zombie. Squirming forward, he clawed my face with long, dirty nails. Damned rifle was stuck in him! He was far stronger than the others, stronger than me.

Thank God I knew Ryan better than his reanimated corpse did. The corporal always carried a 10mm pistol in a back-draw holster. I reached behind him. *The gun was there!* I drew the piece, stuck the business end in Ryan's mouth, and squeezed the trigger.

His death grip combined with the pool of blood underfoot pulled me to the floor. It was too slippery to get up easily. While I freed myself, I tried real hard to assimilate the latest data. If zombies were holding a weapon when they died, they still used it. But the intelligence required to remember a hidden weapon was beyond their reach.

Slipping and sliding on the blood was distracting . . . and then I realized that I was sobbing. Having given myself strict orders to keep emotions under control, I felt betrayed. At least I held onto the pistol.

Standing up, I realized with disgust that the real reason I was weeping was because I had temporarily run out of enemy. All the zombies were dead-dead, and the monsters who had been watching over by the wall of skulls had run off. This was worse than being interrupted in the middle of making love. I really felt that. I had good reason to be crying like a baby.

"Pull yourself together," I ordered Yours Truly. "I mean it. Cut the crap, right now!" I wasn't going to put up with any insubordination.

"Damn you all!" I screamed at the universe. "How long am I supposed to take this, over and over?" It was a good question, but nobody had any answers. I kicked a zombie's head, angry that he wasn't contributing his part to the conversation.

Zombies weren't the only inanimate objects around; I found a metal cabinet that I tore off and flung at a console. Great sound effect. I would have moved on in search of glass to break—an even better sound—but I noticed my little tantrum had actually led to something useful. As the forest fire raging in my brain toned down to a mild fever-delirium, I vowed never to say anything bad about dumb luck again.

A hidden drawer in the console sprang open. I investigated, hoping to find a weapon. Instead, I found another of those computer key cards, the very same cards I had sworn not to use again while I had my trusty rockets . . . the very same rockets I no longer had. Buck Rogers, back to square one. I picked up the translucent, blue computer disk. Waste not, want not.

A rifle in one hand, pistol in the other, and a key card clenched in my teeth. Not having pockets was becoming a major pain in the butt.

Why didn't I simply field-strip a corpse? I don't know; I guess my brain wasn't rolling on all tank treads.

One direction seemed as good or bad as any other, so I went back the way I had come. As the frenzy of the battle wore off, I was starting to feel cold again. The red platform was appealing as the only source of heat I knew about around here, the next best thing to a roaring fireplace. It felt great as the heat warmed my cold, naked skin.

Then, as idiots have asked themselves throughout history, I asked the magic words "Why not?"—and rubbed my hands over the thing.

A million flashbulbs exploded in my face.

By the time I finished blinking the world back into focus, I realized I was *not* in the room I just had been.

My mouth dropped open. *Fly, you gorm,* I thought, *I think you've just discovered your first teleporter!*

That square, red platform just *had* to be the "teleport" pads I had heard about when they posted Fox Company to Mars. They were just big enough for a man to stand on . . . assuming he felt adventurous.

I was dubious about the whole thing from day one, and so was Gunny Goforth. If I were surrounded by trolls and out of ammo, I'd decided, I *might* try one; nothing short of that would tempt me.

The teleport pads were already there when humans first arrived, presumably built the same time as the Gates and gravity generators. Practical folk that we are, we incorporated them into the design of the base; UAC used them to transport heavy ingots and equipment. I don't think many *people* used them; most of us worried about things like souls and continuity of consciousness and all that crap.

Trust Corporal Fly Taggart to render the whole philosophical discussion moot by tripping over his own feet into it!

As I stared stupidly at my new surroundings, a swarm of zombies poured around the corner. As the first one fired a round that took me in the shoulder, several thoughts whizzed through my mind. First, as I fell to the floor, I thought of writing up the careless dolt who'd triggered a teleporter by sticking his paws where they weren't supposed to be. The second thought, as I rolled onto my back, was more ironic: moments before, I'd been *unhappy* over running out of zombies. My third thought, as I sat up, stunned, was: *I'm shot!*

My Sig-Cow was out of reach. I'd let go of it, along with the key card. I opened fire with the 10mm.

A nearby stone platform provided me cover; the zombies were too stupid to do the same. They reminded me of Army privates.

Taking my time about it, I aimed and fired, aimed and fired. The bullets went in, the blood came out. I took them one by one, killing the very last at point-blank range.

This time I wasn't sorry I'd run out of zombies. The bullet in my shoulder made me groggy. There was nothing I'd rather do at that moment than lie down in a nice, warm pool of blood and sleep forever.

Nothing suicidal; sleep was good. Rest was a sacrament.

Willing my reluctant body to move, I got up.

16

By now I must have looked like a zombie myself. I felt like one. Being honest about it, I had to admit that I didn't know how a human being crossed over into the zombie state. I hadn't seen the process. The talkative monster implied that he could control zombies, but he never said a word about how they were made—he simply lied about not reworking me if I surrendered.

I wondered . . . was *this* how the others became what they were, fighting a never-ending war that finally drove them mad? Wasn't a sign of insanity the conviction that everyone and everything is the enemy? That was the way I'd been living since I left the cafeteria and the two Rons and began my assault on Phobos Base and . . . and wherever the hell I was now.

Turning a corner, I was greeted by a sight not calculated to reassure a man doubting his sanity. A gigantic skull, half the length of a full-grown man, glared at me through empty sockets. It seemed to be made of brass. I stared into its eyeless sockets before allowing my gaze to lower. The giant, metal skull had a tongue; a curving, snaky, metal tongue.

There was no way this was standard-issue in a UAC refinery!

Of course, the skull's tongue had to be a lever.

"I can't help it," I said, "I'm a born lever-puller."

If I were already dead and in hell, it hardly mattered what would happen if I pulled the lever. I still had my curiosity. And if I were still alive, trying to save humanity from an alien invasion, then I had even more curiosity.

I pulled the lever. It was ice cold against my already chilled flesh. A metallic, grinding noise riveted my attention. It sounded like all the old, abandoned automobile plants in Detroit had started up at once. And with all that sound, one stupid box rose from the ground containing another pair of skull-tongue switches! I pulled the next one in line and heard a click from the wall directly in front of me.

Moving to investigate, I saw a crack of light in the wall, then another and another until the yellow lines had formed a perfect square. Secret doors were losing their appeal for me. If this one were going to improve my opinion, then it had better offer something better than the usual collection of monsters. I shoved open the door with one mighty heave.

A bloody, naked figure held a gun pointed directly at my face. By reflex, I shoved my own piece right between its eyes.

"DROP THE GUN!"

"DROP THE FREAKIN' GUN!"

"PUT IT DOWN, I SWEAR TO GOD I'LL BLOW YOUR FOOL HEAD—"

"—WHERE I CAN SEE THEM, PUT YOUR HANDS UP—"

"—AND DON'T MOVE OR—"

"—GROUND! ON THE GROUND, MOVE!"

Her eyes. Her eyes were alive. And she spoke . . . *words.* By now we both stood, each pistol pressed against the other's face, eyes wide with fear, wonder, and hope— Was it? Could it be? Could *she* be?—shouting at the top of our voices in pain, rage, and desperate need.

My hammer was cocked, but my finger outside the trigger guard; I had just begun to suspect, just begun . . .

Something clicked in my brain. The penny dropped. I recognized the bloody, disheveled, pallid creature.

A dream come true—*if* true—in a world that specialized in nightmares. Panting before my face, watching warily, ready to fire off half the magazine if necessary, stood the reason I had come this far and hadn't yet given up.

I wanted to say her name, but I couldn't. We were each locked in a perimeter of silence, holding a gun against each other's face, doubts and paranoia having the only voice. One of us would have to say something.

She went first. "Drop the friggin' gun!" The command came from a lifetime of giving not an inch or trusting without two forms of picture ID . . . and that had been back on Earth! She'd worked hard, her every friendship based on a sense of honor. She'd kicked her way onto the Mars mission. And this is what she'd found.

But she'd survived. And I'd survived. She'd kept me alive with every A.S. and arrow; and maybe her fantasy that I'd come after her kept *her* alive—why else use our private code, a link between just the two of us?

But now there was no room for sentiment, only for certainty.

"You are a dead man if you do not drop the freaking gun *now.*"

Oops. My arm and hand had been through too much to even consider it. My body was wired for instant responses. The same as her body if she were still the old Arlene. The only reason I hadn't blown her away automatically was the time spent praying she was alive, and a willingness to take a risk right now that she wasn't really a zombie. No zombie had ever spoken before. And somehow, covered with mud and gore, she looked too damned bad to be a zombie. Only the living could look that fried!

"Arlene, your ass is mine," I replied. "I've had the drop on you since I opened the damned door."

Zombies didn't talk that way, either. They didn't tease or smile a moment later when awareness crept across a human face. She returned that smile, and I knew everything would be all right.

"Your finger wasn't even on the trigger, big guy. I'd have blown you away before you fumbled around and found it." She was wounded, disheveled, filthy, terrified, naked . . . and totally, totally alive.

"You're alive!" I shouted.

"No, really?" she shouted back.

We slowly lowered our weapons simultaneously, mirror images of each other. Grinning.

Staring me up and down, she commented, "Nice fashion statement." I'd forgotten I was buck naked. My damned reflexes insisted on embarrassing me, and I reflexively covered myself.

Well, I guess it was one more proof I was still fully human. I doubt that zombies are modest. "Turn your back, for Christ's sake," I implored.

"I will *not*," she answered, eyes roving where they shouldn't. "You're the first decent thing I've seen since this creep show began."

If we kept this up, maybe things would get so bloody normal that the monsters would simply pack their suitcases and leave.

Arlene could dish out a hard time when she wanted. I decided to get dressed, and *finally* I noticed the corpses and stripped one. She reached out a hand. "No, Fly; don't put those on yet. Please?"

My right foot was halfway into a boot far too small to fit. It stretched, conforming to the size of my foot: one size truly fits all. Arlene turned as red as the crimson wall. "Jesus, I'm sorry, Fly. You're my buddy; I shouldn't have made you uncomfortable. Forgive me?"

I finished dressing. It didn't take long. Now it was my turn to look her over, which I did with a lot more subtlety than she did with me. I kept my eyes moving where she'd let hers stop in embarrassing places. God, she looked good. All the dirt and blood almost gave her the appearance of being dressed in a weirdly hip-punk outfit. Her slender waist, tight, firm thighs, medium bust, and long arms made me think of more than the undeniable fact that she had the body of the ideal orbital pilot—her ultimate goal when she'd earned enough in service to take a hiatus, get a degree, and take a commission. Space travel needed the occasional boost in morale.

She finally got the idea. There were plenty of corpses around with uniforms waiting to be stripped. I watched her from the corner of my eye as she followed my example. The best aspect of these form-fitting uniforms was the way they conformed to every contour of the human body. She looked just as good in clothes.

I tried to think of something appropriate to say, then grunted, punching her shoulder middling hard. *"Now* I forgive you," I said with a grin. The grin didn't last long. I'd completely forgotten about the bullet wound in my shoulder. The pain finally caught up with me as the adrenaline wore off.

"Jeez, that looks bad," she said. "Maybe there's some Medikits around here. You mind holding still while I do some alterations on your shoulder? Meanwhile, tell me where the hell you came from."

Seemed like a fair deal to me. "Long as you tell me what happened to you, A.S. You and the company. And what the hell were you doing hiding in a cupboard?"

She made me go first. I recapped everything that had happened since I left Ron and Ron behind in the mess hall. She'd been through the same crap; I didn't need to be overly detailed about the killing. It would be nothing more than a sentence completion exercise.

While I told her my adventures, hoping I wasn't boring her, we weren't standing still. With the soft suction sounds of our boots on the cold, stone floor, we went hunting for medical supplies. "I'd rather go up against a dozen zombies than one of these monster aliens," I was telling Arlene as she yanked open a closet door.

Dozens of shotguns cascaded down on us like bales of hay . . . heavy, painful bales of hale. Fortunately, they weren't loaded.

Staring at the pile of weapons for a long moment, I put

DOOM

on my best annoyed face and asked Arlene: "Can't you keep your space neat and tidy?"

Rolling her eyes, she scooped up one of the weapons and tossed it to me. She took one, too. I regretted leaving behind such a beautiful pile of weaponry. But Arlene and I only had four hands between us. We still needed a Medikit, and Arlene was starving. With the burning sensation growing in my arm, the Medikit was first on the list.

Then I was going to get my Recon Babe out of this hellhole. I'd e-mail her, if that's what it took to pack her back to Mars. No, Earth.

"Get your crap together," I said, "and take mental notes."

"Notes?"

"We've got to give a full report when we get back. We're blowing this popcorn stand."

Arlene smiled wanly. "You have any good ideas on that one, Ace?"

"I left a land-cart back at the entrance; we can hot-rod it back to the air base and take the troopship back to Mars. Or even Earth . . . it should be able to make it."

Arlene looked around, studying the architecture.

The architect must have been hired by the Addams Family. Nothing seemed normal. The surface of the walls was rough, twisted, the sickening color of internal organs. Skulls, monster faces, and decay dominated everywhere I chanced to glance.

Arlene coughed politely. "Just two problems with that plan. First, we're not on Phobos anymore, Toto."

"Huh?"

"We're on Deimos, and there ain't no land-carts, or rockets, either. We used all the ships to bug our people out four years ago. Fly, we're stuck here, and we don't even know where 'here' is!"

I must have looked blank; she continued. "Look, Fly, don't you remember when Deimos vanished from the screens?"

"No, actually. What the hell are you talking about?"

"Whoops. I guess you were already in custody when we got word from Boyd that Deimos had disappeared from the Martian sky."

The idea that a moon could vanish bothered me for some reason. "Wouldn't there have been gravitational effects?" I asked.

She laughed before asking, "Are you kidding? Do you know how small Deimos is? It's even smaller than Phobos."

"I knew that." These chunks of space rock were so small that their *real* gravity was theoretical, notwithstanding the alien gravity zones. Although I'd become used to fantastic events lately, a little nugget of skepticism scratched at my capacity to believe just *anything.* "How do you know we're on Deimos?"

"'Cause I've *been here,* Fly. I did a TDS as a yeoman right here while I was waiting for an opening in the Light Drop."

"A *yeoman*? But the Marines don't have any staff positions, only line positions."

"On loan to the Navy. Technically, I was still a rifleman, but the only weapon they issued me was a word processor."

I had to think about this. The implications were definitely bad. And the image of Arlene Sanders as a secretary was astonishing.

I looked up. There was a skylight in the ceiling, and where Mars should have been, there was nothing. Where stars should have been, there were no stars. The black of space was missing, too. All I saw was a gray mist, not to be confused with clouds; the texture was all wrong.

Having a gift for the obvious, I said, "We're not in orbit around Mars, are we?"

She smiled and patted me on the head. "Congrats, Fly. You win the Nobel Prize. You don't see a pressure dome up there, do you? But we're still sucking air. I know we're on Deimos; I recognize all the stuff that H. P. Lovecraft didn't redecorate."

Who, I wanted to know, was H. P. Lovecraft? If he'd had anything to do with this, I wanted to punch his lights out.

"No, Fly," Arlene said. "He was a fantasy writer, early twentieth century American. Obsessed with hybrid monsters and underground labyrinths. Always describing ancient menaces as *eldritch*."

I'd never heard the word before, but it sounded just right. "This situation has got eldritch coming out the ass."

"You can say that again," she agreed. "And this *is* Deimos, *muchacho;* only thing is, these bastards have taken it somewhere."

"Great. So what's number two?"

She looked puzzled for a moment, then she frowned. "I don't want to hurt you, Fly."

I licked my lips, feeling my stomach contract. I never liked anything from a girl that began like that. "What?"

"You've always been more loyal to the Corps than I was, my friend."

I stiffened. "What's wrong with the Corps? The Marines have given me a lot, babe, in case you've forgotten."

She smiled and shook her head. Arlene hadn't forgotten my father, a pathological liar and petty thief who ended up doing twenty-five to life for his fourth felony conviction . . . trying to run down a state trooper with his pickup truck. He died in Vacaville two years later, from a cerebral hemorrhage, they said.

My father was the pettiest, lowest, meanest man I ever knew. He couldn't even understand the word "honor." He never knew why I joined the Corps, never would have understood if I told him I did it for him . . . so I would never *be* him.

All right, I confess. Father, forgive me, for I have sinned. The Corps was the world to me.

"There's nothing wrong with the United States Marine

Corps, Fly. But damn you, there's something a bit more important."

"Like what?"

"Like the human freakin' race!"

She had me cold. So I got pissed. "Hang the human race! 'It's Tommy-this, an' Tommy-that—'"

"Oh, don't quote Kipling at me; I'm the one who gave you the book. Fly, what do you think the whole purpose of the Corps *is*?"

I didn't say anything. I didn't like where this was leading; I knew what she was going to say. But I couldn't figure where she was wrong.

"You're so much into honor and duty, Fly. Don't you know what duty means? We're the ones on the wall, kiddo. They might not know we're there; might not even know there *is* a wall, might not give a hang. But that's what we're here for.

"Fly, this thing is bigger than just getting us both out alive. We're the only ones here, only ones who know about the invasion . . . the only ones who might be able to throw something big and heavy into the gears. And damn it to hell, *I'm not going to bug out until I do it*!"

I glared at Arlene. I wanted to protect her, get her out of there. I was a man, she was my—

Bull. I was a Marine. And so was Arlene. I understood what she meant about the wall; somebody had to man it. Who else?

I lowered my gaze. We couldn't just bug out, even if we could find a transport on abandoned Deimos. We had to get to the bottom of all this—and if Deimos was like Phobos, I had a bad feeling that meant getting to the bottom of the Deimos facility. For some weird reason, the alien monster demons preferred "down."

Besides, her point number one still made sense, too. *We don't even know where "here" is.* Deimos had been yanked away somewhere . . . we were stuck, no rocket, no clue where we might be . . . only that we weren't in orbit around Mars anymore. "Up" meant—what? Empty space? Nothingness? The *only* way out—if there was one—was "down," following the levels of Deimos to the bottom.

I glared up at her again; her eyes were as cold as steel, as warm as the sacred heart. "Well don't expect me to say I'm *sorry*," I muttered.

17

While we'd been talking, we came across an undamaged crate that looked promising. All that stood between us and it was one of my fireball-throwing buddies.

This one never got a chance to warm up. Arlene whirled and blasted him; the demon went down without a chance to hock and spit.

The label on the crate promised Medikits and comrats. We opened it and found a full pantry.

Arlene insisted on playing nurse before I played chef. She examined my shoulder; the bullet had gone straight through. Score one for my side. She injected universal antiviral/antibiotic and wrapped a bandage around my shoulder, while I gritted my teeth and groaned like a big baby.

When she finished with my arm, I heaved a sigh of relief. God, I hate medical crap! But I was premature; I'd forgotten about my burns.

Arlene didn't forget. The cream she applied on my forehead, cheeks, and chin hurt worse than the arm injections! It hurt so bad that I started hunting for any serious cuts or burns Arlene might have . . . something that would require my delicate attention—and lots of cream. Despite her appearance, she was disgustingly healthy.

Now it was her turn to tell a story. "Fly," she began, pausing to gulp water from a bottle we'd extracted from the crate, "I don't want to see anything like that first assault ever again."

She sat with her back to a wall, and I stood where I had a good view of anything coming or going. I had to find out what happened to Fox Company. Munching on a bland, fast-energy bar that tasted as fine as a steak at that moment, I gave her my undivided attention (and a chocolate bar of her own).

The situation had been as bad as I imagined. The assault simply fell apart. Seeing the zombies was enough —the guys didn't even need flaming-snot demons to drive them off the deep end. Walking, staring, drooling, rotting human corpses proved sufficient to make them forget every combat lesson they'd ever learned.

They went crazy; they broke ranks and charged the zombies. Fox was full of fighting spirit, all right; it just lacked a plan, strategy and tactics, a command structure, and a snowball's chance in they-should-have-known-where as soon as they let themselves get isolated, cut off from each other. The fire-hocking spinys picked them off one at a time.

I couldn't really blame my buds. I'd had the same reaction, the same rage to rip the zombies apart with my bare hands.

Arlene was saved because she wasn't as affected by the male berserker fury. It must be a male thing; testosterone, maybe? Jesus, did that sour-lemon odor actually stimulate a testosterone and adrenal rush overdose?

Then again, she might simply have had better self-control than a guy. I interrupted to say, "You're a better man than I am, Arlene."

"Shush, Fly, if you want to hear the rest of this." I shushed.

"I found a cupboard and hid out," she continued. "I could hear them moving just beyond the door. Sometimes hearing is worse than seeing."

I nodded at the truth of that observation. "Like this ugly demon," I said, kicking the brown hide of the creature she'd dispatched. "They hiss like giant serpents. Scares the piss out of you in the dark."

She laughed. "I wouldn't call *that* a demon! I've seen some others that more deserve the name."

"Yeah," I agreed, remembering the minotaurs. "I guess those hell-princes you warned me about with your skull and crossbones are a more traditional demon design."

"I wouldn't know," she said. "I never saw them. You're talking about the pentagram room?"

"You didn't see them?"

"I put one foot into that room and heard one of 'em scream. I guess it saw me, but I didn't stick around to see it! What do they look like?"

"Eight feet tall, bright, flaming red, with goat legs and huge horns. They fire some sort of electrical-ball lightning from wrist-launchers."

She shook her head. "Nasty. But the thing I call a demon is a huge, bloated, pink thing with tusks. Maybe we should call it a pinkie?"

"Does your pink demon make a pig sound?"

The way she shuddered answered the question before she nodded. She wasn't kidding about what you hear being worse than what you see. I didn't press her for further details. I had a sinking feeling that no description was necessary. Before this was over, I imagined we'd be seeing lots worse nightmares, a full menagerie from the lowest pits of hell.

"So what happened after you left me the warning?"

She smiled, happy to oblige. "I ran like the devil." She interrupted herself, uncomfortable with the expression. The way things were going, there was no telling who we might meet next. "I ran," she said, "and found the crack.

I had enough paint stick left for a final warning. I want you to know, Fly Taggart, that taking the time for that Do Not Enter sign was the stupidest thing I did all day; while I was making like a public information booth, one of those hell-princes, as you call them, came tromping down the hall."

"You've got guts," I piped in, and didn't care if she shushed me this time. Instead, she insisted on my going back into the narrative and giving all the gory details of how close I'd come to cashing in when facing these monsters.

Then she resumed: "While I was writing as fast as I could, I studied that crack in the wall, wishing I could make it larger."

"I couldn't squeeze through."

"I know. I felt like dog dirt. But what could I do? I didn't have a jaws with me, and no time to crank the crack wider even if I did have. I wormed my way through, leaving a few layers of skin behind, and hoofed it for the Gate."

She stopped to catch her breath.

"You must have been surprised when you came through stripped bare," I said.

She sighed. "I was surprised to still be alive, which is how I've felt every leg of this mission. There was a corpse-reception committee waiting at the other end; but at least they weren't zombies. While I picked my way through all those bodies, a metric ton of zombies started teleporting in. There were too many of them to handle— so I dived into that secret cupboard you found . . . and somebody pressed a switch, and the freaking door slammed shut! And then you showed up, looking. . . " —she struggled for words—"not a helluva lot better than the zombies, Fly."

"Thanks," I said. She always had a knack for compliments.

Sometimes I suspected she liked toying with me. I pointed at the brown carcass of a spiny. "So if you don't want me calling it a demon," I said, "how about a spiny?"

"How about an imp?"

"An imp?"

"Why not? I had a book of fairy tales when I was a kid with goblins and things. The picture closest to this critter had the caption 'imp.' It was playing with magical fire."

Our game was becoming fun. We didn't have a lot of entertainment at the moment. "I dunno," I said. "Something about the head reminds me of an old monster movie about a fish-guy who lived in a lagoon."

"He's an *imp*," she insisted, reminding me that tough Marine or not, she was still a woman.

My mother didn't raise any fools. "He's an imp," I agreed.

"We should name the others, too," she said, encouraged. "We've got zombies, imps, demons or pinkies, and hell-princes. What do we call the rest?"

I laughed. "That's pretty biblical, isn't it?"

She stared blankly. Not everyone had enjoyed the benefits of religious schooling. "Anyway, it's a great idea, Arlene. If we ever find a functional radio, we'll need to report to someone. We might as well play Adam and Eve and name all the beasts."

She relaxed, convinced now that I wasn't making fun of her, so I continued. "One of these imps talked to me—" I started, but Arlene cut me off.

"Talked?" This was the most surprised I'd seen her yet. We hadn't exactly duplicated each other's adventures.

"He tried to get me to surrender, promising if I did, I wouldn't be reworked—uh, zombiefied. But the son of a bitch was such a liar, I wouldn't trust him for the time with a clock stuck to his face."

The way she laughed made me laugh. Finding her had changed everything. I wanted to *live* now as well as fight, report back to Mars or to Earth, do my duty for the survival of homo sap, the home team.

"Are those all the monsters we've discovered so far?" she asked.

"No," I admitted. "There's something around here that's partly invisible. I was thinking of them as killer ghosts."

"Specters," she corrected offhand. If we got out of this alive, I would recommend Arlene for the job of an editor. On a religious magazine. I had a sense of justice. "I haven't run into them yet," she added.

"And some flying skulls. What should we call those?"

"Flying skulls."

"Right. What do you want to call them?"

"*Flying skulls,* you lamebrain! Call 'em as you see 'em."

I found out she hadn't run into any of the mysterious blue spheres, either, so far the only good thing to come out of the Gate. I had the feeling that before this was over, there would be much more of the naming of names.

Now it was back to business. Lunchtime was over.

It was a brief rest; we needed real sleep. We needed to find somewhere secure so that we could take turns sleeping and watch-standing. And we needed real food.

"Something feels weird about this place," she said. Something about Deimos was creepier than Phobos. The place was colder, but that wasn't it. The odors were about the same, but a bad taste seemed to go with it. Maybe we were closer to the source of the sour-lemon stench that hung around the zombies. Whatever it was, a cloying odor underrode everything, something very slowly rotting.

"I hate looking at it," I answered her. If lesser demons were in charge of the other Martian moon, then Old Nick himself had drawn the blueprint here. The skulls were starting to get on my nerves. They were everywhere, all different sizes and shapes, always more evil than a normal human skull.

As we explored, the color we noticed most was red,

darkening into the shade of rare steak. The little voice wanted to know why it wasn't getting hotter. Red was hot. Hell was supposed to be hot.

The floor became moist with the hated ooze, not yet deep enough to require slogging through a river of the stuff. I wondered if Arlene and I were exploring the great intestine of something so gigantic that I was going to have a hard time ripping out its guts.

It seemed like the deeper we went into hell, the closer we got to the life force. Screw that. The Martian moons were more appealing as desolate rocks exposed to the cold of space.

"Bad news," said Arlene, pointing at a teleport platform at the end of a corridor. We had no choice: use it or go back. Along with all the normal maps I wanted, I now wished for a map showing where all these grids connected up. How many shopping days before Christmas?

"Somebody's got to do it, Arlene."

"Do what?"

"Recon these teleport things."

She placed a firm hand on my shoulder. "Nice of you to volunteer, Corporal. Rank before beauty."

"Pearls before swine. I was about to *delegate*, PFC!" I looked around. "The layout's different here than on Phobos."

Looking back, I observed the vista of emptiness we had walked through to get to this point. I had the feeling that the walls were squirming when I didn't look at them.

"More dead ends. I don't like jumping into a fire when I'm getting fat and happy in the frying pan. But we're *humanity's vanguard*, right?" It sounded sarcastic, but I didn't mean it to be. "We've got to find out what's happened and communicate with someone up the chain."

Whenever Arlene smiled, it felt warmer, nicer, than when we'd just been palling around. War brings out something good in a certain kind of person. I didn't know about me, but I was sure about Arlene.

"Besides," she elaborated, "best way to stay alive is to be on the offense. I'm coming right behind you." There was no one I'd rather have backing me up.

"Give me thirty seconds." They wouldn't be my famous last words, I hoped.

The teleporter sensation, now that I was ready for it, was similar to the Gate, but quicker, less disorienting. My clothes stayed on and the weapons didn't disappear. I was ready to secure the beachhead.

I'd arrived on a platform virtually identical to the one at point of departure. I should have jumped off right away, but I was distracted by the sound of heavy pile drivers, coming closer and closer. *Jesus and Mary,* I realized, *they're footsteps!*

18

Abruptly, I remembered where I stood. I leapt off the platform just in time; Arlene had counted the full thirty seconds before following.

"Clear?" she asked as she sparkled into view.

"No," I answered. "Listen to that." Light as a cat, she pounced down beside me. The thudding sound wasn't getting any softer.

"Poke your head around the corner," she suggested. "I have a pretty good idea what's making all that racket."

We took our time approaching the corner. Arlene gestured that she would go first. I don't argue with a lady. When she glanced back at me, her face was stern. "You've been wondering what I call a demon," she said. "So take a good look."

I did. And as Gunny Goforth might have said, she wasn't just a-whistlin' Dixie.

A whole box of demons marched around atop a two-story platform that looked as though it might lower any moment. One of the "pinkies" started making those pig sounds I found so disgusting. But as I paid close attention to the anatomical details of this thing, I decided the Porker Anti-Defamation League might disagree with my description.

These monsters were the most massively concentrated collections of muscle power in the whole zoo. They were about six feet tall, with mouths that looked like they could swallow Cleveland . . . and probably had. They were demons, all right. She had me there. So long as these guys were wandering the corridors, nothing else deserved the name. Their flesh was a dark pink; Arlene's nickname for them was accurate.

They didn't see us yet; but it didn't look as if we'd be going anywhere if we didn't deal with them. There were no other doors; eventually, that platform would have to lower so we could ride it up.

They stamped around on short, stubby legs, like shaved gorillas with horns and saw teeth. "Do they have any projectiles?" I asked Arlene.

"What do you mean?"

"Fireballs, lightning, anything like that?"

"They don't throw anything at you." She noticed my body relax a little. "Don't let it fool you," she warned. "They're deadly if you get anywhere near them."

"Can we pop them from down here?" I asked.

"Not likely. You need concentrated force, like a .458 Weatherby or a twelve-gauge at ten feet. I saw an imp go after a demon, and the pinkie took three fireballs in the face and *swallowed* the imp whole! It burped out the bloody spines."

Data point: imps and demons, like imps and zombies, don't get along.

"Fly, if we're going to progress, we've got to lower that

platform. There's no other way to kill them with what we've got."

I noticed I'd been leaning against something hard and metallic. It was another skull switch, just begging to be flicked. I started reaching for it but Arlene butted my hand away with her shotgun. That hurt.

"You don't know what that's going to do," she protested.

"I can't help it . . . I'm a born lever-puller." I flicked the tongue. With a loud groan, the platform lowered like an elevator. The demons wandered off. They snuffled their pig snouts and evidently scented us, for they made a beeline.

As they came for us, we scutted back around the corner. The demons didn't seem able to run, but they could power-walk with that *thud-thud-thud* pounding through our skulls.

Arlene and I both had shotguns and a serious attitude problem toward demons. I found their open mouths an irresistible target. The first one ate my powder, and the back of its head opened up like a watermelon. There is always something to say for close range. Arlene took hers out with a well-placed blast to the chest.

If we were acting like a team with our backs to the wall, the pinkies were dying as individuals, marching forward two abreast to receive their quota of shotgun death. The corpses piled up, providing sufficient time for us to reload and do it again.

As an added bonus, none of the monsters made that snuffling pig sound. They were too busy roaring as they died. The roaring was loud, but it was the mark of their defeat. I started feeling good about my bloody work.

"Like shooting drunks in a barrel," I said to Arlene.

"Don't get cocky!"

She was right. *Hubris.*

The ranks of the enemy finally diminished. We'd stumbled into a finite number and we were using up our demons fast . . . about as fast as our shotgun shells.

"Don't discount them," Arlene warned me. I wasn't about to discount her experiences. "So long as you can keep them at a safe distance, this is all right. But I saw what happened when a buddy got his arm bitten off; and then it ate his head. He avoided being a zombie, only to wind up as demon food."

Good things come to an end, even in a paradise like Deimos. A bullet came very close to ending the career of Yours Truly. This tipped me off that someone was shooting at me.

"Look out!" I shouted at Arlene; but she was already down, crouching behind the wall of demon bodies.

During the precious seconds I spent saving myself from whoever was playing sniper, the last demon charged like a runaway bulldozer. I turned to find myself staring into a meter-wide maw.

I thought I knew what a bad smell was before that moment. A square mile of human cesspool might come close. The odor was so bad it was like a weapon. My eyes watered so I could hardly see.

Arlene shouted something, but I couldn't make out her words. She was busy with problems of her own; the sniper was still at it.

One of those bullets, clearly meant for Arlene or me, connected with the back of the demon. It had the same reaction as a human being would have . . . if stung by a mosquito. While it tried to scratch at its back (and I wondered how it could accomplish such a task without ripping itself to ribbons), I swung the shotgun back into action. The target came forward, and the bore of my weapon literally went down its gaping maw. I pulled the trigger.

My eyes filled with stinking monster blood; not a desirable state of affairs when trying to avoid the persistent rifleman. I could hear Arlene, though, shouting, "That's the last of them," as her shotgun finished speaking for her. She had to be speaking about the demons. I could still hear the ping-ping of rifle fire over my head.

But it was a relief to know that no pinkish mouths would chew my tender epidermis.

Arlene crawled over to me and started rubbing the blood out of my eyes. I could manage that on my own. I just hadn't gotten around to it. "Spread out," I ordered, "don't make one target!"

She didn't argue with my superior combat experience. She rolled away without a word while I finished clearing my vision. Whoever was trying to shoot us had taken a break, probably just to reload. I was certain it wouldn't last; he had the high ground, beyond where the platform had been. We needed to alter the situation in our favor immediately.

"Platform!" I shouted, then charged the lowered lift. It had its own switch, which I flipped. The lift started up, and Arlene finally realized what was happening. She ran and leapt, barely catching the edge. I pulled her up; we crouched back-to-back and took a little trip.

On the next level, we rounded a corner and came face-to-, well, you couldn't call it a face really—we ran right into another demon. I didn't know about Arlene, but I found the situation very annoying. We'd just been through all that. We were so close that, as it charged, I fell back on my butt and fired a round between his legs. This staggered the demon, and Arlene finished the job, plugging it head-on and killing it good and proper.

Now we could return to the more traditional task of trying to find out who was shooting at us.

Past the platform we saw two doors. Exchanging glances, we approached. One had a blue border and the other had a red border. Of course, they were both locked. I missed my rockets.

I extracted my blue key card and inserted it into the proper slot, swiping it across the mag reader.

The door opened with a clean, whistling, hydraulic sound. At the other end was a teleport. Deimos had a "thing" for teleports, all right.

"The lady or the tiger?" asked Arlene.

"What?"

"A story I read once. We've got a red door and a teleport. Which one?"

"Yeah, too bad we don't have a red key."

"Hell, Fly, all you had to do was ask!" She produced a key card and presented it to me. Arlene liked to play when working. "I found it in the secret room while waiting for you to rescue me," she said with a wink.

"I'll pick the lady," I said, and started to insert the red key.

Marine training comes in handy. I heard something on the other side of the door; and there was nothing wrong with Arlene's ears, either. I swiped the key through the slot, then skipped to the side, scattergun ready. Arlene took the opposite side.

The moment the door opened, she discharged a shell, killing a zombie on the other side. He was holding a shotgun just like ours. He wasn't the sniper. The zombie standing next to him had a Sig-Cow, and I wasted him. We cleared the room, each covering 270 degrees.

The room was really more of a walk-in closet. It was empty of more zombies. But I was already worried about something else: if the one with the rifle had been shooting at us, then had ducked in here, it had all the signs of an ambush. But zombies didn't think! An ambush suggested tactical thinking . . . thinking!

I hadn't yet had an opportunity to confide in Arlene my suspicions of an overall Mind guiding the invasion, using a great number of mindless opponents against a few human survivors to learn our limits.

She probably wasn't in the mood for a quiet, analytical discussion right then. There was too much blood on her, on me.

Now it was the lady's turn to find a switch. The room was flooded with clean, white light. We had found a treasure chamber . . . medical supplies, more com-rats, and ammunition, lots of it. Best of all was another of those handheld video things.

"Fly, you know what this is?" exclaimed Arlene in excitement. I let her tell me. "It's a computer map of the entire floor plan!"

The medical supplies allowed me to return the "favor" Arlene had done me. She'd been winged by the sniper. She wasn't carrying any bullets around with her, but one had grazed her shoulder. And she had other cuts and bruises from our last battle.

"I'm your doctor now," I said.

Eyeing the self-heating tins of food and coffee, she sized me up through slitted eyes and said, "I'd rather you were the cook."

"Chef," I corrected her. "And what's the difference, anyway?"

"Between a cook and a chef?"

"No, between a doctor and a cook!"

"You win. Feed me, Fly."

I bit my tongue. "Doctoring first." She didn't argue, but continued working on the computer map as I tended her wounds. I found a tube of the same cream she'd used on me; but she didn't grimace. I used the hypo to inject the antiviral; but she never flinched. She really *was* a better man than I.

We didn't have any disagreement until I insisted we get some sleep. "You've got to be kidding, Fly. I'm not about to close my eyes and lie down in a rotting pile of zombie corpses!"

"We can carry them out and pile them in front of the door."

"Oh, great—an announcement that we're in here."

"All right. I'll throw them onto the last teleport platform."

"We'll throw them." As simple as that, sweet reason had prevailed.

The job took twenty minutes. We didn't bother with the teleporter; we spread them like speed bumps among the demons. Maybe visitors would think they had killed each other.

Then we enjoyed our first real meal together. The snack had only kept us going; this was a veritable feast by comparison.

I insisted that she sleep first. She'd been on the go longer than I. While I was still being nursemaided by the Rons, she was at risk, in battle, up to her eyeballs in demon guts. She would sleep first, whatever it took.

Turned out all it took was getting her to put her head down "just for a moment." I let her sleep for four.

When it was my turn, I went out like a drained tallboy. She woke me with a gentle hand on my shoulder and a beautiful face to appreciate. We'd both been too exhausted for nightmares. We were living them.

I hated to leave that room. The same way I'd felt about the Phobos lab infirmary. No, that was wrong. This room was better than that. I'd shared the time with a woman whose survival turned my universe from empty muck back into gold.

Blinking away pieces of sleep, I slung the Sig-Cow across my back and we returned to the blue door and again faced the teleporter. "Same routine as last time?" I asked.

"Nah. Let's go together."

"Why not?"

"What the hell."

We found ourselves in a room with no doors, no windows, and one of Arlene's big, pink demons.

"Mine," I called, and pounded a shell before Arlene could argue.

"I have a feeling there's plenty to go around," she said.

I was almost starting to like the pink bastards. Their lack of projectile weaponry made them favorites in my book. Of course, I hadn't seen them chow-down on a comrade the way Arlene had.

I took point, positively greedy for my next demon kill. I moved well ahead of Arlene.

Oh, Fly. *Hubris, hubris, hubris! Pride goeth before destruction, and a haughty spirit before a fall.*

Turning one of those treacherous corners so common in both Phobos and Deimos, I stepped right into *The Wizard of Oz*. What else could you call a giant, floating head?

19

This head wasn't handsome enough to be a movie star. Its grotesque skin was made of millions of squirming, knotted, bloodred worms stretched over a huge, inflated balloon. For an instant I thought of the floating blue sphere.

Staring into the single red eye of this floating pumpkin with a tube for a mouth, I doubted it would make me feel like a million . . . years old, maybe.

I dived sideways as the pumpkin spit a ball of lightning out the tube mouth, burning my scalp and hair as it sailed past. It exploded against the wall, producing a million slivers of blue-flickering electricity that had every hair on any part of my body standing at attention.

"Mary, Mother of God!" I cried. "Another one that shoots stuff!"

I ran back toward Arlene, shouting, "Run, run, run!" With pain and surprise still fresh, I couldn't think of anything else to do.

But the floating head hadn't been in Arlene's face; she was still in control. The red ball floated around the corner, and she let it have a blast from behind.

It rebounded from the blast, roaring in pain, then slowly turned to face her. While it did, I caught hold of myself.

I blasted the floating pumpkin from my angle. As it turned back to me, Arlene skated to the side and blasted it again.

Now we both knew what to do. We dropped naturally into a standard Light Drop tactic—move, fire, move again, fire again. The ball did a lot of bouncing. Whatever life force kept it going hadn't left it yet. But we kept firing.

Then it died the messiest monster death I had seen so far. One moment the ball was bouncing against the walls; the next, there came a spray of sticky, blue goo that smelled like caramelized pumpkin pie and sounded like an overripe squash dropped ten stories. I seriously considered losing the lunch I had struggled so hard to ingest.

"Oo-rah!" exulted Arlene. "Smashing pumpkins into small pieces of putrid debris! What the hell was that?"

"Um. I was going to ask you the same question."

I couldn't take my eyes off the disgusting, deflated remains. We should have been expecting brand new monsters, but this floating beach-ball thing was so weird, it meant *anything* was possible.

That scared the hell out of me. It meant we might run into something indestructible, or at least unkillable.

"What, ah, do you want to call this one?" Arlene asked.

I'd forgotten our little game. It was a good question, but my mind was blank. "Call it a pumpkin," I suggested at last.

Arlene wasn't impressed. She wrinkled her nose as if smelling limburger cheese. "I didn't mean that as a serious name, Fly. We need something more . . . frightening."

"All right, then, *you* name it."

"No dice, Fly. First person who sees a monster has to name it. That's the rule."

I was about to demand to know why *she* got to make

138

the rules; I stifled myself in time. Of course she made the rules—she was the female.

"Then it's a pumpkin, Arlene." I put my foot down. *Maybe I'll get lucky and she'll dislike my name enough that the rule will change.*

We secured the corridor. It was monster-free. It wasn't ooze-free, but the stuff didn't look deep until pretty far along. Ahead lay a small ocean of the stuff with an exit at the other end.

"Best way to get through shallow goo is jogging," she said. "Eats away your boots, but you last longer."

"Sure beats swimming in it," I agreed.

"Don't be silly. That would kill you."

I made a mental note to brag to Arlene about my swim.

I searched the immediate vicinity for any life-giving blue spheres, but we were alone in the sea of green. "So what does your computer map say?"

Arlene zoomed the room we were in, and we noticed a couple of switches and a teleporter.

We threw the first switch, and stairs slid into view like shark fins rising from a tranquil sea. We hoofed it to the next switch, then went straight to the teleporter. We did not pass GO, we did not collect 200 monsters.

"My turn to go first," she declared; I knew better than to argue.

"I'll count to thirty."

Her trim form faded from view, and I started the count. ". . . Twenty-eight, twenty-nine, thirty."

Weapon up, I followed, ready for almost anything—except what I actually saw: a whole bank of shiny, new, undamaged radios! "Bank is open," said Arlene.

"I guess they missed this room," I said, checking the corners for possible ambush. There was nowhere to hide, and we seemed to be alone; but I didn't let down my guard. The invisible ghosts were reason enough not to completely trust the old eyeballs.

Arlene fired up one of the radios then whooped for joy

when it hummed and came on-line. But no matter what frequency she typed, we heard nothing but crashing-ocean static.

Arlene took her time, running carefully by five mega-hertz jumps up the entire spectrum; then she tried the same procedure with different radios. The results were the same.

"Fly, this doesn't make sense," she said finally.

"They couldn't be blocking the signal somehow?" I asked.

"These antennas stick half a kilometer off the surface of Deimos! Whatever's blanking the signal must be enveloping the entire moon."

Time to put on the thinking cap. I even paced. "Arlene," I said at last, "every radio I came across on Phobos was smashed."

"Same with me."

"Now here is a vitally important communications room that they couldn't possibly miss . . ."

"You're assuming an intelligent enemy here," she said.

"There has to be, Arlene! Phobos and Deimos are part of the same invasion. Why leave this room intact, but not the ones on Phobos?"

"Fly, Deimos was abandoned four years ago. I was present when the Marines picked up everything and left. Budget cuts, reduction in force, and a lack of tactical imagination sent us packing."

I nodded, sitting on the floor with my back to the wall, at an angle where I had an unobstructed view of the door. "A big mistake," I said.

She was on a roll: "What if the aliens invaded *back then?* Or some time ago—weeks, months, or longer. They could take their time spreading through the facility . . . and there'd be no reason to smash the radios here on alien-controlled Deimos."

We listened to the symphony of white noise. "So why can't we reach anyone now, Arlene?"

When enough crazy stuff happens all at once, the

imagination is free to float off like that damned pumpkin. I didn't know if it was inspiration or not, but I asked the trillion-dollar question: "Maybe Deimos is no longer in orbit around Mars?"

I was so used to the way she liked to watch me through slitted eyes that when she stared at me wide-eyed, she looked like a different person. "I never thought of that," she said. "It would explain Deimos vanishing from the screens. I just assumed it was destroyed somehow."

Having started down the twisting path, I ran to keep up. "You said Deimos is so small that gravitational effects are negligible. It's more like a giant spaceship than a planet."

We stared at each other. Inspiration can be catching. "But how do you remove an entire moon instantaneously," she mused, "even one as small as Deimos?"

I don't spend all my time on target practice and working out; sometimes I read. "By shifting it into a different dimension?"

She smiled. "Fly, you've been watching too many sci-fi trideos."

"I don't know about that, A.S.; but special F/X will never be convincing again after facing the real thing."

"What makes you think we'll ever see another movie?" Neither of us spoke for a bit; then Arlene continued.

"So suppose they've turned Deimos into a giant spaceship," she said. "Where would they be taking us? Back to their home world?"

"With us as prime specimens?" I said, not feeling the least bit comfortable about the idea. "Whatever the destination, I've got a bad feeling about this."

"Any destination is probably bad for us," she agreed.

"We could be in some kind of artificial wormhole on the way to hell."

"As if this weren't hell already! Besides, I'm not religious, Fly; I didn't go to any parochial school."

My mind's eye conjured up old images from the Chapel of Mary and Martha. Sister Lucrezia, who taught us Dante's *Inferno,* acted as if she'd just returned from a special tourist-class trip through the infernal regions and couldn't wait to share her Bad News for Modern Man. One July weekend at Saint Malachi Summer Camp, I saw her in full regalia, standing up in a rowboat and pushing off from the dock with a long oar. I thought I'd seen a vision of Charon the Boatman, ferrying lost souls across the River Styx. I doubt any monster here could beat her out for the job.

I was half convinced I was already on a one-way trip to the real place. But the idea that Arlene was coming along drove me mad with anger. I wasn't about to let one stinking demon-claw touch that noble soul of hers.

Arlene stood up from the useless radios. "I've been trying to get a fix on the enemy, some handle; but all I'm doing is drawing blanks. I've had the experience of running down corridors before," she confided, "with dozens of armed men out for my blood. Sometimes your best chance for survival is to go right into the rooms and corridors they hold and destroy whatever they came for. We made our way into the embassy vault and burned all our important documents . . . and the KPLA left. You know what I'm talking about?"

"I'm glad you got out of there, A.S. It was a real hellhole."

"Yeah, I wouldn't miss *this* hell pit for the world."

I stared at the radios myself. Yep . . . that's a radio, all right, I thought, which is about as far as my education in electronic communications gear went.

Why on Earth—on Deimos—would the Corps give up such a strategic position as this station? By Executive Order number whatever, the Marines had military jurisdiction on all extraterrestrial planetary surfaces; the Navy had deep space; the Air Force had atmospheric; and the Army had Earth itself.

Mars, Phobos, and Deimos were surely ours to the bone. The only reason I could imagine us giving it up was if the other services conspired to cut our space-ops budget . . . with pretty disastrous consequences. Wonder if anybody felt shame about that, or would if we lived to tell anyone?

"Round of ammo for your thoughts," she said.

"Nothing important. Politics back on the old home planet."

"At least there's no politics here. Unless you count that swastika."

"You saw it, too?" I was beginning to wonder if I'd dreamed that damned crooked cross. "That's not politics; it's a bad joke."

"You think they put it there to scare us, huh? The way they—what do you call it? *rework*—the physical buildings gives me the creeps."

"Nothing from Earth scares me after what I've seen, Arlene. What's next, a hammer and sickle?"

"A what?"

"Never mind. You're too young to remember. I'll make you a bet that we don't find any other symbols from the home planet."

We shook hands. "You'll lose," she said. "You *are* thinking too much about politics. I win if we find *any* symbols, including religious symbols . . . and there've been plenty enough of those."

"Damn, you're right. I lose. All the Satan stuff."

She could sound like a professor when she wanted to: "Maybe the demons—the *aliens*—were confused by Hollywood into thinking the swastika is a satanic symbol. It sure seems suspiciously like somebody had an official list of Things that Scare Westerners . . . like they knew it would be seen by UAC workers and Marines, not by Native American Indians or Japanese. Wonder if they'd change the symbols for different humans, say using the letters kyo or oni if they were invading the Nippon Electric space station?"

"In any case, the religious symbols are terrestrial, so you lose, Corporal."

Now it was my turn to grin. "Well, Arlene, if you are

going to lose a bet, it's good to find out before you set the amount." She gave me a playful punch in the shoulder. We started out while I massaged the numbness out of my arm. At the next inverted cross we passed, I'd pay anything she wanted. Within reason.

20

The video map showed us how to get to the central elevator for all of the Deimos installation. We were very near. All that separated us from our goal was a wall.

The wall had a switch, a full-body bas relief of a cloven-hoofed alien. And it wasn't his tongue that required flicking.

My face flushed. "Um, you'd better take this one, PFC Sanders.

"And here I thought you were a born lever-puller." Arlene flicked the switch; the blue-gray wall cranked down into a slit in the floor, revealing a spacious lift. "Deluxe service," Arlene said, pointing at the labeled bank of elevator buttons. We'd made it through the Containment Area. Below us was the Refinery, then Deimos Lab, the Command Center, the Central Hall, and three levels below that which were unlabeled.

"Basement? Skip the crap?" I said.

"Hm. Yeah, well, maybe."

"Maybe? Makes sense to me. Every time that door slides open, we run the risk of being stormed by giant vampire slugs from the planet Pornos, or being machine-gunned to death by Nazi *schutzstaffel.*"

"Fly, these lifts didn't work too well even back when we had people maintaining them! They got stuck all the time. If the sensors detected anything in the shaft, you stopped at the floor above. If a door was open somewhere, the whole elevator could freeze. Go ahead and push the basement button . . . I'll bet you a month's pay we won't make it more than a couple of levels; then we'll have to find another lift somewhere."

I looked at her and snorted. "You're so full of good cheer. Well, ready or not, here goes nothing."

Here went nothing, all right.

I pushed the button; we started with a jerk and ground downward, skewing back and forth dangerously. As we descended toward the refinery, I saw that the lift didn't take us there directly, but to a warehouse section we'd have to pass through first. In the distance we had an actual view of the refinery through large, gaping holes in the floors and ceilings. Some kind of fighting had gone on here.

We had descended some fifty meters. What we could see of the refinery was laid out like an open maze; it was possible to see in the distance an expanse of pink, moving objects that looked like fleshy cubes or blocks. I hoped they weren't alive, weren't the next creatures on the hit parade. They were gigantic, reminding me of the "organic ladder" and the pulsing walls back on Phobos. Then we'd moved past the point where we could see the refinery. Our descent brought us to a more normal scene.

"Normal" in this case meant a warehouse area stuffed with UAC boxes to the height of twelve feet or more and so densely packed as to create their own pseudo-corridors. We'd noticed a number of humanoid figures with the familiar brown hide and white spikes scurrying for cover . . . back in imp country again.

The lift stopped, not quite all the way to the floor; we had to jump down about three meters.

Arlene peeked over the edge. "You owe me a month's pay, Corporal Flaggart."

"Did I take the bet? I don't recall saying any such thing."

"Native American giver."

We hopped out onto the ugliest, puke-green marble I'd ever seen; but it was still good to have something solid underfoot.

"All right, PFC Sanders, let's do this by the numbers."

"Sure, Fly. So which box is number one? And how come we never do stuff by the letters?" I threw her a withering glance, like an older brother to a pesky sister. We were ready to rock and roll.

Fighting demons had spoiled me. I liked an enemy that didn't shoot back. We popped through the warehouse like nobody's business, pulse galloping, keyed to instant reaction. The refinery had its share of toxic ooze. We didn't pay it any mind, but so far, there were only a few sticky regions instead of slime beach. I looked for barrels of the stuff, my favorite way of dealing with imps; but there were none.

The first fireball missed us by a country klick. The second came too close to Arlene to suit me, so after I killed the imp, I wasted ammo . . . and killed him again to teach him a lesson. They were smart enough to duck in and out of the natural defenses provided by the stacked boxes, but not enough to gang up on us or show any other sign of working together. None of these guys were talking.

Still, there were a lot more of them than there were of us. One almost got me from behind. If he'd had a partner, I'd have been dead meat. Instead, Arlene slid in behind the both of us and used her bayonet like a can opener. Busy as I was staying alive, I could appreciate the sheer grace of Arlene, back to the wall of boxes, cradling her shotgun like a baby; never mind dogs as "man's best friend."

With hand gestures I indicated who would take which section. Another fifteen minutes and we were back in the same place. She'd killed more than I had. The warehouse area had been cleared.

I was tired enough to wish one of those magical blue spheres would make an appearance. I hadn't told her about that because it seemed too unbelievable, even in a place like this. But Arlene the mind reader had brought a small black case back with her. It looked medical. I'd have to start calling her "Doc."

Opening it, she produced a syringe filled with clear liquid, labeled "cardiac augmentation stimulation unit." I held it for a second, then carefully passed it back to her as if it were a loaded weapon.

"Can't believe I found this," she said. "It's synthetic adrenaline to be used on patients who are in the throes of cardiac arrest."

"What would it do to you or me?"

She paused, biting her lip again. "In a normal person, the adrenaline rush would make you super strong. There's a drawback, though; it could also give you tachycardia and kill you."

"Just say no to having an edge," I commented, taking the black package and its contents and adding it to my collection.

"Fly, maybe we should toss it. That stuff could be too much of a temptation."

"Hey, if push comes to shove, we can inject one of them with it, right up their monster fundaments. All in the interests of science."

The only unlocked door led to a huge, green marble chamber with a collection of weird, red pillars. Pulsing veins stretched around these pillars like living ropes. The sharp, cloying odor of perspiration combined with the sick-sweet stench of rotting meat. Mechanical stuff was fine with me, even organic stuff like the arboretum. But I didn't like it when they combined, and I couldn't tell where one part left off and the other began. The throbbing of the veins matched the throbbing in my head.

I was almost grateful for the appearance of a number of imps. At least they took my mind off the architecture. Then some more imps . . . and some more after that. Too much of a good thing.

"Check your six, Fly," said Arlene.

I looked behind me, across the room; sure enough, even *more* snot-spitting spinys.

My gratitude faded fast. I made out a dozen imps.

I started the donnybrook with a well-aimed shell; between their fireballs and our shotguns, we had one serious firefight. I thought the pillars would catch fire, so thick were the red flames and black smoke.

I killed two. Arlene killed three. The survivors were better than the previous imps at dodging behind the pillars, and even our shotgun extender mags were running dry. They forced us back into a corner, pinning us down. Mexican standoff time. I wanted to bail.

Then I pumped, and the slide locked! Nothing up my sleeve; nothing in my gun.

Now what?

Time to even the odds. Arlene was watching the imps, firing off a shot now and then, looking down at her mag window and frowning.

I reached inside my vest, pulled a hypodermic and studied it. Intravenous? No, intramuscular. Well, that was easier, at least. But could I actually do it? To myself? Jesus, what a dilemma.

For a moment it was like being back on Phobos. That needle bothered me more than flaming mucus in my face. Without question, the next scientific revolution should move beyond the need for needles. But more important, could I risk a heart attack if I had a bad reaction?

Jesus, Mary, and Joseph, I'm a Marine! Semper fi, Mac. I gave myself the shot.

At first, nothing; then the stuff stimulated my adrenal glands; and in a minute I was filled with red rage! The world turned crimson and my breath was fire. My heart beat so fast that it spun in my chest like a gyroscope. I drew my bayonet from my webbing and bolted from the corner; if Arlene yelled after me, I didn't hear it.

All that mattered was to kill, getting in tight and cutting the steak. Blood-rare—God, how I loved imp blood, thick as red ink from a shattered paint stick, communion wine splashing on the floors of eternity.

Every motion was a target to strike. Flesh was too easy. Bone was the real work, the blade sticking in the cartilage, the cracking and crunching inspiring me to greater efforts. I hardly noticed the blood splashing in my eyes. The world was already a red haze; liquid salt was trivial pain as I swung my blade in the center of adrenal agony.

The more I killed, the heavier the weight in my arms. But exhaustion spurred me to greater fury. I no longer saw the Chinese-mask faces of the imps, only a blur. Their claws rent my flesh, but we were too tight for them to use their best weapon.

Dimly I realized that I was bleeding from many wounds. That was fine with me. Blood kept me warm, theirs, mine, anyone's . . . just so that I could continue to swing a blade and slay the bastards. Motion must be met with motion.

An imp exploded in front of me before I could even reach it. Only one imp left now.

"Fly!" A voice called my name, near at hand. I hadn't expected any of these imps to speak, especially not in a high, almost feminine voice, calling my name. I was so surprised that I hesitated for a moment, blade poised over the last imp.

"Fly!"

My vision began to clear. My arm was a bar of lead, my chest a sharp pain, as the old heart slowed to merely fast. The fury slowly lifted from me like a thick, red, trideo theater curtain drawing back. The hazy shape before me grew solid and took on familiar features, Arlene's features.

I was very glad that I hadn't killed that last imp.

21

They're all dead," she reported. "Are you all right, Fly?"

"Thirsty," I croaked. My own canteen had split open during the fight, spilling its contents. She shared water from her supplies.

"Better?" she asked.

I nodded, utterly spent.

I almost fell as she helped me out of the room. She set me down, held my arm. My mind still raced, but my body was exhausted.

Arlene made me rest twenty minutes, then reluctantly helped me up so we could move on.

We walked past the secure area, beyond the pillar room, and faced another closed door. It was hardly worth kicking. On the other side was a shimmering floor of the noxious slime, across which was a console with a blue key card. "Doesn't look too promising," Arlene said.

I was never optimistic where toxic goo was concerned; but my head was still flying from the adrenaline, a perfect recipe to make a volunteer.

"I'll go," I said. "I could use the exercise. Jogging is just what my heart needs right now."

"You need to rest, Fly!"

That was thoughtful of her. I appreciated her sentiments as I evaded her grasp and stepped into the gunk, my boots making shunk-shoosh sounds, slowing me down and eating bit by bit through the thick soles. Then I stepped on something hard and felt it shift under me. Heavy machine sounds came up through the slime, followed by something more substantial. A section of floor rose through the toxin.

Staggering was not a good idea. I didn't want to fall down in this. I regained my footing as I saw a wire-mesh platform rising to match a set of blue-paneled lights directly overhead. I was just about to take steps when Arlene brushed past, turned, and stepped to the right to follow the path that was under those lights.

As she ran out of the pathway an odd thing happened. More wire mesh rose to meet her footsteps, corresponding to the lights above, winking like the stars I hoped I would live long enough to see again. I followed her. A major improvement over the normal way of crossing the slimelands—did any other spills have such shortcuts installed, I wondered?

When we reached the "island" on the other side of the green ocean, Arlene said, "You may have something with that rats-in-the-maze idea."

"No human would design this, except maybe a game show host."

"Game is right. I wonder if the entire moon has been reworked?" She reached over and grabbed the blue key card.

We found a door with pretty, blue trim; the key card popped it open. Inside, I whooped with pleasure to see my old buddy, the rocket launcher, with lots of little battery rockets as well as another AB-10 machine pistol.

The body of an imp lay in a corner. "Think that one died of natural causes?" Arlene asked.

"Unnatural more likely."

"Say," she said, "if imps are smart enough to talk, why don't they use weapons?"

It was a good question . . . one of many that had started to gnaw at me. "Maybe because it wouldn't be fair," I said.

"Excuse me?" Arlene's eyebrows shot skyward. "I

DOOM

must have misheard; it sounded like you said they don't use weapons because it wouldn't be fair."

"Let me rephrase . . . it would be a *fair test* of our defensive ability. The mastermind—whoever, whatever —wouldn't learn much except what we look like when we die . . . and God knows, it already knows *that* well enough."

After a moment of silent thought, Arlene whispered, "I don't like it, Fly; it makes me feel like we're being watched."

"You think I'm paranoid?"

"I didn't say I didn't *agree;* I don't like the implications, that the whole invasion of the Martian moons is just practice, a war game, just the prelude to . . ."

"To what?"

"We'd damn well better find out, Flynn Taggart."

Arlene took the AB-10. I took the sweet darling that could kill minotaurs and open doors.

We didn't run into any trouble on our way to the other lift on this level; it was clearly marked on the video map. Maybe that was because there was so much trouble in the refinery. There must be a Law of Conservation of Tsouris. But the buttons for all levels below the next were inoperative. It was a local shuttle only. Arlene made triumphant noises, but I reminded her that we never did have a bet on.

Only way out is down, I repeated, and pressed the button. Whatever Arlene said, I still thought my primary duty was to get her the hell out of hell; but at the moment, her path and my path were the same: we both needed to burn deeper into the nightmare.

"I don't like the look of this place," said Arlene as we stepped from the lift into a vine-covered hallway.

"What's not to like? Rows of skulls, walls covered with squirming, writhing, fleshy ivy . . . should be like high school by now."

We gave the tendrils a wide berth; they looked like they

152

might loop around our throats and strangle the life from us.

"Fly," Arlene whispered, "I see another lift right through there." She pointed to the left, at a gap in the ivy on that side where I suddenly realized there was no wall—only the squirming expanse of "plant" life.

"Uh-oh," I said. There was more on the other side than a room with a lift in it. There were our old friends, the demons . . . imps, too.

We dropped back from the window while the imps began to hiss and heave flaming spitwads. Then my pal Arlene froze my marrow with a professionally calm voice in my ear: "Fly, I think we're going to need the rocket launcher, too."

I was already getting ready to rock 'n' roll when I turned to see a pair of giant, floating pumpkins trapped in a cage ahead of us. I could have sworn that spot was empty when we first came in here! Maybe the cage had been lowered just now.

If it had been demons, we could have ignored them; but the bars were spaced far enough apart that the pumpkins had all the space they needed to fire their deadly ball-lightning.

There was no telling why these heads were locked up; but it meant no more security for us than caged machine gunners.

The air crackled above us; electrical discharge ran thousands of prickling little fingers down my head and back, and our hair stood at attention. Arlene looked like a Goosh Ball. Focusing my concentration on the single task of standing up and firing, I heard her shout, "I'll take our nine!" referring to the maddened imps and demons to our left, at the "nine o'clock" position, ripping through the ivy.

We ducked as the fireballs seared the same area where the balls of lightning had played electric hairdresser. I wished the imps and pumpkins were only closer together, so that the fireballs and lightning balls might cross paths and wipe out both monster lines.

I nearly got my wish. Arlene opened up with the AB-10; when the imps returned fire, they hit their demon buddies . . . the rest was history. While demons swallowed imps, who did their best to give a horrible case of heartburn, I squeezed the firing ring, turning the pumpkin cage into an oven to bake pumpkin pie.

"Are you all right?" I asked. I could tell from the way she was shaking her head that she hadn't been this close to the rocket explosions before.

"As soon as the phone stops ringing between my ears," she answered.

"Pack a wallop, don't they?"

I was still worrying about the giant blocks of flesh as we skirted the cage and entered an empty, gray room. "They used to use a lot of chambers around here to crush ore and refine the liquid," Arlene explained. "Be careful . . . lots of dangerous equipment." Indeed, I could hear some heavy machinery really earning its keep right nearby. But what?

No platforms or lifts, no rising staircases; then Arlene won the prize by looking straight overhead.

"Holy ore-crusher, Batman!" she yelped.

The damned ceiling was descending on us. Not too fast, but fast enough. "Didn't I see this in a trideo?" I asked, edging back the way we'd come.

"It's just too Edgar Allan poetic," said Arlene.

We backed out before turning into grease spots. "Now what?"

"Hate to say it, Fly . . . but there ain't no other way to book. There must be a door or something in there—if we can find it and pop it before they have to scrape us up with a spatula."

The ceiling hit bottom, then rose again at the same stately pace. "We could hunt for another route past this garlic press," she said hesitantly. "But I'm pretty sure this is the only direct route around to Sector Nine, where we were looking through the ivy window at the other lift. At least, that's how I remember it from when I was posted here.

"Look, Fly, let me go in and hunt; I know what this place is like better than you."

I hated the thought—Arlene under the crushing ceiling while I waited outside, "guarding"! But . . . she had a point.

Flashlight in one hand, Arlene ran to the opposite end of the room while the ceiling was still rising. She rubbed her palm gently across the smooth surface.

"How are you doing?" my voice was strong enough to call out.

"I can't find any switches!" she called. Worried, I started pacing in front of the Poe chamber, a restless sentry. Arlene found nothing . . . but would you believe it? *I* triggered a motion sensor, causing a door to slide open near her. It was pure, dumb luck.

"Come on," she shouted. The ceiling had reached the top and was descending again. I ducked my head like a halfback center-punching through the line and bolted across the room through the door—which had already begun to close as the ceiling fell.

The door led to the room I'd seen from above, with huge, fleshy cubes rising and falling, an alien mockery of the ore-crushers.

But the blocks weren't just flesh; they were *alive*. Twenty-five pink, fleshy pumping platforms completely covering a room seemed more pointless than disgusting. They made high, whining sounds like newborn infants.

"What the hell are they?" I asked.

"Wonder if they can move out of those holes in the floor?"

"Christ," I added, "what do they *do?*"

Arlene edged closer to one block. She squatted and rose with it, following it down and up. "This isn't just random flesh, Fly; this is muscle tissue. Human muscle tissue."

I approached another block. "This is a heart or liver or something." I tracked along the edge of blocks. The last of the five blocks comprised convoluted ridges and furrows, folds in a grayish, spongy medium. "Unless my grandma's been lying all these years," I said, "them there's *brains,* A.S."

"Yecch." We backed away. "All right . . . muscles, brains, some kind of organ meat—this suggest a pattern to you, Fly?"

"Several." None of them pleasant.

"Are they farming meat, human flesh?"

"That's the best-case scenario, Arlene."

She looked at me with eyes widening. "And the *worst*-case?"

I smiled grimly. "They're farming *humans.* They're getting the hang of growing human cells because they're trying to genetically engineer zombie-soldiers, better than the pathetic ones they have now."

We watched the blocks rise and fall a couple more minutes. Then Arlene upspake. "Corporal?"

"Yes, PFC?"

"Permission to hose their research?"

"Permission enthusiastically granted. You have something in mind, Arlene?"

She did. There was a row of torches along the wall we'd entered by. We blew them out, then upended them, spilling the oil as we hopped from block to squishy block. At the far end, I let Arlene light the ceremonial cigarette lighter. It was her idea, after all.

We left the flesh blocks joyously in flame. I supposed the bone block would survive. Well, let the bastards animate skeletons, then!

We bolted down a corridor and turned the corner; there I halted in astonishment. Arlene plowed into me, then she too stared.

Fifteen demons had arranged themselves in a semicircle, backs to us, and they were grunting in unison, giving the impression of speech. Over to the right I noticed a barrel of the ooze.

"Have I ever told you about my barrel trick?" I whispered.

"Back up around the corner." I followed her, then peered around, lined up my shot very carefully, and gently squeezed the trigger.

The world exploded. The heat blast pressed on my right eye and right hand as I pulled back. The explosion even drowned out the screams of the demons.

When the debris settled and the last piece of pink and red demon flesh flopped to the smooth floor, Arlene nodded. "Impressive," she pronounced.

Then we found out what the demons had been doing crowded into that semicircle. They had been worshiping.

Out of the smoke and flame strode a hell-prince . . . and it was as mad as its name. It burst through the wreckage, throwing pieces of demon and chunks of masonry in all directions, a state-of-the-art minotaur with one hell of a 'tude.

The hell-prince roared defiance and began firing dead-ly bolts at us from its wrist launchers.

22

Run!" I shouted as I started loading the rocket launcher. She wasn't listening. Her AB-10 was rattling off hundreds of shots that harmlessly bounced off the hel-lion. Our only chance was the rocket launcher.

I fired off the first two rockets as I was dancing

backward; the force knocked me into Arlene and sent us both sprawling. The AB-10 skidded across the floor, and Arlene went after it on hands and knees. An energy bolt flashed between us, searing my eyeballs for a moment. I didn't care if I could see, so long as I could feel the smooth, metal surfaces of the little D-cell rockets and finish reloading. Just as I finished loading, my vision cleared; the eight-foot hell-prince bore down upon us, surrounded by smoke and stinking of brimstone.

I'd promised myself never, ever to fire off rockets this close to the target! But a good look at that green gorgon face with the ram's horns was all I needed to reassess my position. I squeezed.

The third and fourth direct hits slowed the behemoth to a confused crawl; but still it stood. I could see again—but now I couldn't hear.

Loading, fingers numb, I didn't bother getting back to my feet; I fired from where I lay. I slid past Arlene, who had picked up her machine pistol and was aiming it.

She shielded her eyes and hugged the ground as rockets five and six pounded the same tough chest that had withstood the previous four.

I closed my eyes while sliding; the force of the sound took me like a physical wave, carrying me down the hall. The weight of Mars pressed on my eardrums as I rose groggily to my feet to reload the launcher. The Prince of Hell stood stock-still, eyeing me with a doleful expression.

I aimed and prepared to fire; but the monster made a loud, wheezing sound—a sigh?—and tumbled over, stiff as a statue, to impact directly on its face.

"What in God's name was *that?*" Arlene gasped, still shaking.

"No naming game for this baby," I said. "Already has a name. You're looking at the same model of Hell Prince you dodged when you slipped through the crack on Phobos, before the Gate. *This* is what was tramping down the corridor while you scrawled a skull and C-bones on the wall."

She shook her head, clearing alien cobwebs and appearing truly weary for the first time. "Boy, if the light had been better, you'd have been on your own, Fly, 'cause I sure as hell wouldn't have wasted two seconds making a mark with *that* mother staring me in the face."

"Oh yes you would have."

"Egomaniac."

We needed all the cheering we could give each other. Picking through the carcasses, it seemed unfair that our only reward would be more ooze exactly where we needed to go.

"Damn," said Arlene, "the whole place looks flooded."

"You came up with the jogging theory," I reminded her. "Let's find out how good it is."

I shouldn't have said anything, for then she insisted on going first, running through the middle of the toxin. I followed close behind, feeling the pain right through my soles. We didn't quite manage to jog, but we did keep up a brisk walk.

The toxin slowed us down with a sucking, gripping quality; each second made me feel like it had been too long since my last checkup. I kept wishing for another of those crazy blue spheres to show up: I was beginning to wonder if I'd imagined the first.

All bad things come to an end. We finally made it around the facility to the other elevator in Sector 9, not ten feet from where we'd started, if only we'd been able to shove through the flesh-ivy. I was beginning to hate the ooze more than I did the monsters . . . except when it was in barrels.

The lift was the antique kind with a lever to start and stop, rather than buttons. We had a hell of a time trying to get it to stop at the next level down.

The level started with a teleporter; not a good sign, far

as I was concerned. "My turn to go first," I said; Arlene didn't argue.

By the time she arrived, thirty seconds later, I was back at work. I'd killed three imps and five former soldiers/ workers, a more dim-witted than usual zombie collection.

"My turn to rescue you," she said; but this was duck soup after the hell-prince. Heck, most of the zombies weren't even armed!

"We're getting good at this," I said.

"Don't get cocky," she warned. I let it pass without remark.

A platform lowered as we approached, as if inviting us into the parlor; still feeling cocky despite Arlene's warning, I stepped aboard. Arlene followed, of course.

At the top, I took a turn and came face to face with *another* hell-prince, holding a blue key card in its claws!

"Get it—get it!" Arlene shouted; I didn't know whether she meant the card or the monster . . . but in either case, I had only four rockets left, not enough!

I jerked up the launcher, then paused, staring. Something was weird. Then I realized: we were nose-to-snout, and the thing hadn't screamed yet.

Or moved. I edged closer . . . It was frozen solid, like it had seen a gorgon from Greek mythology. Turned to stone.

Heart pounding like a pile driver, I stepped close and gently plucked the blue key card from its claw. Then I rejoined Arlene on the floor, still shaking.

Toxic waste literally surrounded us, the dry space where we stood like an island. The light was good enough to see other raised machinery platforms making islands in this sea.

Arlene found a pole of thin metal. She tapped around for shallow parts and traced a crossable path to the first "island"; then she repeated the process until we made it through the toxic goop and into blue-glowing corridor.

At least the color of the corridor made me glad to have the blue key card. On cue, we ran into a blue-trimmed door at the end of the corridor. We crossed into a narrow corridor with red-glowing walls, floor, and ceiling, so bright that it hurt our eyes. We heard a familiar thud-thud at the end of the hall; it sounded like more flesh blocks.

Variety is the spice of life, even on Deimos. The sounds came from a piece of stamping machinery that didn't seem to be the least bit organic. I was grateful for that.

"Oh, great," said Arlene, "some jerk has tossed another key card onto the base." The implication was that we couldn't walk away from something so valuable as another computer key card.

A giant, metal piston repeatedly smashed down to within a few centimeters of the base, stamping anything on the base into powder. "Arlene, why would anyone put the card out for us, except as bait? We don't need it."

"We used the blue card to get this far," she insisted. "What's behind the mystery yellow door?"

"But Arlene . . ." She was through listening. The only way to get the yellow key card was to slide across the base, grab it, and roll off the other side before the stamping part came down to turn the contestant into paté.

She backed away, measuring the piston's rise and fall with her eyes. I was about to stop her and tell her about the patented Fly technique for opening doors; then I remembered my meager supply of rockets.

"At least let *me* do that," I said.

"You? Corporal Two-left-feet on the drill field?"

I opened my mouth to angrily protest; then I realized she was right—understating it, if anything. I never could get the timing right on anything more complicated than dress-right-dress or point-and-shoot.

My heart in my mouth, I watched Arlene count, timing

the piston. Then quickly, before she could think better of it or I could object again, she jumped just as it hit the low point and started to rise again.

Arlene sprinted across the room and threw herself into a face-first baseball slide, scooping the key card in her arms. She slid to a halt . . . but she was still on the base!

For an instant she froze. I couldn't possibly reach her in time—and a horrible image flashed through my mind.

If Arlene died, in the next cycle, I knew I would jump on the machine and die alongside her.

Thank God I didn't have to make that decision; at the last second she made a panic roll off the platform.

Arlene left the key card on the stamper, near the edge; but it was a simple matter, when the piston rose, to scoop it off from where she stood.

She pocketed it . . . and good thing; past the stamping machine was a thick airlock door, tough as a bank vault, surrounded by yellow lights. I doubt a rocket would even have scratched the chrome. Maybe a SAM.

The yellow key card let us into a central, circular corridor surrounding a giant, cylindrical room. We took a lift down into the room; once inside, the lift moved up again.

"Uh, Fly, I don't see any switch to bring it back down." Damned if she wasn't right.

From inside, the lift door looked like a spine with ribs coming out of it. Once again, no human would ever have made anything like this. The aliens were definitely re-working Deimos, and had been for some time.

"I don't like their interior decorator," she said, as if reading my mind. She tilted her head in the direction of the latest attraction. A row of what looked like red spittoons stretched out of sight, and on each one there was a skull bathed in red light.

"If these were human minds, I'd say they were psychotic," I commented.

"You know something, Fly? Every monster we've seen

has a head too large or strangely shaped to be mistaken for a human head."

"Yes."

"Then how do you account for the skulls? Whether they're designs on walls or ceilings or whole skulls like these, they're all human."

"And they couldn't have been taken from us, not all of them; with all the zombies and unbeheaded corpses, who'd be left?"

She touched one. "This isn't real," she said. "More like metal than bone."

I turned it over, looking at it from different angles. "I'll bet it's meant to scare us, same as the freakin' swastika. Well, we're past being bothered by Halloween."

I instantly regretted my choice of words. No sooner would I toss a challenge into the air than it would be answered. Was someone watching our every move?

This time it was a horde of imps, zombies, and a couple of pumpkins coming around the curve of the room, screaming doom in our ears. Fortunately, they were only coming at us from the one direction. We would have had no chance if attacked from both directions.

Arlene dropped flat, and I let fly with my last rockets. I ignored the imps, concentrating on the two pumpkins, the greater threat.

Somebody got careless on the other side, and soon all the monsters were mixing it up among themselves.

We drew back around the curve and waited for silence; then we slid back and smoked the survivors with shotgun and AB-10. I still had one last rocket.

In the course of the fight, somebody—us or them— accidentally activated a switch in the floor that caused part of a staircase to rise. When the last pumpkin smashed into orange and blue slime against the ruined head of the last assassinated imp, we started up the steps. Arlene activated the next switch.

Another set of steps rose, and we took them to the

third switch and set of stairs. At the top we found a teleporter.

We stepped aboard one at a time, me first, teleporting to a long corridor with barred windows looking outside. Arlene bent over for a closer view and pulled back with a gasp.

"Let me guess," I said. "You didn't see the stars or Mars."

Swallowing hard, she motioned for me to look for myself. She wasn't in the mood for humor. Blood had drained from her face, a reaction I'd never before seen in Arlene. I put my face against the window.

As a child, I'd seen a painting in a museum that gave me my first nightmare. I hadn't thought of it in years; but now it came back to me.

Beyond the window was a river of human faces, hundreds of them, each an island in an ocean of flesh. Each face had a horrified expression stamped on it, each a damned soul.

The spectacle achieved its purpose. We were both distracted. Otherwise we wouldn't have been so careless as to allow a stomping, single-minded demon to get close enough to clamp its jaws on Arlene's back and shoulder.

Her cries were echoed by each face in the river of damned souls, each screaming Arlene's pain and torment.

23

Arlene!" I shouted. I grabbed the monster with my hands and literally pulled it off her before it could position itself to take a second and certainly lethal bite.

It stumbled clumsily. I grabbed the AB-10 and pumped two dozen rounds into its open, blood-caked maw. It didn't get up.

I was almost afraid to touch her. Blood pumped out of the horrible, fatal wound.

Arlene was dying.

Her face was sallow, eyes vacant and staring. One pupil was dilated, the other contracted to a pinpoint. There was nothing I could do, not even with a full medical lab.

But damn her, she was *not* going to die here and join that river of faces.

As gently as I could, I lifted Arlene's bleeding body in my arms and carried her out of that circle of hell. Her rasping breath was a call to arms, a signal that life and hope still remained in the young gal.

I set her down at the end of the corridor; the lift door was blocked by a river of what appeared to be lava. Hoping the red stuff was at least no worse than the green stuff, I dashed across into an alcove where a single switch mocked me.

I flipped it, causing a path to rise up through the "lava." So far, so good. I ran back, grabbed Arlene, and walked across the path as quickly as possible.

At the last step before reaching the lift, I heard a grinding noise from behind. I paused and looked back: a *new* path rose slowly, leading to an alcove hidden from view except from where I now stood.

The cubbyhole contained another one of the blue-face spheres that I thought I'd never see again, the one item that I had hesitated to tell Arlene about because it seemed so incredible.

The sight was like another of the adrenaline bursts. Quickly, before the path could lower again, I powered her across, not bothering to stop and pick up pieces of equipment that fell from us, some landing on the path, some lost in the lava. I had a great terror that the sphere would fly away just before I got there, like a carnival balloon just out of reach.

I reached it, hesitated for a moment—then literally *threw* Arlene onto the sphere to make sure I wouldn't be the one to touch it first.

With a nearly audible silent pop, the blue liquid was all over her; and the red liquid on her body, the blood, evaporated into the blue. Arlene sat up and coughed, looking like someone coming out of a deep sleep.

"How do you feel?"

"My shoulder hurts like a son of a bitch. What the hell happened?"

"Pinkie decided to have you for a midnight snack. I put him on a diet. You sure you're all right?"

Standing up, she shook her arm, staring in wonder at the shredded sleeve and tooth marks. "What in God's name did you *do* to me?"

I figured the time had finally come to tell her about the magical blue spheres. She had no trouble believing me.

Only my pistol and some shotgun shells had been lost to the lava. Weapons in hand, we slid into the elevator and pressed the only floor button, labeled Command Center.

The lift had barely begun to grind slowly downward

when suddenly Arlene reached past me and pushed the red "kill" button. The elevator stopped, falling silent.

"Why did you kill the power?"

She stared at me before answering. For a moment I had a terrible fear that something had gone wrong with the blue sphere and she was going to turn into a zombie in front of me. Instead she asked, "Fly, are you starving, or is it just me?" I shook my head. She continued: "Maybe it's that blue thing, but I'm so famished I could swallow one of those pink demons."

"How about floating pumpkin pie for dessert?"

"And I'm suddenly exhausted. Fly, I need some sleep." I had completely lost track of the supplies. Arlene hadn't. "Don't you ever listen to training videos? Never wander into battle without MREs." She demonstrated the truth of her maxim. Suddenly, I realized I was hungrier than I thought. A Meal Ready to Eat sounded like the finest, gourmet cuisine in the solar system.

"A stopped elevator as a secure base. I never would've thought of it."

"Next best thing to a Holiday Inn," she added, raising an eyebrow. Arlene showed a domestic side that surprised me. While we talked, she took the packages of freeze-dried food and mixed them in the water of her canteen. "Sorry it'll be cold," she said as I watched her shake the contents with the skill of a bartender preparing the perfect martini.

"That's all right, beautiful. I like cold—" I picked up the package, glanced at the title. "—cold beef stew."

I also liked the fact that Arlene was alive. As we chowed down, I felt the strongest emotions since finding her on Deimos.

Maybe she sensed the inappropriate feelings coming off me in waves. She lowered her head and blinked rapidly, as if stopping herself from crying by main force.

"What's wrong?" I asked.

"Don't want to tell you."

"Why not?"

She hesitated. "Willy," she said. "PFC Dodd."

"Oh." I squirmed uncomfortably.

"I've been forcing myself not to think about him. He's dead, isn't he? Or . . . worse."

"You don't know that! I thought *you* were dead or reworked, but I found you alive."

"Find anybody else?"

I didn't say anything.

"Fly, I've accepted the fact. That he's dead, I mean. I don't think I could face—the other possibility." She looked up, her eyes moist but not tearing. "Promise me something."

"Anything possible."

"If we find him and he is, you know . . . and if I can't do it . . . will you? Promise? And don't mention him again."

I nodded, not trusting myself to speak. Funny lump in my throat. *Yeah, babe; I'll be happy to blow away my rival for your hand if he should happen to turn up a zombie. No problemo!*

She changed the subject, wrenching my mind back on the primary issue. "Fly, I think it's pretty likely that the aliens we're fighting aren't the same ones who built the Gates."

"I was wondering about that myself," I said. "All this weird stuff, skulls and satanic symbols—there was nothing about the Gates themselves that hinted at this. The Gates don't look like a Vincent Price movie."

"There's nothing eldritch about the Gates," she said. I was starting to like that word. "So let's assume these aliens found the Gates and discovered a way to turn them on from the other end. But why do they look so much like human-style demons?"

"Genetic engineering?" I suggested. "They could be deliberately designed to look like our conception of hell, particularly the hell-princes. They're the dead giveaways."

"Can't you find some other word than dead?" she begged, a fleck of red tomato paste on her lips.

"The hell-princes are just too much like medieval drawings of the devil to be natural."

"Unless they really are hell-princes," Arlene said.

I shook my head, unwilling to consider that possibility. So we sat in silence for a moment, finishing our food and drink. Much more thinking along these lines and I'd be ready to take communion again.

"I was never really afraid of monsters as a child," Arlene finally said. "Grown-ups were scary enough by themselves."

"Why invade at all? What is this for?"

"Good question," she said. "Here's another: If they can genetically engineer imps and demons, why do they need human zombie-slaves? And why grow human flesh?"

"Maybe they want super-zombies, more powerful than these dead excuses for lemmings, but still able to pass among us undetected."

Arlene yawned, struggling to show enthusiasm. "But that may be their weakness, Fly. The zombies don't amount to much. You and I aren't scared by skulls and evil symbols. What if there is a finite number of the actual monsters and they can't easily recreate them? What if the monsters too are 'reworked' from other creatures, creatures the mastermind has to breed and raise? That would mean every horrible creature we kill is one fewer to invade Earth if they can't be replaced. Until the new, improved pod-people come on-line."

I liked it. "Arlene, if you're right, all we have to do is kill everything . . . and we end the invasion."

We didn't have anything for dessert, so we used imagination to sweeten the conversation. "I've been thinking about the idea they're using Deimos as a spaceship," I said. "How can you move something as large as a whole moon?"

"I was thinking some sort of hyperspace tunnel. Yeah, I know; I've been reading too much sci-fi, Fly."

I didn't say it. At least it was something, a hypothesis. "Maybe there's some way to break through the tunnel walls?" I asked.

"Maybe. But it could also kill us. We don't know if 'outside the walls' has the same physical laws; and even if it does, if there's even any air."

"It could also disrupt what's happening, maybe destroy Deimos and everything on it."

"Including us? But that would throw a monkey wrench in their invasion plans," she said with a smile that turned into a yawn. She wasn't bored. Her eyelids were heavy from exhaustion.

"If these creatures run the moon—the ship," I said, "then what horrors guard the tunnel wall?"

"Those faces couldn't be real, could they? I hated those faces . . ." Her head nodded forward and she snored. It wasn't a very loud snore.

The elevator was as secure a place as we were likely to find. I sat watch and let her sleep. There was an eerie silence despite the faint vibration. After four hours I woke her up.

"Your turn," she insisted, rubbing pieces of sleep from her eyes.

"Don't let me sleep more than three hours."

"Fly, sleep! I command you to sleep," she said, making hypnotic passes. I slept . . . not because of the mystic passes, but because of a mud slogger's ability to sleep anywhere.

I could have done without the dreams.

The river of faces touched something deep in both of us, the place where you store up all your fears and regrets. Going to sleep meant sinking right into that place.

I was tangled in long, sticky fibers like a giant spiderweb, but at the center of the web was a face made of a hundred different faces. I didn't want to look at it; but the face came closer, slowly rotating like a planet, showing different faces spread across its surface, smiles melting into frowns, rows of eyes like so many beads of glass, noses creating an uneven mountain range stretching to the horizon.

Then the sphere of blue faces was pressed right against mine, and it had stopped turning. In the center was the face of my long dead grandfather as I had seen him in the open casket. His toothless mouth was working, lips twisting, but no sounds came out.

I knew what he was saying, though: "Dinna let them rework me, Fianna Flynn, me lad . . . dinna never let them rework us all, b'Gad."

The sticky fibers became tendrils sliding up my nose and into my mouth, choking me. The truth is out there . . .

I woke up in a cold sweat. Arlene was shaking me hard. "Fly, are you okay?"

"Sleep is overrated," I gasped. I was just as tired as when I'd put my head down. Standing, I felt dizzy. Probably running a fever, but I didn't want to mention it. There was nothing to be done anyway. I pushed the button back in to reactivate the power; then I pushed the floor button, and the elevator continued its trip to the Command Center.

It was a good thing we'd eaten and tried to get some rest. The moment the doors opened, we were in another damned firefight with zombies, imps, pumpkins, and a specter.

The ambush trapped us in the lift. We used the lift doors for cover.

By the time we worked our way out, we'd cleaned a huge room with stairways at either end, leading up to a split-level. There were six pillars; each had its designated nasty hiding behind it.

Pushing through a door at the top of the split-level, we

found a gigantic indoor garden or arboretum. The air was thick with pollen from a jungle of fleshy plants overgrowing where some breed of computers used to be.

Arlene sneezed repeatedly. I lucked out. I was so exhausted that maybe I wasn't breathing as deeply. "You can say one thing for the greenhouse," I observed. "Plants are plants here, and not combined with machines."

Blowing her nose—allergies—Arlene added: "And men are men, and so are the women." All that was missing was a handsome horse and blazing six-guns.

The absence of monsters was reason enough to explore. We could breathe later. The primary motif seemed to be a blackish, oily wood that sure as hell never originated on the old home planet. Periodically, the wood bubbled and popped, like ulcerated sores in whatever monstrous trees had produced it. I imagined a three-headed Paul Bunyan with ax-handle hands cutting the planks.

The ground squished underfoot as we walked; I looked closely and saw incredibly long, wafer-thin insects scooting out from under our feet. We finally reached the end of the arboretum and the vegetation ran out against puke-green marble, just as we'd seen back in the warehouse.

"Will you look at that?" said Arlene, pointing at red-orange curtains of fire crackling beyond the high walls, at a sufficient distance that we weren't roasting.

"Now that's bad taste," I said. "Next they'll have Lieutenant Weems in a red devil suit pop out of a cake."

"Complete with pointy tail?" she asked wryly.

"You have a twisted mind, PFC Sanders."

The better to explore with, I added mentally. I hoped this situation wasn't like those science fiction stories where the terrifying menaces are taken telepathically from the greatest fears of the human beings involved. My worst fears couldn't be this corny!

Arlene found a switch that opened a hidden room; we went with the flow. Entering the chamber, we marveled at how different it was from what we'd seen before. The entire room was constructed of that black, oily, ulcerating wood. There was one object in the room, placed at dead center: a bas relief of a demonic monster more horrible, or more ridiculous, than any we'd fought. Every physical attribute of the thing was exaggerated so that it almost seemed to be a cartoon. The largest protuberance of all was its penis, sticking out at a 45-degree angle.

"They've got to be kidding," said Arlene.

"I hate to bring it up, but that's probably another switch," I suggested.

"I've handled worse," she admitted.

24

As she flipped the switch, we heard familiar heavy, grinding sounds outside in the marble chamber. Being nearer the door, I took a look-see. I wasn't the least bit surprised to see a set of stairs rising up in the marble room leading straight up to one of the walls of fire. Arlene joined me in pondering this new development. Neither of us seemed to be in a great hurry to run up those stairs.

"Do you feel fireproof?" she asked me.

"I left my asbestos pajamas back on Earth."

"Maybe there's an opening we can't see from down here."

"We can only dream," I sighed. I went first. She was close behind, though. As soon as it became too hot, I had every intention of stopping. I didn't feel any heat at all.

Arlene noticed as well. "This isn't a bit like Campfire

Girls," she said. "By now, all the marshmallows in my pocket should be screaming out: 'Put me on a stick!'"

"You have marshmallows?"

"No."

"I don't think it's a real flame. Wait here, Arlene. If I catch on fire or die of heat stroke, you'll know there was something wrong with my theory." Another ten steps up the stairs convinced me that I was definitely on to something. Ten more steps and I was becoming certain. I still wasn't hot as I walked right up to the curtain of seething flame and very slowly put my hand out.

The hand went right through the fire, disappearing from view without causing Yours Truly the least discomfort. I didn't even get a blister. "Arlene," I called out, "the fire is an illusion. Come on up."

I walked right through, then turned around where the fire should be . . . and there was nothing there but the welcome sight of Arlene coming up the stairs. "Arlene, can you see me?" I asked.

"No," she answered, staring right at me. "You've disappeared behind the fire."

"For my next illusion," I announced with my best stage magician's voice, and stepped back through where the curtain had to be, "I pull something cool out of my hat."

"Like a beer?" she asked, taking the last steps two at a time so we stood on the same level.

"No beer, but I do have a surprise." She was curious, and I bent from the waist, gesturing through the curtain. She preceded me to the big surprise.

"Oh, no," she said, "not another teleporter."

We were both pretty worn-down by this point, but a new teleporter meant we had to make a decision. What we needed was a map to show us the location of all the frying pans and fires. "So should we bother with this one or not?"

She sighed. "We'd better try it, Fly. We've got to find a

way off this moon, and this is pretty carefully hidden away. Let's give it a shot, hon."

"Who's first this time?" I asked.

She hooked her arm in mine. "Let's do it together again."

Weapons out, we stepped aboard. With a flash of light, we zapped to a huge room shaped like the spokes of a wagon wheel.

Six hell-princes surrounded us.

Six monstrous mouths opened.

Six monstrous throats emitted guttural screams.

Twelve angry, red eyes burned at us in the dim light.

The hell-princes were not the only ones screaming. Arlene and I screamed, too. This was a sight to make anyone howl at the moon. As the green fireballs began exploding all around us, we simply lost it—running around like chickens with their legs cut off, shooting wildly. There was nowhere to run, but we sure as hell tried!

"Duck!" we shouted at each other at about the same time. The balls of energy made fireworks over our heads. Our gunfire was nothing more than a quiet popping in that chaos, mild raindrops, but we kept firing, me with my shotgun and Arlene with her AB-10.

I found a door by pure, random chance. Praying for a miracle, I hollered for Arlene and yanked the door open . . . and now I was surrounded by a dozen floating pumpkins! Frying pans and fires—definitely frying pans and pumpkins.

Arlene screamed something from the chamber with the hell-princes, but I couldn't hear her over my own screaming. This situation was fast becoming unacceptable.

There were too many pumpkins even to think about shooting; death, doom, and destruction from all directions! I ran as fast as I could . . . right back into the room with the hell-princes.

I wasn't thinking very clearly, but Arlene still had her head screwed on. Her hand snaked out and grabbed me. She'd stepped inside another of the spoke-chambers and now hauled me inside with her. I imagined wall-to-wall demons waiting for us, zombies stacked like cordwood to the ceiling, imp tartare . . . but inside, for the moment, was nothing but Arlene and Yours Truly.

She held a finger against her lips; I braced myself for the Bad Guys to come after us and imagined the absolute worst. A tidal wave of sound crashed on us—roaring, screaming, crashing. But all that came through that doorway was sound. The pumpkins and the hell-princes collided in a torrent of blood and vengeance.

There were so many monsters that they took a long time to die. At least fifteen minutes Arlene and I crouched in our little closet of safety as the pumpkins splattered themselves against the horned heads of the hell-princes. Blue balls of energy evaporated against lethal lightning bolts. Blood flowed thick on the floor. We stayed right where we were.

Finally, there was beautiful silence. We heard each other's breathing. "Who goes first?" Arlene whispered.

"What do you mean?"

"Who takes a peek?"

I raised my hand as if I were back in grade school. Cautiously I poked my head outside the star-pointed hideaway. A single hell-prince remained on its feet. I pulled back inside our hideaway and reported.

"Then why isn't he at the doorway threatening to rip our lungs out?"

I looked past her. The hell-prince loomed in the doorway, waiting to . . .

It looked like yesterday's lunch today. Arlene saw my face, followed my eyes and saw it.

I grabbed for my rocket launcher, but it was gone from the webbing—dropped in panic in one of the two rooms, of course!

Arlene pointed her AB-10. "That won't work," I

shouted. A peashooter against the most powerful monster we'd run into! Had she gone insane?

She pulled the trigger three times, and thrice the hammer clicked on an empty chamber.

She stared as the mauled, bloody beast staggered forward like Frankenstein's monster, clutching at her. Winding up like the Mud Hens' star pitcher, she heaved the gun into the minotaur's ugly face. *Good God. I'm watching an old episode of Superman!* I thought.

It blinked. The horned head shook slowly back and forth, left to right, as if trying to remember something.

Then it fell, straight as a toppling redwood, to the cold marble—dead.

"And I didn't even know he was sick," said Arlene. We both burst into hysterical laughter—stress released.

The floor was slippery with slick, tacky pumpkin juice, and we almost slipped several times. Clambering across the body of another hell-prince, Arlene pushed into the pumpkins' room and shouted, "You won't believe this!"

"What?" I was hunting for my good pal, Mr. Launcher.

"Get your butt in here! Um, *please* get your butt in here, Corporal." There it was! I snagged it and clambered after her.

The light was flickering, but I could see well enough. Crucified on the walls were the mutilated bodies of four hell-princes, with spidery trails of dried blood extending from their hands—if those hams with claws on the end could be called hands.

"Jesus, Mary, and Joseph! What the hell is going on here?" *Blasphemy!* chanted my memory-nuns... *demons crucified in mockery of Our Lord.*

The hell-princes were killed a long time ago; the dried blood told us that much. We made a circuit of the chamber and found plastic spheres with cracks so that they could swing open or close as easily. All the spheres were empty... but they were just the size to hold pumpkins.

"Pumpkin nests," said Arlene.

I stared awhile longer at the four crucified bodies of the minotaurs. "My God, it must have been the damned *pumpkins themselves* put the princes up there! They must hate them worse than they do us."

It was a religious revelation for both of us. "No wonder it's so easy to pit them against each other," said Arlene in awe. "They despise and loathe each other so much, they proudly display each other's ripped carcasses." She looked up at me, face lighting up. "Jesus, Fly, we have a chance to win!"

I saw where she was headed. I had thought that the monster-aliens were simply so bad-tempered that when a zombie stumbled in the way of an imp fireball, or a demon took a bullet meant for one of us, they lost their concentration and turned on each other with mindless ferocity.

But "mindless ferocity" didn't explain the cold, deliberate crucifixion of hell-princes by pumpkins, did it? Such a contemplative act required a deep, abiding animosity or hatred, and the single-minded determination to torture.

Something, the "mastermind," held them together; but left to themselves, the natural inclination of each monster would be to hunt down all the other kinds and kill them.

The thought certainly suggested our tactic: kill the damned mastermind, and let nature take her course!

Now the only question was where in this hell that mastermind was.

We continued searching the pumpkin room. We found it stuffed with ammo, everything from rockets to shells to rounds for Arlene's depleted AB-10; the various firefights had run us dry. After loading up, we pushed past one of the crucified hell-prince bodies and checked out the rest of the wagon wheel.

Not a creature was stirring, not even a zombie.

"Shall we teleport?" asked Arlene.

"After what happened the *last* time we teleported?"

"We going to spend the rest of our lives on this karmic wheel?"

"Après vous, Bodhisattva."

We teleported together. Appearing on a platform in a metallic room, we saw a door with blue trim that sure as shootin' required a blue key card. Arlene went over and put her ear to it. "I hear what might be a lift operating; I guess we go thataway."

"Key, key, who's got the key?" I asked. "Another typical day on the job. Teleport. Get a key. Open a door. Find a teleport."

Arlene smiled. "I guess we're in a rut."

25

Nothing remarkable about this area, except one dark section that was just begging for a flashlight. I went up, cast a light, and saw twisty passages that suggested a maze. The light was curiously muted, dying out after only a few feet.

"You want to poke in here?" I whispered; whispering seemed appropriate.

"Um . . . no. Maybe we don't need to; and I don't like the look of the place. It's dark—not that I'm afraid of the dark!"

"Really? I sure am, especially recently. All right, it's pitch-black, it's a maze, and the ceilings are low and claustrophobic. Pass." I mean, why? Life is short, especially on Deimos.

I was still staring into the blackness when gunshots yanked my attention back to Arlene. I raced down the hall and saw her pumping slugs into tiny, emaciated demons, so small I almost didn't recognize them. "Look what I found!" she exclaimed, kicking the tiny bodies aside. Reaching behind their corpses, Arlene extracted a blue key card.

Tiny demons? I wondered . . . were they mutants? Failed experiments? Or did demons shrink when they starved? Other possibilities were more disturbing: Were these child demons? Were demons born or hatched, or created whole somewhere? I shuddered; whatever they were, they gave me the creeps more than their gigantic counterparts.

She sprang the door with the key card, and we went right through, smooth as you please . . . only to discover *another* door right behind it, this one requiring a yellow card! "Egah," I bellowed, and by God I meant it!

An hour later we had traded a bunch of ammunition for a shiny, new, yellow key card. Don't ask.

We shuffled back to the mystery door, and Arlene inserted the card.

It slid. Revealing . . . Yet another door: red.

"You know," I said, "there's only one section of this whole place we've avoided."

"The dark, mazy thing we passed? Fly, we don't even know there's a key card in there, or that if there is, it's red."

"Well . . . I shot a door open with a rocket once."

"How many rockets we have?"

"Now? Six."

"How many does it take to kill a hell-prince?"

"Usually six."

Arlene sucked air through her teeth. "Maze," she voted.

I understood her concern; if we used one or two rockets to open the last door, then encountered a minotaur on the other side, we'd be out of luck. I shrugged; maze it was.

As we entered the pitch-black corridor, our flashlights barely penetrated the darkness. "There must be some kind of neutralizing or damping field," Arlene whispered behind me.

This bit was too close to that Jules Verne movie, where the members of the expedition get separated in the dark. I wasn't going to let that happen to us.

"Fly—didn't I see a pair of goggles of some sort back in the yellow-key room?"

"Did you? What of it?"

"Could they be light-amplification goggles?"

That sounded like a good excuse to get out of the dark. Actually, *anything* sounded like a good excuse to get out of that dark maze; I had the creepy feeling that creatures were shadowing us . . . creatures that didn't *need* light-amp goggles.

We returned the way we had come, and sure enough, the goggles were there. Arlene was right: one pair. "Will these even work in the energy-sucking field?" I wondered.

Arlene shrugged. How else could we find out?

At the mouth of the maze we hesitated. Who was to wear them? We settled it scientifically: my vision was 20-40, barely good enough to avoid glasses; Arlene's was 20-15, better than "perfect." In other words, she got the goggles.

Besides, she was the girl. I don't know why that occurred to me then; she seemed to get the goggles an awful lot.

She put them on and adjusted for ambient light, then led me back into the tunnel of darkness. I don't even like haunted-house rides at amusement parks. "Oh, spit," she said.

"Don't give me any bad news."

"Battery's low."

"I told you not to give me any bad news."

"The goggles keep fading in and out." She'd stopped walking forward and I bumped up against her again. "Or maybe it's because of the field; but they're lower power than the flashlights, and they do work . . . sort of."

She started moving again, and dark as it was, I made believe I was her shadow, hand on her shoulder. "Tell me what you see."

"Everything is green and fuzzy. It's like looking at the world through a Coke bottle."

About five minutes into the maze Arlene dived to the side, bowling me over. An exploding ball of energy lit up our surroundings for a fraction of a second; but all I saw was the back of Arlene's head.

"Hell-prince!" she shouted. "Fly, use the launcher!"

"Can't we run?"

"No," she said, strangely insistent, "we've *got* to fight it!"

I unslung and waited, staring wide-eyed into the black. "Where? Where is it?"

"I'll guide you," Arlene said, voice lower, more in control. Holding her shoulder so she wouldn't be between me and my monster, I tried to aim the rocket launcher with the other hand. I couldn't do it!

"Still—stand still, beside me," she urged. "Right. Now listen . . ." Another lightning ball scorched the air, pounding the wall just above my head, and I dropped the damned weapon! She didn't miss a beat. "It's right at your feet, Fly. Bend down, pick it up.

"Why don't *you* take it? You can see!"

"Fly, *I don't know how to shoot it*—never checked out on it. Now shoulder it, damn you."

"Aim me." I was becoming impatient, but I knew she was working as fast as she could.

"Left, to the left, more, more; elevate . . . shoot now!" I squeezed the firing ring. The flare of the rockets lit up a cone of vision around us but I still couldn't see the attacker. "Where is he? Where?"

"Never mind—you winged him, Fly! Glancing blow to the stomach, knocked him down."

"Aim me again."

The second shot scored a direct hit. Normally that wouldn't stop a hell-prince. He'd only redouble his efforts. But this one must have gotten lazy in the maze, only encountering victims occasionally, and no resistance worth mentioning. Suddenly I realized we were facing a minotaur in something like its natural habitat.

Aim me—fire!—aim me . . . I loaded my sixth and final round. "Where?"

Arlene waited a long time. "Fly . . . you knocked it to its butt in a chair thing with your last shot; it's still breathing, but it's not getting up."

We waited; the situation remained static. "All right, kid," I said. "I guess we're officially clear."

"And now I can officially tell you why we had to fight. Look at this—whoops, I mean feel this: a key card, though I have no idea what color; they all look green to me. That slime had it in its claws."

"You mean it was there while I fired rockets at the hell-prince? I could have destroyed the key, too!"

"Well, that's why I kept it a secret. Now aren't you glad you saved those rockets?"

"I guess so," I said, not bothering to point out that if we hadn't gone into the maze at all, just used one or two rockets on the door, we'd be out of here by now, and richer in rockets, to boot.

We started trekking back, and with the unerring instinct such items have, the batteries chose that moment to burn out.

Arlene tipped me off with, "Damn it to hell!"

She pulled the goggles off and shoved them into her pocket. "God, Fly, I don't want to die in the dark." I thought she had a perfectly reasonable attitude. The idea of being caught and torn to shreds when you can't even see to fight back didn't appeal to me, either.

I had a vague idea of the way we must return. I took her

hand and led her as fast as possible in that direction. Even found time to pray again. The nuns always knew the power of a dark room to inspire piety.

After all that, I really was in no mood for a damned imp waiting for us when we'd almost made it through the maze. It hissed, and we stopped cold . . . we could hear it—but where *was* it? Hands shaking, I spun left and right with my scattergun, afraid to shoot lest I give away our own position. Or worse, hit Arlene!

"Jesus!" Arlene shouted, finding religion as a fireball careened over our heads. What a dolt—the imp, not Arlene; the fireball lit our surroundings, and in the glare I fixed Arlene and the imp. When the fireball faded, I shot where the imp was. Arlene didn't kill time when she could kill a monster instead; she fired just as I did, and the imp was toast.

We were back in the light in short order. We returned to the three-door stack. I performed the honors of opening the last door, popping through, finding the lift, pressing the down button . . . and asking Arlene if she didn't enjoy the music of screams and explosions behind us as the monsters took care of each other. They were running out of humans.

"This is a hell of an invasion," she said.

"You can say that again."

Deimos must have been listening and eager to confirm every prejudice we had. As the lift door slid open at the next level down, we found ourselves staring into the hugest, hairiest, foulest, and *pinkest* butt I'd ever seen.

One of the demons, Arlene's "pinkies," was standing with its backside up against the lift door. It hadn't even noticed that the door had opened. Cautiously, I raised a machine gun and Arlene raised a shotgun. We gritted our teeth against the noise and fired simultaneously. A Light Drop rectal suppository.

But on the other side of Demon One was Demon Two—and it did not take kindly to our prescription. This one charged like a *hausfrau* on speed in a megastore.

We hadn't been able to see it originally because its buddy had blocked the view. Now it dived through the door after us.

The big silly got itself stuck. We took our time blowing this one to oblivion at point-blank range. Oh, our bruised eardrums!

As Arlene wiped demon gunk out of her eyes, she took a gander at her clothes and asked, "Does this come out or is it like gravy?"

"Don't ask me. I was never much of a house husband."

Although we felt good about our most recent bout of carnage, we couldn't help but notice that we'd trapped ourselves between two demon bodies, each of which probably weighed over five hundred kilos; a half ton per baby. We'd have to climb out between them.

"How are you at mountain climbing?" she asked.

"How are you at spelunking?" I asked back.

She owned I was right; we didn't so much climb over the bodies as burrow our way through them. It took a bit of wriggling and writhing, and breath holding, but eventually even I made it.

The next problem consisted of some imps. Mighty monster slayers such as Arlene and myself could no longer be bothered with something so trivial as a few imps. We mopped up the floor with them on our way

"I think we're getting a bit cocky," Arlene said.

"We earn the right to wear the haircut of our choosing," I shot back, and she laughed louder than ever before.

We entered a warehouse through an open door and around a couple of corners; this one was stacked wall-to-wall with pinkies, none as large as our elevator pals. They charged; having nowhere else to go, I leapt up, grabbed the edge of a huge box and hauled myself onto the top, then stretched out my hand for Arlene.

The way the demons screamed and growled and pounded on the box, you'd think they didn't appreciate initiative and quick thinking. They were so upset they made the box shake violently. I was afraid we might be thrown off, but by God, we hung on. Then we aimed, squeezed, and eventually the box stopped shaking. We didn't have any trouble getting down.

Now we had a moment to enjoy the new decor. The motif here was gleaming chrome and intricate, blued enamel. The appearance was rather sci-fi, actually . . . utterly misplaced, considering the monsters inhabiting it. But then, I didn't subscribe to *Better Homes and Demons*.

Then we kicked the door at the far end—well, *I* kicked it—and found the spawning vats themselves.

Huge, metal containers they were, a heaping helping of pure evil; cisterns containing a weird, toxic-green junk, but not thick like the slime; inside each container was the body of a half-formed monster.

Arlene, on a whim of personal revulsion against the aliens, shot one of the partly formed torsos. The wound sealed up with a giant sucking sound, and the creature continued cooking. "How do you stop something like this?" she asked.

"I wish I knew. We can give up the hope of a finite number of the things. They must be genetically engineered soldiers. The alien mastermind, whoever or whatever it is, must be stealing our nightmares and producing them wholesale."

"Uh, yeah. I wonder how long it takes for a vat to finish producing a newborn monster?"

Arlene held up her watch. Six minutes later the one she'd shot was finished, and none the worse for wear. She shot it again as it stumbled out of the vat. Again and again. Now the bullets worked. We repeated the experiment several more times at six minute intervals.

"The fluid is life-preserving as well as life-producing," I said. "But when a critter is born——"

"In other words," Arlene said, "we can't do abortion, but we sure as hell can nail 'em as newborns." She wrinkled her brow. "Let's do a rough calculation: at six minutes to cook a monster, that's ten creatures per hour per vat. Say sixty-four vats in the room, means 640 monsters per hour just from this one room. Christ! That's fifteen thousand per day."

"There, ah . . . there could be scores of rooms."

"In a few days they could have an army of millions," Arlene said, finishing her number exercise.

"We still have one chance, Arlene. Find the alien mastermind and destroy it."

"Yeah, that's all we have to do," she scoffed. "Piece of cake."

26

Too many, too many monsters, monsters, monsters," I muttered.

"Monsters, monsters everywhere," she echoed. "I don't suppose it matters if there are any new types. We're doomed no matter what."

"Don't say that, Arlene. We've been able to kill everything we've come up against so far. That matters. The weapons and ammunition give us a fighting chance."

"Rats in a maze," she said in a tone of voice new to her. She sounded defeated. I didn't like that one bit. "You were right, Fly. Even if we always find enough ammo, it won't save us. There are *millions* of them. They *are* testing us."

They are!

At a moment like this I realized how important it was that we had each other. I'd experienced this same sense of defeat on Phobos, and for less cause. Now it was my turn to encourage the natural fighting spirit that burned so deeply in her.

"Then how we respond to this is part of the test, as well. We won't defeat them by firepower. That's only to buy us time so we can reason out a solution."

She looked at me without blinking and asked, "Fly, what if there is no solution?"

"Don't believe that!" I urged, and in so doing helped convince myself. "If they were unbeatable, they wouldn't need to collect data on us."

That took some of the shadows out of her dark mood. "Don't worry," she said. "I won't let you down."

She'd been my buddy, my pal. We'd been careful not to confuse the issue by trying to be lovers. But this was the right moment to take her in my arms, bring our faces close together and whisper, "It's you and me. We'll go to the end together. We'll make them pay for everything."

"Outstanding," she said breathily, transforming the traditional Marine bravado into something very different. A moment passed between us that reminded me of the time we *could have been* lovers and chose buddies instead. Now I kissed her hard and she responded. We might not have another chance. And we weren't going any farther than this; not in a place where we could so easily be reworked into dead meat, still on the hoof.

"I'm feeling better," she said. "My brain is working again. You know, we're in a good spot to do some damage."

"Go on."

"The bottom level of Deimos, directly below us, is one huge tank that was eventually going to be filled with liquid oxygen."

"What the hell for?"

She flashed her sneaky smile. "You'll love this. The UAC was thinking of using the entire moon of Deimos as a spaceship, too."

"You're kidding!" I said, but I could tell she wasn't.

"The idea was to move it to the asteroid belt and use it

188

for a mining base," she said, finishing the news flash. "When I first realized we were moving, I thought some of us might be back in charge here. Then I suspected the more horrible possibility of a human-alien alliance."

"Jesus, what a morbid imagination! How is it I never heard about this plan even in casual talk?"

"There's secret, there's top secret, and then there's 'rat us out and we'll push you out the airlock.'"

"Point taken. If we're going to find out what's really going on, then, I think we need to go the same way as before. Down."

We hunted through the level, but couldn't find an exit, a secret door, anything. While we were searching, Arlene's mood improved. That we were still alive was a miracle. Any monsters who tried to have us for lunch would get a bad case of indigestion. No matter what we were up against, I was going to bet on human unpredictability. We hadn't spent a couple of billion years clawing to the top of the food chain for nothing.

"Fly, have you noticed how this section is shaped?" Actually, I hadn't. We'd been working our way along the inside of the wall in search of switches. "It's shaped like a skull," she said.

"These guys are running out of ideas," I answered.

"Those two pillars over there," she said, pointing, "are the eyes."

"Cute," I said. Less cute was the pumpkin that suddenly came out of nowhere and began firing at us. Arlene and I hadn't shot anything in whole minutes. We deflated the pumpkin; and this one acted more like a balloon with the air let out that any of its brothers, as it zigged and zagged on the way down.

We chased it beyond the two pillars, where we found its limp and leaking remains sitting like a cork on a narrow ladder-tube leading down. "At last," she said, "a guidepost."

"Just what the place needs," I concurred.

And now what? Should we still continue "down"? Or

was it time to settle once and for all whether we were bugging out and reporting or going after the mastermind ourselves?

I stared at the tube. So far as I could tell, down was *still* the only way out. So far, our paths still coincided.

But there would come a time when one of us would have to prevail: either Arlene's romantic sense of duty to the entire human race, or my more practical duty to her as my buddy, as a Marine, and—all right, let's face it—and as a man to a woman.

We popped the "cork" and climbed down what seemed like two hundred meters, down into the heart of the lox tank. The climb was long enough to make us tired even if we weren't carrying all the crap that was necessary to keep us alive. By the time we reached bottom, my hands were aching and my right knee was acting up. I could imagine how Arlene was feeling from the way she tottered on her feet. I hurried over to catch her if she fell, but she recovered herself and made no comment.

We found a cozy room with four doors and a single switch in the center. "Do you hear that?" Arlene asked.

Until she mentioned it, I hadn't heard anything but our heavy breathing; but then I noticed something so unbelievably loud that a deaf man should have felt it; concentration is a funny thing.

It sounded like the World Trade Center taking a stroll just outside.

We rotated slowly, tracking the noise, and I thought about that movie with the tyrannosaurus stomping around.

"Well, Fly, what now? I doubt we could climb back up again."

I looked up; the hole we'd climbed through was far over our heads. "We already know there's no way to get us out in that direction. We're here; if an exit exists, it has to be through one of those doors."

"Besides, we came here to do a job, Fly, even if that means fighting Godzilla."

I shrugged; what else was there to say? "One switch; four doors. Which one does it open?"

I went to a door at random and tried to open it manually. Nothing. It wouldn't budge, even when I kicked it. The behemoth still marched back and forth outside, shaking the entire building with every step.

"I can't help it," I said at last, "I'm a born lever-puller."

"You're repeating yourself," Arlene repeated.

She flattened against the wall as I slapped the switch, then joined her. All four doors opened smoothly, simultaneously.

"Move out!" I shouted.

As fast as we could, we bolted through the door and entered a tiny, garagelike room looking into a brilliantly lit, silver and white, chrome-covered keep—the size of Texas. Wings from the central room extended like an X into the huge tank.

We slid outside on the double. The sound of the walking skyscraper inspired speed on our part—and that was without even bothering to look behind to see what was making all the ruckus.

Halfway to one of the wings, I couldn't stand the suspense; like Mrs. Lot, I looked back.

I thought I'd seen everything. After imps and demons and pumpkins and hell-princes, I'd be able to handle anything else they threw at us! At least that's what I thought.

I'd also thought the hell-princes were giants when I first saw them. My scale was in for a rude awakening.

"Mother Mary!" I shouted involuntarily. The others weren't monsters any longer, not compared to this!

It stood five meters tall, with piston-driven legs supporting a body that must have weighed hundreds of tons. Deep within its massive structure came the grinding of many gears. The arms were also piston-driven, and the left arm ended in a huge box that didn't look anything like a lunch box.

"No!" This time it was Arlene who had glanced behind and echoed my opinion. Now that we'd had our turn at making noise, it was time for the colossus to speak.

The scream of rage that came out of its mouth was so loud that it was as if the two long horns—one on each side of its head, and growing out so far as to end over the muscled shoulders—were actually 50,000-watt stereo speakers amplifying the sound so that everyone could hear it from Deimos to Phobos to Mars.

While it roared, the arm with the box on the end pointed at us. That broke the spell. We were both very good at noticing anything pointing at us.

We ran like hell itself was on our tail, up the left wing seconds ahead of a terrific detonation. A miniature cruise missile had missed us, impacting against the far wall. Even at a distance of two hundred meters, the explosion knocked us off our feet.

We ran as we'd never run before. All the eighteen-wheelers in the universe were coming at us on a down-grade to doom. We needed an exit ramp.

"Look!" Arlene screamed, pointing at a narrow hole where the wings joined the central building we'd just exited. She dived through without a hitch. Me, I got stuck—it was Phobos all over again! But I wasn't going to waste an opportunity, even with the wits scared out of me.

I turned and loosed a few rounds from my trusty rocket launcher. I figured, *Why the hell not?*

The rockets struck dead-on—with no apparent effect.

The titan roared; a good translation, I guess, would be, *"Now it's my turn!"*

27

The steam-driven demon returned fire, striking the wall of the wing, blowing us to the ground. The good news was that this finished the task of getting me through the hole.

We were so stunned, we could barely pick ourselves up from the floor; a floor that was shaking from the approaching leviathan. "Get up!" I said, grabbing Arlene by the arm and pulling her to her feet. The colossus stomped straight toward us, and I knew that a flimsy piece of wall would be like a piece of Kleenex to the thing even before he ripped through it without slowing down.

We staggered in the other direction, up the other wing. "My right foot's numb!" Arlene hollered. "It's asleep!" I heard the fear in her voice. I'm sure she could hear the fear in mine, too.

"Wake it up," I said, and while she stomped her foot, forcing the blood to circulate, I fired a few more rockets at the monster. There was no effect worth mentioning.

"This thing won't die!" Arlene shouted as we ran.

"Not without something heavier," I agreed. Arlene stared at the far wall and started mumbling to herself, obviously making thumbnail calculations. I added one and one, and got two human beings crazy with terror.

As we rounded the corner of the next wing, we heard the steam-driven demon crunching after us. At least he wasn't moving any faster than a brisk walk. At his size, if he didn't tire, that walk would finish us. I didn't want to think about the missiles he could fire. We turned another corner. So long as we heard him but didn't see him, I figured we were doing our best.

"Fly!" Arlene cried. "Near as I can figure, this room is much larger than the Gate gravity field the aliens set up." She took another deep breath, coughed, continued: "The periphery of the room should be at normal Deimos gravity."

"Close to zero, you mean."

"Yes."

I froze, staring at the far wall. Something was nagging at the back of my brain. This was no time to ignore hunches, instincts, or sudden revelation. "Arlene, we've got to lure Godzilla out of the anomaly and into the normal gravity zone."

She didn't ask why. She had a better question: "Which one of us?"

She was right. The only way to do this was for one of us to get into the zone and taunt the creature until it charged.

Arlene did some quick mind reading. "There's only one choice," she said. "I'm faster, you lumbering ox."

I couldn't argue with her about that. I was already a lot more winded than she. I used to kid her about having the fastest cleats in the Light Drop; now it was life or death riding on her foot speed. She must not have liked my expression. "Fly, it has to be me! Besides, you're a much better shot with the rockets."

"Lot of good that's done us."

"It's the only weapon might even slow it down," she insisted; and there was no arguing with logic. She stopped running and so did I. She put her hand on my cheek and it was warm and damp. We were both sweating like mad. "If I don't make it," she said, forcing her breathing to slow, and the words to come out slow and easy, "it's been a cool couple of years. Take care, Fly, and when you start firing those rockets, try not to mix me up with the big guy."

I wanted to say too much, so I only nodded and kept my mouth shut. She jogged toward the distant wall, looking back over her shoulder once. I felt like a heel, but she was right. Got sweat in my eyes, too.

Then the biggest monster in the universe rounded the edge and loped by. It walked right by me, sniffed the air with nauseating nostrils, and stopped! That unbelievable head slowly began to turn in my direction. I gave myself up for dead . . . but Arlene had other ideas.

She made so much noise she could have been a three-piece band. She caterwauled, taunted, laughed, pointed, howled and hooted, and tap-danced for a big finish. She passed the audition.

The big mother raised its missile arm. Arlene, back against the wall in the corner, planted her feet firmly and shoved off, like a kid shoving off in a pool to get a head start at a swim meet. Darn near zero-g could be fun.

She streaked sideways along the adjacent wall, and the missile impacted astern of her, pissing off the steam-demon.

"Roaaaarrrrrrrrrrggggggggrrrrrraaaaaaaauuughghh," it complained, stomping after her. She crouched, safe in a corner, watching every move the enemy made. When Godzilla stopped halfway and fired another three missiles, she was ready for it. She timed her leap to take her farther along the back wall, out of the blast radius.

As the demon pumped after her, I had a clear view from behind, and noticed that a whole rack of small missiles was built into the creature's back! What did that say about the thing's creators?

Then, one cannonball-crashing step past the invisible line did the trick, and the big guy launched into the air, smashing against the high ceiling. "Welcome to the gravity zone, sucker!" I yelled, then stepped out of cover and fired a barrage of rockets at a target that was just too damned big to miss. Hell, Lieutenant Weems could have hit this one.

The rockets exploded against the demon, knocking it farther back against the wall. This got its attention. Eyes big as dinner plates looked at me in an unkindly fashion. The demon raised its arm, but didn't fire. This was because it was slowly rotating in the air like a windmill. Good old zero-g!

Every time it lined me up for a shot, it had shifted again. And while it was unable to steady itself, I kept firing rockets. By the time it managed to stabilize itself and line up a shot, I had pumped a total of fifteen rockets. Fifteen, and it didn't give a spit!

Realizing that sooner or later the steam-demon might get off a missile in my direction, I made plans.

The essence of virtually every martial art—and they taught us a lot in the Light Drop Infantry—is to use the other guy's own weapons against him. Like, what the hell? What did I have to lose except my life, and all Earth?

I stood perfectly visible and stopped shooting; I *wanted* that titanic SOB to finally bring its missile launcher to bear. Sounds stupid, I know . . . but it really was all part of the plan.

I *meant* to do that!

Behind me the walls came to a point, and there was another hole in the wing just begging for me to fill her up. I waited until the steam-demon drew a bead on me . . . then I dived into the slit as it fired. By the time the cruise missile impacted against the wing wall, I'd rolled on the other side of it, protected.

What happened next was in the hands of Sir Isaac Newton.

The force of the shot threw the demon backward against the wall with such terrific force that five meters of solid monster was torn to shreds.

It sounded as if an entire supermarket had been slam-dunked into the side of a mountain. The next sound was music to my ears: Arlene giving a war cry of such glee and joy that I wanted to join her around some prehistoric campfire to gloat over the dead enemy and marvel at our own survival.

I still exercised some caution as I peeped around the wall. A few lights still flashed and flickered on the demon as it feebly tried to crawl. But this baby wasn't going to bother us anymore.

"Shall we put it out of our misery?" asked Arlene as she rejoined me.

"Does it deserve so merciful a fate?" I asked. She raised an eyebrow in surprise. Sometimes I think she underestimated my intelligence. What, only girl Marines can get away with sounding pompous?

"Best to play it safe," she said. "I don't want to get back on that merry-go-round."

I nodded. It only took the rest of my rockets, fired point-blank, to turn the prone body into cotton candy. "Whose turn is it to name the new monster?" I asked when the job was done.

"You saw it first," she said.

"All right, then: steam-demon. That's what I kept thinking when I watched it move."

"Not bad, Fly. You're getting better at this. Maybe you could be a writer."

"No need to be insulting," I said, patting her on the head in a patronizing way. This time I could get away with it. I felt good. It's not every day you trick an unstoppable force into an immovable object.

We explored and found a huge, round manhole in the floor near where the demon was originally standing. Perhaps it had been performing guard duty. Arlene did the inspection and laughed. "You're going to love this," she said, standing up.

"Let me guess. It needs a key."

"You don't like having to mess with keys, do you?"

"Not when I'm fresh out of rockets." But we had plenty of time for a scavenger hunt. Great. Whoever came up with the need for all these keys was on a par with the guy who invented cross-merging back on Earth. No torture too severe.

"I'll bet I know where it is," Arlene said. Following her lead, we returned to the still-sparking, burning body of the steam-demon. Arlene found a key stuck in a slot in the creature's belly. So he had definitely been the guardian. She started to pull it out and quickly yanked her hand away, cussing.

"What's the matter?"

"It's freakin' hot!" Being careful not to burn herself on the quickly slagging metal, she gingerly extracted it, shielding her eyes from the heat with her other hand. Wisps of steam rose off the purple computer key card, but it retained its shape. She grinned like a kid who'd just gotten the prize in the cereal box.

We ran to the door in the floor, the hole for a mole. Arlene plugged it into the slot. The hatch rose, then rotated open. Through this opening we saw a brilliant, eye-hurting red. A rickety, wooden ladder descended out of sight. "I can hardly believe it," she said.

"Believe what?"

"Has to be, babe. Fly, we're looking right at the wall of the hyperspace tunnel itself."

We looked long and hard. "Now what?" she asked.

I shrugged. When there's no data, flip a coin. After all, the ladder wasn't even charred.

I reached my naked hand down into the red-red-redness. I touched a color. Arlene touched my shoulder.

"What does it feel like?" she asked.

I told her: "You'd think it would be hot, but it isn't. It's ice-cold."

"Weird," she said, and put her hand down next to mine. "So what's outside a hyperspace wormhole?" she asked.

"Outer space?" I suggested. "That river of faces we saw earlier? Heaven and hell? Death?"

We glanced at each other and nodded. Holding hands, we took a deep breath and stepped into the redness.

Crimson red. Fire-engine red. Rose red. Bloodred. Lipstick red. Martian red. The color curled around us like cold, smothering, arctic water, filling our brains with the redness of death. We were on fire! But I felt no pain.

The experience was not pleasant. The flames burned away our clothing and weapons, but not our skin.

The ladder vanished; it was only in our minds, anyway. For a while we slipped and slid as if we were at a crazy amusement park; but at least we could see. No matter how bad a situation, I was always grateful for light.

28

The red tunnel was bathed in the kind of hazy glow you get in a dark room when you're developing photos. So long as I could see my hand in front of my face, I wasn't going to freak. But that was the only good thing about the situation.

Then we fell into a room. Room? Some sort of internal organ . . . the walls, floor, and ceiling were pink, pulsating flesh, ribbed and liberally coated with slippery mucus.

Once again both Arlene and I were naked as jaybirds. Instinctively, I covered myself again, just as I had before.

"Oh, come on, Fly!" Arlene complained. "You're a human being, thank God. We have little enough to remind us of who we are and why we're here . . . we don't need you being shy on top of everything else."

I slowly took my hands away. But I tried not to look to hard at Arlene—I didn't trust myself. We were buddies; I wanted it to stay that way.

"This place stinks," Arlene said. Maybe my nose had stopped working. I counted myself lucky; the organ was diseased, sickly, and I was glad I couldn't smell it. There was a downward slope that wasn't so steep as to cause us to lose our footing altogether, but I wasn't comfortable as we stumbled through the giant organ. I had a disturbing sense of what organ it was . . . a place we've all been before.

"I just had a bad thought, Fly; I hope whatever burned away our clothes didn't also burn away all the microbes in our guts that help us digest food. Without them, we'll die of starvation no matter how much we eat."

"I doubt it," I said, my voice shaky, as if I hadn't used it for decades. "I don't feel ravenously hungry, so evidently the Gate left the MRE food in my stomach. Probably left the microbes, as well . . . anything organic."

We both jumped when the demonic uterus started contracting. I had always hated amusement parks. Then we were sliding out of control. I grabbed Arlene's hand and she squeezed hard.

The contractions pushed us along the floor to a "door," a giant, semitransparent cyst membrane with a doorknob in the middle. The knob was made of some kind of cartilage. I pushed my arm into a wet opening all the way to the shoulder and turned the knob.

Two corpses were on the other side. They'd only been shadows seen through the membrane; we couldn't tell what they were.

One was male, the other female. After our experience with déjà vu, I experienced a momentary shock of thinking the bodies were our own! They weren't, but they could have been related to us—similar body types, similar faces.

I sure as hell knew who they *were,* though: one was the

third woman in Fox Company besides Dardier and Arlene, Midori Yoshida.

The man was Lieutenant Weems.

I felt a curious lack of emotion, looking at the pair. They lay in an awkward position, head-to-head, each with a pistol in the other's mouth. It was pretty clearly a suicide pact—I supposed because of finding themselves in hell.

Arlene leaned down to separate them, and we made a horrific discovery: they weren't just lying tête-à-tête; their heads were *joined together,* fused at the crowns, the scalp flowing smoothly from one to the other . . . like Siamese twins joined at the head. The hair color faded continuously from blond (Weems) to black (Yoshida) without seam or break.

"Jesus and Mary," I gasped.

"I don't guess there's any question why they blew their brains out," Arlene whispered, dropping the bodies.

Arlene silently pointed to bloody imp prints all around the bodies. We both knew the shape of an imp footprint when we saw one. Judging from the depth of the heels, the bastards had been dancing around the bodies of their human victims. I spat at one of the footprints. Arlene gripped my shoulder.

"Fly, please don't think I'm a ghoul—but goddamn it, we need those pistols! And much as I like looking at your . . . your manly chest, I think we need the clothes, too. Definitely the boots."

She had a point. A stomach-turning, revolting point; but still one against which I couldn't argue.

We spent the next several minutes robbing the corpses and throwing up in the corner. But afterward we each had a pistol and twenty-six rounds.

To exit the room we had to squeeze through a narrow opening that looked exactly like . . . well, I didn't like to even think about it.

I volunteered to go first, and she didn't object. "Fly," came her voice as we wriggled and writhed through the orifice, "do you ever get the feeling you're being born again?"

I'm not a huge fan of morbid jokes; this time all I could do was shudder. "Arlene—maybe we shouldn't be pissing off the only friend we've got down here by blasphemy."

The moist, decaying walls pressed in around my shoulders, but I could still push through, and where I went it was easy for Arlene to follow. The thought crossed my mind that the passage might narrow so much that I'd become stuck. I wasn't completely rational about this one.

I was so glad to pop out the other end that I barely minded the seven imps waiting on the other side. For one truly insane moment I wondered if that would make Arlene Snow White! Then I was busy again, doing my job. Arlene was right behind me, doing her job. We only had a brace of pistols. The sons of bitches didn't stand a chance.

As was the usual case after a good killing, we took advantage of the opportunity to do more sightseeing. Not once did I regret that neither of us had thought to bring a camera. "So this is hell," Arlene said.

"What they want us to think of as the infernal regions," I replied. Hell was made of fleshy walls, an open field whose ground was a mottled scalp with comically giant, prickly hairs growing out of randomly scattered tufts, rivers of fire, a black and red swirling sky . . . and air that stank of urine, decayed flowers, and bitter lemons. There may have been a hint of old cat boxes mixed in there as well. "Come to think of it," I continued, "not a bad try."

"One of their more creative efforts."

We saw a single door, sagging with moldy, rotten timbers. The stonework lintel was crumbling. Arlene strolled to the unpromising portal and made a close inspection. "Fly, come look at this."

I went, but my stomach wished I hadn't. There were mites or larvae eating away at the stone, the wood, the fleshy walls, everything! "Quite an attention to detail," Arlene said as if evaluating an artwork.

The next moment she stopped being an art critic. A cloud of the tiny creatures came off into the air as if we'd pounded on the door, but neither of us had touched anything. They settled on her. More followed and they settled on me. Holding up my hand, I could see dozens of little specks spreading across my flesh . . . and there was a very slight itch.

"Damn it, get off'n me!" Arlene shook her arms wildly, but enjoyed no more success than I. We ran, rolled, and still the little vermin hung on. They were worse than lint.

"Ah, the hell with it," I said. "They don't seem to be killing us. First chance, we'll take a bath."

"Or go through a teleporter," she said.

"Being living organisms, they would probably go through with us. No, we'll look for water."

"Or flea dip." She probably had a very good idea there. But her voice cracked; she held on by main force.

"Can't stand here forever," I said. "Let's pop it."

I cracked the seal. Surprise! A pair of larger than life pumpkins floated out. At least they weren't going to crawl around on our skin. They were up high enough that we ducked and managed to avoid being seen. They sailed past, looking for hoops and nets.

The pumpkins saw the dead imps and floated over to investigate, providing us with the opportunity of darting through the doorway. Inside we found a single shotgun and a few shells. Arlene picked it up and tossed it to me.

I was touched. We soldiered on.

To the left we saw a rickety, wooden walkway over a pool of boiling, red stuff that seemed to be a cross between lava and the traditional green toxin. Annoyingly, it was the only way to go. As we began to cross cautiously, the path started to give way. For some reason, neither of us was the least bit surprised.

There was nowhere to go but *forward* before the pathetic bridge collapsed into the evil fluid below. We ran like hell. But at the end we were blocked by what appeared to be a solid stone wall.

I threw myself at the wall, hoping to grab a handful, and Arlene could grab me. Instead, we ended up very much alive on the *other side* of the illusion. There was no wall.

If we were startled by the turn of events, the imps we had landed on were downright stunned. The shotgun lost its virginity then and there. Arlene took care of a few stragglers with her 10mm.

This time, when we lifted our eyes from the carnage of the moment we were in for a real surprise. Right in front of us was the figure of a human being wrapped in something sticky and suspended from the ceiling by his feet.

We could tell by his clothing that he was a UAC civilian. We could tell from his groans that he was *alive*.

He was tall, nearly two meters. He was overweight and suffering a lot more because of it, the stomach hanging at a painful angle, his belt about to come loose. Blood trickled down his wrists from where he had tried to free himself.

"God, he's still kicking," Arlene said, focusing on the only important thing.

I looked close; the man appeared to be wrapped up in *spiderwebs;* the web suspending him from the ceiling was thick and didn't look like we could easily break it.

"Is there a knife anywhere?" We pulled UAC boxes over and rummaged through them; no knife, but a bottle would break to serve the purpose. Arlene sliced, and I cushioned his fall as he came down, grunting at the weight. Good thing there were some medical supplies in the UAC boxes; the man was in shock. Arlene pushed some D5W saline to pump up the volume; after a while his eyes opened. He stared at us without comprehension. I expected that.

"Can you hear me?" I asked, and got nothing. "If you understand me, nod your head."

That took a moment but he finally nodded. Arlene massaged his neck and I held a finger in front of him until he focused on it. "Are you all right?" Arlene asked him at last.

"Unh," he grunted in a low, husky voice, carrying all the pain.

"Who are you?" I asked.

"Bill Ritch," he said, groggily.

"How long were you up there?" Arlene asked.

Further proof that life was coming back into him was the way he shuddered. "Long enough that I thought I'd died."

"Who put you up?" I asked.

"The—goblin," he answered. "Spidermind."

Oh, great; a whole new nomenclature. That narrowed it down to any of the monsters. If we ever reported to Earth, we would need to settle on a common terminology.

"Congratulations," said Arlene.

"For what?" he asked, half turning to her, still dizzy.

"Surviving." It was a big deal finding another human who could move and wasn't a damned zombie! We would have opened a bottle of champagne and celebrated if we'd had the time . . . or the booze. As it was, Ritch was stunned to receive a mouthful of cold water, if still a bit confused.

Following a corridor that looped around, we wound up back at the same damned central entrance. I would never enjoy an amusement park again. Peeking cautiously around the corner, I saw we had company, tired of inspecting the dead imps outside. Pumpkins in the air, pumpkins everywhere . . .

They roared in frustration and shot their nasty little balls of electricity at each other. Important datum:

pumpkins are immune to their own weapons. And I made a note to see how they responded to being baked in a pie.

"Were those the goblins you meant?" Arlene whispered to Ritch. He shook his head, but his grim expression left no doubt that he'd encountered pumpkins before.

"They're so freaking stupid," said Arlene contemptuously.

"You'd think something that was all head would have more brains," I added.

The next step was obvious for those of us *with* brains. We dashed across the corridor to another closed door. I opened it a crack while Arlene kept watch, making sure the pumpkins didn't float back. Ritch obviously hadn't received military training, but he caught on fast. Considering what he'd been through, he was a quick study. He kept pace, which was all we really needed from him at the moment.

Through the door I saw two pumpkins on the inside as well, hanging with a bunch of imps. Taking a deep breath, I waited until a mob of spinys marched between the door and the nearest pumpkin. Then I stepped out and fired five or six unaimed rounds. These guys didn't merit any wasted shotgun shells. Having done my damage, I popped back and braced the door. Arlene and Ritch helped.

One thing you can say about pumpkins: they don't let a little obstacle like imps stand between them and a target.

And one thing you can say about imps: they don't like being shot by balls of electricity.

We left them to each other's mercies. Over the sound of carnage, Ritch shouted at me. "How'd you get them fighting each other?"

"We do it all the time," said Arlene, smiling. "It's the Iago tactic."

"I'm impressed."

I watched for the two in the hall; but they'd gotten

tired of shooting each other and returned to shoot the imp carcasses.

When the sounds behind the door died down, I slowly cracked it. I saw a lot of dead imps on the floor and the remains of one deflated pumpkin on top. I assumed the other one must be on the bottom of the pile. That's when I made a huge mistake.

29

Stepping inside, I didn't think to look behind the door, straight up, the logical place for a surviving pumpkin to be waiting in ambush. And that's exactly where the bastard was.

"Fly!" Arlene shouted. She was paying attention. She never used that tone of voice except when it was life and death—and in this case, the issue was my life. I threw myself on the floor just as a lightning ball fried the tip of my scalp. A run of 10mm rounds got my attention.

I flipped over to see Arlene blasting away, then scrambled to my feet and pumped my shotgun at the floating head. She split left and I right, and we kept firing.

When we were done, that was the deadest pumpkin I had ever seen still floating. It was almost like one of those old cartoons where the character hangs in space for several seconds before it remembers the law of gravity, then quickly plummets to the ground. All that was missing were the sound effects.

"Incoming!" yelled Ritch, outside the door. We hadn't forgotten the other pumpkins. We'd hoped they might have forgotten us, though.

"Get in!" Arlene yelled, pulling at Ritch's sleeve. He didn't need another hint. The moment he joined us, we slammed the door shut and jammed the latch with Arlene's pistol. The latch immediately rattled; God only knew what the pumpkins were using for hands.

"Look," Ritch said, pointing. Protruding from under a dead imp were the pieces of a box of shotgun shells, along with shells.

"They may be covering all kinds of supplies," I said. The prospect didn't appeal to me, but I thought I should set a good example. Getting on my knees, I pulled the corpse away from the box, and dozens of shells went rolling as Arlene and Ritch collected them.

Then we all got busy moving the dead monsters and stacking them in one corner. We received our just reward. There was another functional shotgun, lots of ammo, even tools: hammers, nails, even a gas-powered chain saw. Maybe the zombies had been used to build condos for imps and pumpkins. We even found an antique revolver for Ritch; I wondered which one of us the civilian would accidentally shoot.

We replaced the pistol in the latch with a handful of nails, then collected all the tools and put them in a neat pile for later use. Weapons and ammo in hand, we explored the room and found it led to a broader plaza area. Then we found a door leading into a narrow corridor.

"I'll go first," I said.

"Fine with me," said Arlene. Ritch was more than happy to bring up the rear.

No good deed goes unpunished. I realized that the moment I heard the familiar pig-grunting noises, the ugly snuffling that always turned my stomach and might keep me from ever eating bacon again. They didn't make us wait very long. The demons came storming down the corridor, pale pink flesh with claws and lots and lots of teeth.

Somehow, though, after the steam-demon, I couldn't take the pinkies seriously.

The narrowness of the corridor meant I had taken point with a vengeance; no one could shoot past me. I loosed a shotgun blast. "Fall back!" I shouted, and heard Arlene and Ritch doing it. Taking steps backward, I never took my eyes off the enemy. I shot a second time, then a third and fourth time, before dropping the first demon.

I didn't like the arithmetic. Despite our extra ammo, there were more demons than we could take down at this rate. My comrades had made it back through the door as I held the corridor. Back to the wall, I kept firing, when suddenly . . .

"Hold fire!" It was Arlene's voice, and I couldn't imagine that she'd gone nuts. I risked turning my head. She stood in the doorway, holding the chain saw. Then with a *chugga-mmmmmm, chuggga-mmmmmm,* she pulled the cord. Third time was the charm, and it kicked to life with an honest roar to drown out all but a steam-demon's scream.

Elbowing past me, she lifted the buzzing blade and let the teeth bite into the nearest demon. "Die, Pinkie, die!" she screamed. It sounded odd, but the results were great: red blood splashed us both, and she kept at it, screaming a war cry that just might scare a fallen angel.

Arlene waded through them, working the saw, beads of sweat and drops of blood covering her face. A demon arm fell to the floor, blood exploding in a torrent. She slipped on the gore, but the movement carried her forward and the saw buried itself in the chest of the next demon, ripping a death gurgle from the creature.

I tried to get to her to help, but the demon corpses were in the way. She worked the chain saw loose but fell backward, swinging it in a wide arc. A large demon swung its claw down hard and knocked the chain saw out of her hand.

Before Arlene could get away, another claw ripped her open. She didn't scream but fell silently.

The sight drove me mad. Somewhere in the back of my mind I'd accepted the likelihood of our being blown to bits; but I wouldn't have us die like animals!

Picking up the saw, I revved it and finished the damned job, shoving the blade into the face of the one who had hurt her. I lost count of how many were left but I kept at it, swinging the chain saw back and forth, covering the walls with gore. Finally, there was nothing left to kill.

The red haze lifted and I remembered Arlene. Turning back, I saw that Ritch was with her, trying to stanch the bleeding with improvised first-aid. My right sleeve was already in tatters, so it was a simple matter to rip off a strip of cloth and use it for bandages. We patched her up as best we could.

Her face was pale and she was weak; but she was alive. "Can you move?" I asked.

"Move or die," she wheezed, "so I'll move." We helped her stand up. I started to pick up her shotgun and pass it to Ritch, but she shook her head. "That's mine," she said, reclaiming it proudly. I wasn't about to argue.

We left the heavy chain saw on the deck and staggered forward into a last chamber. There were disgusting things lying around, but as nothing was moving or alive, I gave it no further attention. In the center of the room was a teleport pad of rusted metal, designed in a heavy and cumbersome manner. It looked like an antique.

"That doesn't look promising," I said.

"We have no choice," Arlene answered through clenched teeth. We hadn't had a good choice in a long, long time. All three of us stepped aboard, arms linked. Ritch must have been religious. He said a prayer.

Maybe because it was an old-fashioned teleporter, the experience was different from the others . . . like the special F/X were provided by a different company. I noticed sounds that were new, a wind tunnel combined with an avalanche; and there was the sensation of falling turning into floating. Then we arrived.

"Wow!" Ritch said. He wasn't as used to this stuff as we were. The terminus was a rock garden. Although the light was dim, we could make out the twisted, curved, and warped rocks that made me think of a giant coral reef, except the color and texture of the formations was the same as desert camo. Met our old friends, the zombies.

Arlene fired first. The opportunity to fight put life back in her again. Most of these zombies weren't armed—ex-UAC civvies—which was fine with me. Ritch got off a couple of shots as well; I don't know if he hit anything. Abruptly, I realized we had a more serious problem than the walking dead crew. I'd almost forgotten the real spooks—the ghost things I thought of as specters.

One touched my face with all the coldness of space. I hit at the horror wildly but struck Ritch instead, knocking him to the ground. It was joined by some of its buddies, those flying metal skulls I hoped never to see again. They dive-bombed us like kamikaze pilots.

Then Ritch found the back of a specter head by swinging his hands; he put his revolver against its skull and squeezed off a point-blank round.

That got the critter's attention; it spun to deal with Ritch, turning its back on me; I blew its head apart with the riot gun.

Somehow the idea of a ghost you can slice and dice appealed to me. I didn't think the nuns would approve. The damned specter went down screaming like a banshee and bleeding something that stank of ice-cold grave-yards.

While I was auditioning for Ghost Busters, Arlene popped the flying skulls. They didn't require as much firepower as the pumpkins. Ritch took care of the remaining zombies.

"Aim for the head, just like the movie," Arlene shouted.

He was doing okay for a novice, and naturally gravitated to the easiest job; but he acquitted himself well. I was happy we had found him.

Finally the wave of bad guys subsided and we could play beachcombers. There wasn't much worth grabbing this time, however—only a bit of ammo and a Sig-Cow for Ritch from the poorly equipped zombies.

Now seemed a good moment to find out more about Bill. Arlene thought his "goblin" might be a hell-prince and described one, but he shook his head. "Not a minotaur; it was more like a giant spider," he said.

"Oh, great," said Arlene, "a new one for the files."

We found out Bill Ritch was a computer programmer. If we found any monsters with laptops, he would prove invaluable. To be fair, he'd done fine killing his quota of zombies.

"How'd you get captured in the first place?" Arlene asked.

Ritch sighed. "Classic case of 'this can't really be happening to us.' When we were—" He stopped, face turning red. When he started up again, I knew he had skipped something important. Later, I thought. "We were studying the Gates, and suddenly one of them on Deimos experienced a marked drop in temperature. It started glowing, too."

"But I thought Deimos was deserted when all this started," I interrupted.

"You were supposed to think that," he said. "When the UAC found alien electronics and started—then we all crowded in to see, and that's when they started coming through, the goblins. Aliens, I mean."

"Which ones?" I asked. "Which ones came first?"

"The first thing through was one of those things you call an imp. It looked at us and grinned, and we were all frozen in total shock. We didn't know what to say or do—our first contact with an alien race, and we were speechless! All those wonderful plans about what we were going to say and how we were going to react—"

"Well, how did the *imp* react?" Arlene was always good at cutting through the plastic to get to the meat.

Ritch shook his head sadly, remembering something painful. "It threw one of those wads of phosphorous mucoid and killed a senior scientist and two Air Force captains. I was in the back . . . thank God. A woman screamed; I think it was Dr. Tyya Graf. Then another one came through, and we panicked."

"Mob scene?"

"Like *Soylent Green*." Arlene mm-hmmed, but I was confused. Must have been another old movie reference. "If I hadn't been such a big guy, I would have been trampled. As it was, I was knocked down. I tried to get up, and they squirted some sort of webbing around me, a neurotoxin that paralyzed me.

"I was out of it for some indeterminate time; when I came to, this spider thing was interrogating me and I was in a huge room, surrounded by hundreds of goblins of different types, and even some of those zombies. I recognized Dr. Graf, but I could tell right away she was dead and her body was just reanimated. And, well, that's the story."

Speaking of which, Arlene interrupted with her own thoughts: "Fly, do you notice there's a lot more zombie bodies here than anything else?"

"Sure."

"So with all the noise we just made, why didn't a lot more come running?"

"Curiosity may have killed the cat," I said, feeling flip, "but never a zombie. Or maybe this is all of them."

"No brains," said Ritch, bending over one of them.

Arlene shook her head. "I think it's because they never do anything they're not told," she said. "They must stay in constant communication with someone or something, and only go investigate when they receive a command. If they've been told to patrol, looking for humans, then they'll attack; otherwise, they might march right by us and not even see us."

"That imp who talked to me made me wonder if imps give them orders," I said.

"Maybe; but we've seen zombies where there are no imps. Maybe they get standing orders. I saw a bunch of imps come running to check out a situation once where all I'd done was get the zombies firing at each other. The imps couldn't control them."

"Well, the pig-snuffling demons don't have any intelligence worth mentioning, either," I said. "If there's any more of them around, they wouldn't hear a battle over their own breathing."

"The skulls don't even have ears," Arlene said. "Look, it's either hell-princes, the steam-demons, or that thing Bill described, the spider thing."

"The spider creature that interrogated me," Ritch said, shuddering.

"We'll keep that in mind." Time to move on. Hugging the right wall, we discovered a narrowing, "natural" corridor with more shotgun shells lying on the floor like popcorn. We scooped them up, but I was disappointed to discover that some were defective or spent. I was preoccupied with a handful of questionable-looking specimens when they spilled through my fingers and I dropped to my knees to recover them. That saved my life. A shotgun blast filled the space where my head had been a moment before.

"Zombie!" Ritch called out anti-anticlimactically. No one ever shot at us with human weapons except former humans. Another shot missed high, but there was no third attempt on Yours Truly.

Arlene turned to fire—and froze! "F-Fly . . ." she whispered hoarsely.

I stared. Jesus; it was Arlene's worst nightmare come true. Wilhelm Dodd, or what was left of him, lurched toward our little group, shifting his twelve-gauge to get a better shot.

30

Arlene stared at him approaching, her mouth open, face pale as a ghost. I didn't want to do it, but she'd made me promise!

Feeling sick, I raised my own weapon. I knew what would happen: I would blow the f'ing SOB away—and Arlene would hate me for the rest of her natural life . . . which might not be a very long time at that.

Then a miracle happened.

Just as my finger tightened on the trigger, Arlene's face suddenly hardened. The color returned. She closed her mouth.

Then she pumped a shell into the receiver, shouldered her riot gun, and blew the zombie-Dodd's face off.

Nobody said anything; Ritch took his cue from our awkward silence. I put my hand on Arlene's shoulder, and she spoke. Her voice croaked like a rusty can tied behind a very old car. "He was already gone, Fly. And I didn't want him to come between my buddy and me."

There was that damned peculiar lump again. I blinked —dust in my eye, I guess—and squeezed her shoulder so hard she winced. But she didn't move to push my hand away.

She knew what would happen if *I* were the one to kill the reworked Wilhelm Dodd . . . and she wouldn't allow that to happen.

Evidently, our friendship was as important to her as it was to me.

I'd forgotten that the zombies had ever been human; I

made myself forget. But the staring face of Willy Dodd wouldn't let me get away with it any longer. He was a man, a Marine, and very important in my life. Now that he was gone—I didn't know what to think about Arlene and me.

Best not to think at all, I advised me; it was good advice, and I took it.

Arlene was taking it hard. Sitting on the floor, she put her head between her legs and took a series of long, deep breaths. I wanted to comfort her but felt helpless. "Arlene . . ." I reached out to touch her. She shook her head and pulled away. Any other situation, I would have left her alone to mourn in private. But there was no privacy on Deimos except the solitude of the grave.

Ritch understood what was going on and kept his mouth shut. I liked him more and more. I glanced at my wristwatch, a pointless act in this place, perhaps; but it helped somehow: a tiny act of useless normalcy.

"Arlene," I said, gently as I could, "we've got to split. You need to pull it together."

"Leave me alone!" she said, keeping her face turned away. "Don't look at me."

This didn't seem like a good time to push the envelope. I'd never seen her this badly shaken; without another word, I sat down, back-to-back with her, and kept watch while she got it out of her system. Ritch stood a little farther up the hallway, gun out, eyes averted.

Every so often her entire body shuddered; I pretended not to notice. When she finished, she wiped her eyes and stood up. "Let's move, Corporal," she said. She was a PFC and I outranked her, but it was all right. The fighting tone of voice was back.

Ritch rejoined us and we pushed on. Up the defile was a rise where we could peek over the rock wall to our left. The architect from hell had been busy again. A huge garden stretched out before us in the shape of a right hand. We were in the thumb.

"Can you believe this one?" Arlene asked.

"Better than a swastika," I said. The hand covered a good piece of territory, with the "fingers" wide spread, each undoubtedly offering a wide selection of motion sensors and other surprises. The "ring" finger had a bizarre, wooden shack right where the ring would have been; I wondered if the "pinkie" finger would be full of Arlene's demons.

We started with the thumb. "Bet the only prints we find are *foot*-prints," Ritch said. I've never liked stupid jokes, either, but Arlene laughed; anything to shake her out of her depression.

I heard a familiar bubbling: the red "lava" liquid. The pool was in a raised, stone structure that could pass as the swimming pool from hell. I thought I saw a switch just below the lava line.

"What's that?" Ritch asked.

"Toxic yecch," Arlene answered. "Haven't you seen it before?" Ritch shook his head. "You've been lucky," she went on. "Fly and I have been through an ocean of the stuff."

"Looks like lava," Ritch said, proving an old adage about great minds and small circles. "Is it hot?"

"Not enough," I said, "but it can still kill you." The switch teased me, like a piece of plastic sticking up from a bowl of red oatmeal.

"You know," I mused, "that switch is awfully tempting . . ." I found a rock and pitched it at the button, jumping back. I didn't want any of that spit splashing on me.

I should have tried out for the majors when the twelve-year strike began. First try was the charm; we heard a loud click, and a door rotated open, revealing our latest take-home pay: another AB-10, and far more important, a pair of beautiful Medikits. I would have preferred another of those magical blue health spheres, but this would definitely do in a pinch.

But my heart sunk when I picked up the first one and saw the telltale signs of imp. This was not a virgin find.

Tooth marks explained why most of the drugs were missing. Apparently the imps liked the taste. A hurried investigation of the kits showed that barely enough drugs had survived for Arlene.

Ritch helped me gather together what we needed. After cleansing her wounds, with special care for the bad gash in her chest, I gave her painkillers and put on fresh bandages. Ritch seemed embarrassed, swabbing at her amble, naked breasts; but titillation was the last thing on any of our minds.

"How's that?" I asked.

"Better," she said, but I could tell from her strained voice and pale face that she was far from perfect. *Better* would have to do.

The dregs of the drugs proved a bonus for Ritch. He didn't look so hot, either. Coming down from the ceiling and snapping out of shock so quickly couldn't be good for anyone, and he'd been holding his own in combat instead of resting.

I wish I could have offered him a needle of the stimulant I'd used back in the marble room, on Deimos; but stimulant seemed to have been what the imps were after—the vials were all empty.

Leaving the thumb, we descended on the palm as if storming heaven and began a serious housecleaning, sliding from rock to rock, blasting anything in our way . . . and scooping up anything useful. The opposition was feeble, hardly worth mentioning except to say that they died quickly.

Arlene lucked into finding a rocket launcher of her very own. Then we helped her locate the little battery-sized rockets that were nearby. She collected seven of the little darlings, and I showed her where to stick them and taught her the forbidden lore of proximity fuses and firing rings.

We were so happy about the find that we must have sent out a subverbal signal. Monsters don't like humans being happy.

We were ambushed by six former comrades at arms and ex-UAC workers, four imps, three demons, two flying skulls, and a partridge in a pear tree. (I'm lying about the pear tree.) In the ensuing carnage, Arlene used up every rocket; but at least she could never again say she hadn't been checked out on the launcher.

Arlene and I barely worked up a sweat. Ritch was getting good at the game; he was a good draft pick. He'd been doing some thinking that he was eager to share with us. Arlene still seemed numb from the discovery of Wilhelm, but I was ready to get to know this new Ritch better.

So, as we surveyed our latest gaggle of ex's, I encouraged him to speak his piece.

He'd already told us that computers were his area, but he'd been overly modest. Evidently, he was a bona-fide computer genius kidnapped from Deimos by the aliens.

"We had already decided that the Gates were hypermass transportation devices; if they really worked and weren't just some elaborate failed experiment from millenia past, it would blow every physics theory we had out the wash.

"We discovered they responded to bursts of high-energy microwaves; their circuits responded for several seconds after each burst—not electronics, exactly, but something involving direct manipulations of particle streams."

As Ritch held court, Arlene perked up and started paying attention. She was getting that expression she wore when a boyfriend betrayed her. Suddenly, her mouth dropped. "You mean you—*activated* the Gates yourselves? You turned them on? Jesus Christ, *you brought those things here!*"

Arlene had a romantic side that tried to believe whatever nonsense officials put out as the truth du jour. I'd gotten over that sort of silliness long before I joined the Corps—it wasn't a long-term healthy attitude for a jarhead.

"I . . . I *think* we brought these aliens through the Gate ourselves, in a way," Ritch admitted pathetically. "But it was an accident!"

"Ah, an accident," I snorted. "Well, that certainly relieves everyone of any personal responsibility."

Ritch continued, not noticing the irony. "I think, now, that whatever these creatures were, they were listening to the Gates. Maybe they were trying to fire it up from their end, and until we 'answered the phone,' they couldn't do it. But yeah, I guess we let them in.

"Anyway, I don't believe these are the creatures that *built* the Gates."

"That's what we figured," I said. "You got anything more substantial than a gut feeling?"

"The UAC has . . . engravings that the Gate builders left behind. They are as old as the Gates, showing what the Gate builders looked like." He paused, trying to find the right words.

"And?" we asked as one.

"You're not going to believe this—" he started.

"After what we've been through, we'll believe anything," I said, launching a preemptive strike.

"Well, they look like something out of H. P. Lovecraft," he said.

"I knew it," Arlene said. She still looked furious.

"Am I the only person in the solar system who never read this guy?" I asked, irritated. "The first one of you to talk about anything 'eldritch' is going to get a rocket right between the eyes."

Ritch looked at me like he thought I might be serious, but a big smile from Arlene put him at ease. He swallowed hard and said, "They have snakelike trunks with multilimbed upper torsos, no visible head; and they'd have to move like sidewinders."

"How big?" Arlene wanted to know.

"Up to ten meters long," he answered. They didn't say it but I just know they were both thinking, *Oooh, eldritch!*

I agreed. "I'd bet my life we haven't met the real intelligence behind this."

Arlene joined in: "Bet something of more value than that, Fly. What value do you think an insurance company would put on us?"

"I don't gamble," Ritch said with a straight face, "and I *have* met the—what'd you call it? The mastermind. That spider thing . . . it's in charge, I'm positive."

"Tell us more," I requested.

He shuddered. I knew how he felt. Theory was one thing, close contact another. "So far as I can tell, the spider thing has real intelligence," he said. "It spoke in clear English." I wasn't about to doubt him after my experience with the imp back on Phobos.

"What did it say?" asked Arlene.

"Well, first it started asking me questions. It started with simple, yes-no, true-false; I tried to lie a few times, but it already knew a lot, and I got caught."

"What was its response to a lie?"

Ritch shrugged. "Didn't seem to care emotionally; but it punished me. Horrible stuff, but all hallucination. You know how you're having a dream, and you dream that you're absolutely terrified? The spidermind thing can do that: I can see why people who encountered one of those, maybe thousands of years ago, could think they'd died and gone to hell." He shuddered at the memory.

"But the fears were all unreal. And after a while I realized I could take it. You just have to accept being afraid like you've never been afraid before; but if it can't break you with fear, it doesn't know what to do next."

"What did it do to you?"

"It started ordering me to reprogram all the Phobos and Deimos equipment. When I refused, it tortured me with more and more Fear Itself, which is what I started calling the hallucinations. When that didn't work, it hung me from the ceiling with its webbing, like it was saving me for later."

"I got the impression it needed to find out more about humans so it could figure out how to crack us. Meanwhile, I think it went looking for a more cooperative programmer. I'm sure it would have killed me when it found one."

"To find out more about humans," I repeated, feeling a chill. "Arlene . . . do you think all this crap that's been thrown against us . . . ?"

She glared at me, then glared at the deck. She knew what I meant; she knew it made sense.

We had been the secondary information sources. Had we given the mastermind anything useful? *Mater Dei,* I hoped not.

"Describe the monster," Arlene said.

Ritch gritted his teeth. "It's like a huge, brainlike thing inside a mechanical, spiderlike body."

"What about the weapons?" I asked.

"Ringed with more weapons than you can imagine," Ritch said. I doubted that. I'd reached the point where I could imagine quite a lot.

Actually I was glad to receive Ritch's news. A leader alien meant we had something to really fight. I was exhausted cutting off the inexhaustible limbs of this army. I was ready for a general. The new information cheered up Arlene as well, bringing color back to her cheeks. She and I didn't need to talk about it. We were on the same wavelength. We shared our theories with Ritch, especially the one about Deimos as a spaceship and what we had discovered about the hyperspace tunnel. He had already guessed a lot.

Then we continued our journey up the ring finger, where we'd seen the shack. We ran into one specter, hardly a match for the three of us. I couldn't help contrasting our casualness now with my terror at seeing my first zombie. Nowadays, I was almost blasé.

We prowled our way up to the ancient, crumbly, wooded hut. Hell needed a facelift.

"Check out the lock," Arlene said, grinning like a girl

with a Christmas of accessories for her favorite doll. "I love these!"

"Why?" I asked.

"They take an old-fashioned key."

"I'll help you look for it," Ritch said before I could.

"Hell with that," she said. "I've already got one!" She dismantled one of the pistols; then she took the gas-expander stablizer spline for a flexor and the fixed end of the magazine-advance spring for a tensor. It took her just five minutes to pick the lock.

"Where'd you learn that?" Ritch asked.

"I read a lot of comic books."

"You need help putting that back together?" I asked with a straight face. I couldn't resist teasing her a little. She rolled her eyes and reassembled the piece in nothing flat. She made us wait until she was good and ready to open the shack door.

Inside was a switch. Surprise, surprise, surprise . . . as our patron saint Gomer might say. Arlene did the honors, lowering the wall ahead, revealing a hidden platform containing a dozen dead, mangled, squashed imps and a teleport pad.

"It's about that time," she said.

"I want a new travel agent," I said.

We teleported and stared, stunned into angry silence.

We were right back where we'd started after crawling down the hyperspace tunnel! The only improvement was we still had our clothes and weapons—and Ritch, of course.

31

Déjà," said Arlene.

"Vu," I said.

"Dejah Thoris," Ritch said, and Arlene snorted. They were speaking some kind of secret code. I wasn't going to worry about it. Starting all over was something to worry about.

As before, I inserted my arm up to the elbow in the membranal switch and opened the door. Inside, we found Weems and Yoshida in the same room, same position, still joined head-to-head . . . and still *holding their pistols* in exactly the same position as before. Clothed!

We stared for a long time, and poor Bill Ritch had no idea why Arlene and I were so stunned; he started to examine the bodies, but Arlene gently pulled him back before he could see what they'd done to them.

"This is worse than the monsters," I said. We passed by and crawled through the narrow tunnel, a very tight fit for Ritch.

When we reached the end, we faced the same seven imps as before, only this time we used shotguns. At least that was an improvement.

We popped the same door. Out came two pumpkins, just like last time. The pumpkins were pretty much the same except for varying sizes. Arlene used the AB-10, and I finished them off with a shotgun, our favorite tactic. Ritch made a comment that was new: "They'd look better with two burning candles for eyes instead of that headlight in the center." No one argued.

We started to bypass the collapsing pier, going for the other door instead; but suddenly Arlene said, "Fly, I have a feeling we should duplicate our actions as precisely as we can."

"Arlene, last time the demons creamed you in that narrow hallway," I reminded her. She nodded, a bit shaky at the thought. She wasn't in any condition to survive a bout like that again. I pursued the point: "We've already deviated by not taking Weems's and Yoshida's pistols and by killing the pumpkins outside."

"I know," she said. "I don't have any good argument except for female intuition." I was about to make a crack about the unlikelihood of that particular attribute in *Arlene Sanders,* but I saw that she was deadly serious. She glared at me until I saw reason.

We left Ritch in the corridor. He wasn't in shape for what we had in mind. Of course, after we cleared a path for him, he could stroll through in relative safety. We ran like bats out of Deimos down the pier, this time charging through the illusory wall of flame and blowing away the imps we knew to be on the other side.

There was another reason I'd insisted we leave Ritch behind, one I kept to myself: I half thought we'd find a second Bill Ritch hanging from the ceiling here.

We didn't . . . and I never brought the subject up to Arlene or Ritch. God only knows whether they thought of it themselves—probably, but they kept quiet as well.

We slipped back by the secret corridor and used the same trick on the pumpkins and imps inside the room. It was a lot easier when we knew what to expect. This time I knew where the last pumpkin would be floating in ambush when I opened the door, and I enjoyed not being surprised. Pop goes the pumpkin.

Crossing the patio, Arlene grabbed the chain saw and revved it up; but she made me promise to start shooting the moment she lost it this time. Except that this time, since she knew what to expect, she didn't slip and wasn't out of position where a demon could knock the chain saw out of her hand. She ducked. She weaved. She sawed all the demons to death. It was hard to believe she'd been seriously injured only a short time before; but having a chance to get it right the second time did wonders for her psychological recovery.

We continued up the narrow corridor to the teleport. "So what happens now?" I asked. "Back to the hand again?

I should've kept my hole shut. We stepped aboard, but instead of teleporting, the walls of the chamber lowered into the floor, leaving us standing behind some pillars in a very wide open courtyard.

A neat row of UAC boxes stretched across the court-yard before us like a skyscraper on its side. Every box held a five-pack of rockets—all the rockets in the world. There was also another launcher.

A silver lining like this couldn't possibly arrive without an accompanying thundercloud. We heard the thunder of the heaviest feet in all monsterdom. Another lovely steam-demon . . . and there weren't any convenient zero-g zones around this time.

"What the hell is *that?*" Ritch whispered, crouching behind a pillar.

"That, my friend, is a steam-demon. Fifteen feet tall, long horns, a missile launcher for an arm—"

"Oh, one of those," Ritch said, nodding.

"You know about them?" asked an incredulous Arlene.

"Sure; I've just never seen one before. They ripped off my programming for an ore-crusher to run the creature." His tone of voice was what you hear in small claims court, offended about business-as-usual.

"Any way to sabotage it?"

Ritch frowned in thought. A steam-demon was large enough to inspire frowns in anyone. "If you can get me around back, maybe," he said. "That's where the missile feeder is."

"Worth a try," I said. I looked at Arlene, and she nodded. We dashed out to either side of the pillars as the steam-demon spotted us. It was as ugly as last time, but not as terrifying when frozen in indecision about which target to attack. While it made up its mind, assuming it had one, Arlene and I fired rockets from opposite directions.

At last the steam-demon chose the prettier target and raised its missile-launching hand. Arlene saw what was coming and dived behind her pillar. Three small cruise missiles struck dead-on, shattering the pillar.

I jumped out and shot the sucker over and over until I got its attention. As the big ugly mother deigned to notice me, I popped behind my own column; Arlene repeated the same process, out from her cover and blasting away. It was kind of like dealing with the playground bully where the stakes were real.

The steam-demon proved that it had a mind by passing our little intelligence test. It stomped closer to the pillars, cutting off our angle. Arlene was ready for this. She ran backward, zigzagging, popping off an occasional rocket.

Time for Ritch's plan.

While all this was happening, Ritch and I were moving into position. When the monster was finally standing with its back to the pillars, lining up a fatal shot for Arlene, I interlaced my fingers, bent down, and let Ritch climb aboard. Heavy as he was, I could barely boost him up high enough to grab the back of Godzilla for the ride of his life.

He shoved his hand into the missile-loading machinery up to the elbow. I ditched him, as agreed beforehand, and leapt to a safer position to try something else in case Ritch failed.

Arlene was still dodging around as if she were an actress at a producers' convention. She was too busy now to even take a shot. Besides, she wasn't going to risk hitting Ritch. As for the behemoth, it hadn't even noticed that someone was riding on its back.

Then Ritch ripped out a cable, and the steam-demon noticed.

It jammed its left arm back at an impossible angle; it could just barely brush Ritch, but couldn't bring much force against him, not enough to dislodge him.

The hand with the launcher had a better angle; the steam-demon got it back, pointed at Ritch, and I held my breath, expecting Armageddon. But at the last moment, rarely used self-preservation circuitry kicked in, preventing the big guy from firing into its own missile supply. The steam-demon alternately swatted at Ritch from both sides until our man finished his task and jumped down.

Then Bill Ritch started running, headed in my direction. The steam-demon turned around with great deliberation and aimed its missile launcher at Ritch's head. This was point-blank range. Ritch would never have to worry about a hat again. The monster fired. We heard a loud, empty click. Nothing happened. Ritch kept running. The steam-demon kept clicking, pointing and clicking, as if it couldn't fathom the situational evolution. It flunked *that* intelligence test.

Arlene didn't waste the opportunity. She started pumping at it from behind. The poor bastard turned and aimed its useless arm at her. Click! I shot it three times with my own compact rockets. I kept at it, squeezing the ring until my palm became numb; after what must have been twenty-five direct hits at least, the titan finally staggered and fell to the deck like a skyscraper under demolition—I kept firing, and it got weaker and weaker.

Then Arlene got smart, ran around back, and pumped a couple into the missile supply; the steam-demon's last words were pretty spectacular. I was surprised the entire hyperspace tunnel didn't collapse.

I was tired. But Arlene and Ritch were still full of fire.

We went back the way we'd come, but there had been a change in the architecture. Walls no longer stood where they had. Floor plans were different. A room that had been a small, empty antechamber was now a huge room with the equivalent of a "beach" against which red waves of toxin washed relentlessly.

"Look!" Arlene said. I followed her pointing finger to the unwelcome sight of a hell-prince wading through the crimson toxic surf. After playing patty-cake with the steam-demon, a minotaur didn't seem that serious—but back on Phobos, Arlene had ripped through a crack to avoid one, and I'd been almost paralyzed with fright. How times change!

But it wouldn't do to be careless. We took it left, right, left, right with rockets until it was slagged. It made one gratifying "Ork!" before dying.

The long, narrow corridor where Arlene had chainsawed the demons was now one edge of a triangular room full of specters. We gave that a pass, rushing through before the lumbering, invisible pinkies could avenge their more-visible cousins; we beat cleats back to the door leading to the central corridor and slamming it, jamming the latch with some 10mm rounds.

We didn't see anything in the corridor outside, so we went back along the secret passage by which we had exited from the room behind the illusory wall. From that room we could see that the lava lake now had a wall at the back, and next to it a corridor that offered the possibility of dry land. I was about to slog across the corridor when Ritch got into the act.

"Why don't you use the toxic protection suit?" he asked, pointing.

"What? Where?"

"See those coveralls?"

Huh! I pulled one on over my armor and boots before making a dash through the crud to the island behind it. There, I found the damnedest rifle I'd ever seen, huge, gyrostabilized, and with a gigantic battery backpack. Hoisting it up, I was pleased that it was a lot lighter than it looked and considerably less unwieldy. Grinning like I'd won a bowling league trophy, I humped back to where the others were waiting.

It was a good thing I followed Ritch's advice on the protective suit; the toxic glop ate away at the material with a consistent low hiss for company. I started feeling lousy by the time I was out of the stuff, but at least I wasn't in pain. Arlene reached out to help me climb from the red pool.

"Get it off!" she said. "Your suit is disintegrating." I eagerly stripped for her. She noticed a telltale bulge under the suit. "What's this?" she asked.

I looked at it. "It's a . . . it's a big, freaking gun, I guess."

"What's it do?"

"I hate to say it, but we'd better find out in combat; I don't want to waste power. Ritch?" He looked at the thing and shook his head.

My skin was tingling after dumping the suit. We three exchanged that special expression that is only shared by those who skirt close to death. We touched hands, more than a handshake—more like taking a secret oath.

There was nowhere to go but back out to the courtyard, and now I was glad we'd already popped the two pumpkins. We found another difference in the pattern: a new door next to the old, this one locked. Arlene dropped to her knees and fiddled with it. "Bad news," she said finally. "I can't pick this one."

That was annoying. I'd about convinced myself that she could handle any of these. Surveying the scenery, I noticed a *third* door on the far side of the courtyard. This place was turning into a hotel lobby! "Let's try over there," I suggested.

We skulked through the doorway and entered a dark corridor. I took point and no one argued. I suppose I'd become careless. I didn't notice the teleport pad until I'd stepped on it.

This one was quick, but it made me feel like I wanted to throw up. Suddenly I was standing on a triangular platform directly behind two pumpkins, not two meters away!

32

They didn't see me. That was a good thing because there was no way I could kill them quickly with a shotgun or pistol. It would take multiple shots to destroy them, and at this range, long before that happened they'd fry me with their lightning balls. And I could forget about rockets, unless I had a "burning" desire to be a burnward poster boy.

This seemed a fine time to give the big freakin' gun—call it a BFG—a shot. Taking a deep breath, I raised this fine piece of Union Aerospace Corporation craftsmanship and pointed it at the nearest oblivious target. There was no obvious trigger mechanism, so I squeezed the hand grip. There was no kick at all. Instead, I heard a loud whine of energy. The pumpkins heard it also and started rotating.

Nothing had come out of the muzzle of the weapon yet; I had just about decided I'd made a big freakin' mistake when a green ball of energy exploded from the sealed mouth of the gun. The light was so bright it seared my eyes . . . the pumpkins screamed and popped like balloons, leaving nothing but smoking, blue and orange shreds.

But my troubles were not over; I wasn't back home with my feet up.

A horde of zombies poured out of cubbyholes that were like eyes stretched up and down both corridors. Funny how I hadn't noticed them until trouble came out. Exhaustion was taking its toll and making me lose my edge.

I'd already dropped to my belly when I heard the unmistakable clatter of machine-gun bullets ripping over my head. Who the hell was shooting now? The attack came from behind. I was tired of attacks coming from behind.

Rolling to the side, staying low, I fired off another BFG blast down the corridor to the left. The results were good—a large bunch of fried zombies. I was ready to institute a firm gun-control policy for all undead: I would firmly control my BFG as I fired it.

Leaping down from the pumpkin platform, I bolted along the corridor to the left end, ducking into a cubbyhole myself. Old rule: when a bad guy comes out of a hole, he's not there anymore. I laid down the BFG and unslung my trusty shotgun, then poked my nose out of the cubbyhole again. Seemed like a good idea at the time.

A stream of bullets came out of nowhere and I ducked back in. And *at last* I figured out what the hell was happening: it was Arlene! She must be firing across the hidden teleport pad . . . and her bullets were being teleported to where I had first emerged. No wonder the zombies were confused. This was enough to confuse someone with a *functional* brain.

She was doing just as good a job of mowing them down as if she'd been present and accounted for. Encouraged, I helped out and shot the ones who ran past my cubbyhole, hunting for an enemy. So specters weren't the only ones who could play this game. Of course, the zombies got mad and started shooting each other.

They were all dead by the time Arlene joined me. She hopped off the pad and I filled her in. Then we returned to the end of the corridor where I had hidden; I'd seen a door awaiting our attentions.

There was no special key required to open this one; of course not . . . a hell-prince waited for us on the other side.

It had a blue key card in its mouth; we took it after making a fair trade: he got a whole bunch of rockets. I'm sure the minotaur appreciated our generosity.

Returning to the mouth of the corridor, we picked up Ritch. We hadn't forgotten him. Ritch never seemed to regret missing out on our repeated exterminations, although he acquitted himself admirably when backed into a corner . . . the perfect civilian. He'd have done well at Lexington and Concord, provided there wasn't a lot of running involved.

The three of us trucked back across the courtyard to the locked door—and none of us was the least surprised when the key unlocked it.

Inside was a single, ornate teleport pad. We blinked into existence in a vast room, a huge, open pit with a narrow catwalk running around the periphery. Our eyes watered from mist in the air. The place stank of boiled rock and the walls were the color of dried blood, and everywhere was the stench of sour lemons.

"This is it!" Ritch said, suddenly excited. "This is the place where the spider, the mastermind, interrogated me."

I'd been getting to the point of dismissing any differences in the hellish architecture. All the chambers seemed more and more identical. But they'd never tortured me, stringing me up to hang halfway between life and death. There was no doubting Ritch's memory after what he'd been through.

We heard a cacophony from below, as if a monster convention was being held under our noses. We dropped on our bellies, hugging the catwalk, and listened.

I heard roaring, grunting, screaming, wheezing, howling, snuffling, and even a weird piping or whistling.

Heavy thumping and thudding left no doubt that some of the big guys were down there. Didn't hear a steam-demon, though; that was the only good news.

"If you want to see the spidermind, now's your chance," Ritch whispered.

"Isn't it special invitation only?" Arlene asked.

"I can't help it," I whispered. "I'm a born Gate-crasher."

She crawled to the edge. "Pumpkins, hell-princes, those crazy flying skulls."

"Did we ever get around to naming them?"

Arlene looked at me with a strange expression, as if I'd just missed something. "Gee . . . how about 'flying skulls'? Any objections?"

Shaking my head, I couldn't help but notice Ritch's expression. He probably thought our little name game the pinnacle of insanity. And Ritch had a gift for it himself: he'd called our steam-demon a "cyberdude," and "spidermind" turned out to be a perfect description for the thing that chose that moment to make a big entrance.

It was worse than all the rest.

If I'd found the steam-demon disgusting with its mixture of organic and mechanical, this completely alien *It* scuttling across the floor down below completely turned my stomach. Numerous mechanical legs supported a dome housing a gigantic, gray, pulsing brain with a hideous, ersatz face formed in the center of the squishy gray matter itself, complete with "eyes" and "teeth." It should have been funny, almost a cartoon—but there was nothing remotely humorous about the living incarnation of a nightmare.

Its appearance was so unnerving that one could easily neglect taking inventory of the most important thing: its weapons. Even from this awkward angle it was easy to see that it came equipped with what looked like an ultraspeed Gatling gun, like a Vulcan cannon. There was little doubt that up close there'd be other unpleasant surprises.

"Listen," I hissed, "suppose we can take this spidermind thing. We'd throw a monkey wrench into the invasion plans right here and now! I could run along the catwalk, drop down in front of the creature and fry it with my new toy."

"Too dangerous," Arlene said.

"It would get you with its machine guns before you got close enough to try," Ritch added.

These were extremely good points, I had to admit. Rethinking the idea, I realized that even if I succeeded, I would be ripped to shreds by the throng of monsters surrounding the boss. Ritch seemed to be reading my thoughts when he said: "We should kill some of the other creatures so the spidermind won't have as much back-up." Maybe this guy could make an honorary Marine after all.

Creeping along the catwalk rim, peeking over the edge, we made slow progress. While finding a more advantageous position, Ritch sneezed. I think he was allergic to monsters.

The element of surprise blown, it was time to open fire and blow them away. Their reward for paying attention. Arlene and I worked through the rockets we'd scavenged from the steam-demon chamber. Good distance and angle to use those little darlings.

There had been so much noise already that plenty of the monsters farther away still hadn't noticed what was going on. They were partying down. Our primary goal was to keep the spidermind from noticing as long as inhumanly possible, so we never shot a rocket in its direction.

We still had a lot of unanswered questions: How well did the brain hear? And were other creatures supposed to report back—and were they in constant communication, by radio or telepathy?

We continued the slaughter. Ritch was proving himself useful again, this time with his Sig-Cow. Finally, the general run of monsters noticed that something was amiss.

Some became agitated and began to run about, their roars more thoughtful, attuned to the condition of the general community . . . communication, obviously. A few even attempted to apply what mentality they had to "investigate" the mysterious deaths of their comrades.

Alas, the spidermind lived up to its name. It detected the trouble and began stomping around, trying to identify the source. But my respect for that great quantity of gray matter declined somewhat as the damned thing got frustrated and started blasting away at random, killing its troops!

Ritch crept over and offered more analysis: "Corporal Taggart, I—"

"Call me Fly."

"Well, Fly, I've been thinking that the amount of energy required to actually move Deimos through hyperspace would be monumental. There's no way they could have snuck such a huge power generator onto Deimos through those fairly small Gates. We're talking many terawatts, thousands of Hoover Dams worth of power."

"Makes sense," I said. Arlene nodded, while continuing to hold down the fort.

"The most likely explanation is that the power is coming from an external source," he said, "and they're beaming it in somehow."

"Ritch," Arlene said, "are you saying cut the power and end the invasion?" For the first time since seeing the spawning vats, I began to think we might really have a chance. So long as they had power, they could produce an endless number of monsters in their damned caldrons.

It was time to cancel their service.

33

    Arlene pointed at a central building, a small pillbox structure right in the center of the monster convention. In all the chaos, *none of the creatures* had gotten anywhere near this pillbox . . . as if they deliberately avoided it.

"Could that be the power receiver?" she asked.

Ritch shrugged. "I don't know, but it seems like the best possibility."

That possibility did as much for our morale as if we'd each been given a blue face-sphere. The spidermind continued firing until many of the other creatures, its own troops, were killed or driven off. It was now or never.

I jumped first, feeling as if I could fly. Arlene followed and I turned to help, but she didn't need a hand. We both had to help Ritch, who wasn't exactly constructed for flight. The three of us made a dash for the central building.

Monster corpses presented a major obstacle; but we quickly turned grateful for the thick-limbed, heavy bodies all over the floor. The spidermind noticed us and opened fire with its 30mm Vulcans. We hit the deck and used the bodies for cover.

The incredible creature charged us, firing maybe three hundred rounds a minute, five rounds a second. In a few moments it would be upon us, firing so rapidly we'd never be able to return fire.

Suddenly the firing stopped. The spidermind was

tangled up in the bodies it had helped produce. The mechanical spider legs were not designed for an obstacle course.

"Run!" I shouted, heading for the building. A quick glance at the location of the spidermind told me what I needed to know—the angles were perfect. "Get between the spidermind and the building—move!"

I bolted hutward and immediately sprawled gracefully over the prone body of a steam-demon—a *steam-demon!* My heart leapt up my throat . . . then I realized the damned thing was under bloody construction. Great, and me without my monkey wrench!

The gigantic monster lay on its belly, face into the deck; the missiles were exposed, and as bullets flew haphazardly over my head I swallowed hard: a couple of good shots might detonate the warheads on those puppies—or, if the warheads weren't yet attached, the fuel cells could rupture and spray us all with caustic and flammable rocket fuel.

"Very adroit, Mr. Leslie," snapped Arlene, yanking me to my feet.

We made tracks. We had crossed perhaps a third of the open territory when a wave of horror struck me like a physical hammer blow.

Nightmarish images of Degas, Bosch, Patrick Woodruff . . . blood dripping from the walls and ceiling, sprays of blood in the distance, blood from overhead sprinklers . . . it probed, trying to find a weak spot: my father lurched out of the building, grinning and slapping his body. "Me heap big chief Kamehameha!" he shouted, then gave a Tarzan yell.

He humiliated me all over again, as he had twenty years earlier; we'd been *in Hawaii* in a museum, before a life-size (huge) statue of Hawaii's greatest king. I shrank away from him, praying to God no one knew he was my father; but he followed me, saying, "Did you see what I did? Watch!" And he did it again!

I was never more ashamed of him in my life. We were

lucky to make it out of the museum alive. But goddamn it, he was *not* going to stop me reaching that building. I pushed on, tuning out the spidermind.

Then I saw myself brought up on charges again, but this time I was tried and convicted, and they ripped the stripes off my sleeve like, what was it, that old television show, two-dimensional . . . *Branded,* something like that. They tore off my sharpshooter's medal, my ribbons, finally the eagle-and-globe that told the world I was a Marine.

But I gritted my teeth, and through my tears I told myself that *I* knew I was a Marine no matter what, and Arlene would never let me forget it even if I tried.

My feet never stopped.

God knows what horrors it sent to Arlene and Ritch; their faces were white, grim, but determined.

The monstrosity realized it didn't have our number psychologically and tried the more direct route: it opened fire. But it was off balance, picking its way through the bodies, and the whole contraption tumbled over. This gave us the time to get into position. Just as we got behind the building, the spidermind freed itself, stood up straight on mechanical legs, swiveled the weaponry into position . . . and started firing. A few quick burps of gunfire probed our way; then it abruptly choked off and there was silence.

"What happened?" Ritch asked.

"It's like it stopped automatically," Arlene said.

"It can't shoot us without shooting the building!" I realized. "The guns were clearly cut off by a circuit breaker."

We had to get inside; but the spidermind lived up to its name. The thing scuttled quickly to the side, trying for a better angle and a clear shot. We kept moving, dancing around the pillbox in a tightening spiral, always keeping ourselves between the spidermind and the building. It was like playing some kind of children's game, only this playground was the killing field.

Then we had a new problem. The other monsters had been considerate enough to stay away, but now the noise attracted them back into the fray. A random sampling of fireballs, ball lightning, and even the hell-princes' green fire creased our bow. Under the circumstances, it would have been rude not to respond. We fired back, while we kept running from the spidermind.

"One rocket left!" I yelled as I fired the penultimate one at a minotaur. I slung the launcher—never know when a weapon might come in handy. But Arlene must've figured there'd be no more rainy days: she blew through her AB-10 ammo and dropped the pistol without a second glance, not wanting anything to slow her down.

Bill Ritch fired his Sig-Cow at the spinys and actually dropped one.

Despite his bulk, he'd managed to keep up with us, although his heavy breathing was cause for worry. I hoped he wouldn't have a heart attack. We still needed him. I wasn't being callous in thinking this; the mission was all-important.

God, did I actually think that? I guess I did. Arlene had converted me . . . and I didn't even know when she managed it. My goal had shifted from rescuing her to fighting the last battle as the last Marine.

I blew the door off its hinges with a point-blank shotgun blast. One of the spinys didn't approve of my housebreaking; it dive-bombed me and flung a ball of burning mucus that just missed . . . just missed *me* that is. Arlene took it out—but then I glanced over at Ritch and saw that the imp had done him serious damage.

Ritch had taken a faceful of the poison and was coughing his guts up. Holding the door open with my back, I racked and fired as fast as I could as Arlene dragged Ritch inside.

Vindication! The room was full of electronic gear, cables, data banks. While Arlene did what she could for Ritch, damned little under the circumstances, I stood guard on all four doors, shooting anything that ventured close. Naturally, the monsters couldn't fire back. I enjoyed the situation until one of the imps flung a spitwad and hit the door frame, missing me by a handsbreadth.

For one moment in the history of the universe, the spidermind and Yours Truly shared the same opinion. The imp's action was ill-considered in the extreme. The spidermind proved it was no dummy; it blew the imp to cutlets.

I drifted from doorway to doorway and nothing shot at me; however, every time I passed within line-of-sight of the spidermind, I caught another faceful of hypnogogic horror. It was the only weapon the critter had left; in a way, you had to feel sorry for it.

Well . . . maybe not.

"How's it going?" I asked Arlene, already knowing the answer. She shook her head. Ritch was in a lot worse shock than when we first found him. The flaming goo had stuck to his face, catching him just as he inhaled; his lungs were fried . . . they could no longer transport oxygen to his blood.

I didn't know what we were going to do; maybe a hospital could save him . . . but we didn't even have bandages or painkiller.

The skin of his face was angry red, and it was bleeding in a dozen spots where enough layers of epidermis had burned away. He must have been in agony . . . and Ritch knew it was hopeless, for him at least; he was a smart man.

Bill was dying.

Arlene propped him against a wall and whispered in his ear. He nodded, making the coughing worse; but she wiped his eyes, and he could see well enough to help us.

In a weak voice he began identifying critical components within the room. He remembered everything from when they forced him to work on the mess. He told us what we needed to know.

Arlene left him propped against the wall and came to

me. In a low voice she said "I wish we had one of those blue spheres right now."

"It's the only thing that would save him," I agreed.

"We don't even have a Medikit. At least I could make him comfortable."

I looked her in the eye. "He told us what we need to know," I said. "That's the important thing."

I felt professional. I felt several degrees colder than mean.

But Arlene was as much a pro as I. "Do you want to perform the coup de grace on this energy conduit, or shall I?"

While I thought about it, she made up my mind for me: "You'd better do it, Fly; we need a *real* sharpshooter's eye to keep those bastards far enough away that they can't reach in and grab us. I suppose even you can't miss a computer bank from two meters away, hey? Even if you can't shoot an apple off Goforth's head." She grinned.

I turned and became a one-man wrecking crew. Raising the BFG, I took a deep breath and let fly at the collection of electronics. The explosion knocked me on my butt. I staggered up and took out the rest of the targets Ritch pointed out in the mass of equipment. After four walloping shots, the BFG fizzled and wouldn't shoot anymore. Out of juice. I finished the job with a dozen shotgun shells.

"Jesus, Fly! Come look at this," Arlene shouted. I came, still shaking, ears still ringing like Christmas.

This was turning into an hour of surprises. The monsters were acting like they were on PCP, wandering in circles and firing at anything that moved—which meant each other.

The spidermind still seemed to have control over its ugly faculties. It opened fire on several of the hell-princes, no doubt with the idea of removing those of its minions most potentially dangerous if there were no way to give them orders.

Naturally, the executions drew the attention of other monsters. They fired at the noise. We weren't cast members in that show, but we took full advantage of our backstage passes.

Fifteen minutes later there was one monster, count 'em, *one monster* left that we could see. For the moment, the spidermind was boss over itself. And it had one other problem besides not being able to get any decent help. The gun cylinders spun, empty. The spider hadn't saved any ammo for us.

"Ritch," Arlene said, speaking quietly but enunciating clearly, "your plan worked brilliantly."

I'm sure he would have appreciated her good opinion of him—if he had still been alive.

The damned, stupid spiny had killed him after all. I stared at the dead face of Bill Ritch, the captivity and torture survivor, comrade, the man who gave us a real chance to defeat the alien invaders. I looked at this brand new corpse and something snapped.

"I'm sick of this," I told Arlene. I shrugged off my beloved rocket launcher and handed it to my best gal-pal. "Keep an eye on me, First Class. You'll know when to use it . . . and *don't,* God damn it, miss."

"Show me the apple, Flynn Taggart, and I'll pop it off your head."

I loaded up my shotgun, for attention-grabbing purposes only, and calmly walked out to face the ugliest alien of them all.

"Hey, spider baby," I called out. "Yeah, I'm talking to you!"

The turret turned. The spidermind and I looked at each other . . . and suddenly I was overwhelmed with the most horrific vision of all: I saw the Earth in flames, burning buildings, fields, oceans of corpses. I saw the demons, not just aliens, but honest-to-Lucifer *demons,* wading through the rivers of filth and blood and urine, laughing in triumph.

I saw mankind under the heel. Collars around our throats, chains on wrists and ankles. I saw collaborators, traitors, quislings, turncoats of every race and culture.

I saw a "Vichy" Earth government.

And I saw in the distance an endless parade of bigger and more ghastly demons. They filled the land from end to end, sea to shining sea.

And I knew this vision was no nightmare plucked from my own subconscious fears. This was reality.

I saw the future. I leaned forward and spat upon the shredded machine mind.

"Remember the imp you had talk to me back on Phobos? That creepy leatherface asked for my surrender. Well, here's my answer, you insect!"

Raising my shotgun, I took careful aim and blasted toward the brain inside the crystal case. Then I did it again. And again. And again. I stopped at eight shots because I'd run out of shells, and because the turret had finally rotated in my direction and was chewing up the deckplates with 30mm rounds.

I slalomed through the heaped corpses, looking for one in particular . . . one body not dead but *pre-born*, as my nuns would say, though in a hell of a different context.

I was looking for my steam-demon, and that had to be a first!

The spidermind scuttled after me; on open ground it could make quite a clip . . . quite a bit faster than a mere two-legger like me. But we weren't on open ground; I chose my route well. I leapt from body to body like Eliza across the ice floes, and the frustrated arachnoid android started shooting the corpses out of the way for clearer footing.

I put some distance between us, and for a moment the stupid thing lost me! Great . . . I should've brought an air horn. Crouching so I wouldn't get clopped by a stray, I loaded up, stood, and fired a few more shells. It spotted me, screamed in triumph—just like you'd expect an insect to sound, magnified a billion times—and charged, Gatling barrels spinning like gyroscopes.

I ran the hundred in world-record time. I flung myself through the air in a graceful swan dive, tucked at the last second, and rolled beautifully—dislocating my shoulder.

I struggled up, shifted the shotgun to my right, weak hand, reached over the steam-demon, and let fly with the last shell.

My cough was answered by a diarrhea of Vulcan Cannon rounds that tore up the iron flesh of the steam-demon like an AB-10 tears up plaster. The bullets ripped the legs apart; they ripped the head apart.

They ripped the missiles apart.

I clenched my teeth . . . now was the moment of truth. If they'd already attached those warheads . . . Well, I guess I'd either go north and meet the nuns, or . . . or stay right where I was—in Hell!

Fifteen seconds and 750 rounds later, sudden silence startled me back to the here-and-now. My ears throbbed and rang, and my skull felt like it was still vibrating; but the spidermind had stopped shooting to see what damage it had done.

I wasn't about to stick my head up, but I didn't need to: I closed my eyes and sniffed deeply.

There is a smell most people don't know, but once you've tasted it, you never forget it. Anyone who's hung around a Marine air base or Naval air station remembers and pilots remember from the airport: it's the pungent aroma of JP-9 "jet propellant," and it tears through your septum, up your nasal passages, and straight into your brain. Think of ammonia, formaldehyde, and skunk-juice swirled together into a malt.

There was no possibility of error . . . dozens of gallons of the burn-juice pooled around the steam-demon; in fact, looking down, I saw it seeping from under the body onto my side, eating away at my boots worse than the green sludge.

My bruised eardrums were trying to tell me something urgent, a sound behind the ringing and throbbing: clicking feet. The spidermind was on its way to investigate!

I backed slowly away, crouching lower and lower to stay behind the steam-demon; then the spidermind loomed, and I could no longer hide.

It screamed again, this time in rage, not triumph, and charged.

It slipped in the fuel slick that it itself had created. It tried to rise and slipped again, skating in the horrible stuff. JP-9 dripped from the spidermind's underbelly, splashed up and down its legs, even sprayed across the crystal canopy.

Time to split that apple, A.S.!

I dashed to the side, waving frantically at the building; I couldn't see Arlene. I pointed at the spidermind, screaming, *"Now, now, you crazy bitch!"* She couldn't hear me, of course, or I never would have said such a thing!

A tiny bud of red bloomed in the black doorway, flowering into the bright-red tail exhaust of our very last rocket. I hit the deck, hands over head, belatedly wondering whether any of the jet propellant had sprayed on *me* . . .

I barely heard the explosion through the ringing, but the force kicked me in my dislocated shoulder. After a moment with my eyes shut, arms locked over my head, I ventured a glance.

The spidermind screeched and skittered, joyously engulfed in bright white flames, like one of Weem's monks protesting the war in Kefiristan by immolating himself with burning gasoline.

I watched for several minutes, keeping low as the last of the spidermind's ammo exploded, bursting off in all directions. Mobility lasted only half a minute, then the intense heat melted the crystal canopy, turning the truck-size brain into a crispie critter in seconds. It took longer for the metal body to liquefy, even longer for the whole mass to bubble through the melted deckplates. At last there was nothing left of the dreaded spidermind but a smoking crater. . . . "Get used to it," I muttered, unable to even hear my own voice. "Think of this as a rehearsal for the next eternity."

A hand grabbed my arm—my left arm. *"No!"* I screamed; then I screamed again in pain as Arlene yanked on my dislocated shoulder.

"Jesus, Fly, I'm sorry!" I faintly heard her voice, as if through a speakerphone across the room.

I rolled onto my back, swearing like a drunken long-shoreman. "Oh," she said, "I see what it is. Hang on, Fly, this is going to hurt—but you'll thank me for it in a minute."

Would you believe she grabbed my biceps, *pulled my arm out of the socket,* and snapped it back into place?

I passed out.

I came to in a few seconds, then cursed her out again, sorting the epithets alphabetically, in case I missed any. I passed through the scatological and had started on the blasphemous when she shut me up by planting a big, wet boot-heel on my mouth.

She sat me up; by then, my ears were starting to recover, and I could hear what she said. "Pretty spectacular, Fly. I guess we won. . . . Ritch would've loved this spread now."

But still I heard the hum of power. The lights remained lit. Something was wrong with this picture.

"I hope you won't take this wrong," said Arlene, staring curiously around, "but why aren't we plunged into terrible darkness, Fly Taggart?"

"I know what you mean, A.S. We can't feel total satisfaction until we're freezing to death in the black night of space . . ."

"And running out of air."

"So what's gone wrong with Bill Ritch's plan?"

She frowned in thought. "I guess that building didn't house the power receiver, after all," she said. "It must have been the communications gear by which the spidermind was controlling all the other creatures."

"You mean all the creatures left on Deimos and Phobos will destroy one another, like these guys did?" I smiled . . . I like that thought.

"The spidermind was barely able to control them as it was," she pointed out. "They have a natural hatred for each other."

I remembered the crucified hell-princes. Then I remembered Bill, dying from the stupid blast from a stupid imp. Now he was gone!

Focus, Fly . . . focus.

We went back in the control room and I threw a piece of canvas over Ritch. We laid his body out in the place that was the most appropriate crypt: the scene of his victory over the demons.

"All right," I said. "I think we should retrace our steps back to the surface of Deimos. Maybe we can figure out how to get back to Mars from there, or at least figure out where in hell we are."

"Watch your language," Arlene said seriously. Hm, Arlene Sanders—with religion.

As we worked our way back up through the levels of Deimos, we found the dead bodies of hundreds, then thousands, of the alien monsters. It was as if the Cosmic Orkin company had come through and done a big special on demonic infestation.

There were a very few live ones, so completely out of it that they hardly seemed worth killing. Somehow Arlene and I found the will to exterminate them anyway.

When we reached the surface, we discovered the pressure dome was cracked, the air rushing out, creating a minihurricane. Of course, we had been adequately briefed on the basics of life in space. It would take days for all the air to escape; we weren't planning to wait around that long.

I looked past the crack—and stopped breathing. I stared so long, forgetting to blink, that my eyes blurred.

I wasn't staring at Mars anymore. Where Mars had loomed, hanging over our heads like a wrecking ball, was a different planet, one that looked disturbingly familiar: blue-green, familiar land masses, cloud cover, teeming with six billion cousins and uncles.

We weren't in a hyperspace tunnel any longer. We looked for several minutes, hoping it was a shared hallucination. At last Arlene said, "I guess we know their invasion plans now."

As I stared at Earth in the skies of Deimos, through a cracked and broken pressure dome, I felt a queer sense of dislocation, as if I were no longer sitting inside my own body—but standing alongside. I shook, as if I had a terrible fever, mindlessly clutching at my uniform—Weems's uniform. "Well," I began feebly, "at least we stopped them."

"Did we?" She reached out, as if trying to pet the planet.

Beyond the domes, amid the bright-flecked black of space, other bright spots flared upon the continents, shining through the scattered clouds. Nuclear explosions would look just like that; other things, worse things, could look like that as well.

"Jesus, they've already invaded," Arlene said, hope draining away from her voice faster than the escaping air.

I took her by the arm and said, "It's not over, Arlene! We've already proven who's tougher. We won't let it end like this!"

But we had no ship, no radio, not even a really long rope. We were stuck in low orbit around Earth, a mere four hundred kilometers away, hanging over our heads like the biggest balloon we could ever hope to play with.

I shut my eyes tight, then opened them. How would we do the impossible? How could we jump four hundred kilometers to Earth and kill the orbital velocity?

We didn't say anything for a very long time. We

watched the white spots appearing over the northern hemisphere, over the hot, blue oceans and cool, green hills of earth.

Suddenly, Arlene gasped; her eyes opened wide. "Fly, I have it!"

"What?"

"I know how to do it!"

"Do *what* damn it?"

Her lips moved, silently calculating. Then she grinned. "I know how to get us across to Earth, Fly!"